# RAGE

## of The Assassin

Russell Blake

First edition.

**Published by**

**Reprobatio Limited**

# CHAPTER 1

*Twenty years ago, Culiacán, Sinaloa, Mexico*

Peals of laughter rose into the afternoon sky from the school yard. The bell had rung a few minutes earlier, excusing the day shift's students in preparation for the evening class's arrival two hours later. Tall palm trees swayed in a humid breeze heavy with the distinctive aroma of the brown river just over the rise mingled with the pungent dankness of the freshly turned dirt of the surrounding fields. Stray puffs of clouds drifted west toward the Sea of Cortez, the final remnants of a morning storm that had flooded the town's streets.

A group of youths in white jerseys and blue trousers stood in a rough circle near the entrance of the fenced yard, where a befuddled boy in the middle of the gathering looked around with a panicked expression as the others taunted him. A few disinterested teachers ambled near one of the crumbling building façades, ignoring the fracas, their job done once they left their classrooms after a long day of mindless repetition.

"What's wrong with you, moron? Can't talk?" Paolo, one of the tallest of the boys, none of whom were older than eight, baited the unfortunate. Paolo spit on the ground by his victim's feet and glanced at the others in disgust. "I swear he's a total retard."

Several nodded at the insight, and one sneered as Paolo took another step toward his prey. "I said I want your backpack. It's mine now."

The encircled child shook his head, eyes wild, clutching the bag to his chest. "N-no," he managed, his voice cracking with obvious desperation.

1

"Why? What do you have in there? Come on, give it up."

"I won't."

The throng closed in and fists flew. The boy with the backpack fell to the asphalt and his assailants kicked him. He curled into a ball, protecting his treasure with his body as blows fell, and then everything went black when a particularly vicious kick struck the side of his head, snapping it back against the hard pavement.

~ ~ ~

"Ynez? What's the big emergency?" *Don* Aranas asked as he marched into the kitchen of his hilltop home, his shoulders square, his bearing erect. Three of his men followed at a prudent distance, the pistols in their belts as common on the grounds as the trees that ringed the hacienda's lush periphery.

Ynez, the head of the housekeeping staff, knelt in front of Aranas's nephew, blotting at his face with a crimson-stained towel. Martin was covered with bruises and had two nasty gashes on the side of his head. One of the boy's eyes was partially swollen shut, and he was pressing a plastic bag filled with ice against a lump on his head.

Aranas took in the damage with a grunt and glowered at Martin.

"What happened, Martin? Damn it, boy, speak up!"

Martin looked away, shame obvious in his averted face, and Aranas scowled as he neared the youngster. The man's deeply tanned face was already lined from a life spent outdoors, as well as the constant stress that came with being the most powerful drug lord in Mexico – the head of the Sinaloa Cartel, the entity that had given birth to all the other criminal enterprises engaged in narcotics trafficking to the United States.

Aranas's voice softened when he spoke to Ynez. "Enough. Leave us for a moment. There will be time to attend to his scrapes later."

Ynez nodded and stood, and Aranas's entourage followed her out of the kitchen. When the last of their cowboy boots had clumped down the hall, Aranas turned his attention to Martin, who had a thin stream of blood working its way from his brutalized nose to the corner of his mouth.

"Who did this to you?" Aranas whispered, reaching out with his handkerchief and stemming the flow of red.

"Boys. A...at school," Martin said, his voice so tentative it was almost inaudible.

"Why?"

When Martin looked up and met his uncle's eyes, the little boy's contained all the misery of the human condition in them. "They hate me," he said with the simplicity of youth. "Because...you know. I'm different."

"Did you fight them? How many were there?" Aranas demanded, his tone hardening.

"Seven. Eight. I don't know. Too many." Martin winced as his free hand probed his ear and came away smeared with red.

"Did you hurt any of them?"

Martin's eyes returned to his scraped shoes and the torn knees of his uniform pants. "N-no."

Aranas stepped back and cleared his throat. "You must not let them pick on you. I can intervene, but that won't help. This is your battle, and you have to show them that they can't do this and get away with it."

Martin licked away a fleck of blood from his upper lip and remained silent. Aranas's eyes narrowed as he considered his nephew – who was indeed different and needed to learn life's harsh lessons early if he was to survive. The first of which was that he wasn't a victim – he was a threat to anyone who would harm him.

"There are two kinds of people, Martin: predators and prey. These boys are aggressive because they are in a group, so they feel powerful. They see you as weak. So you need to find a way to prove to them that you're stronger, and that to hurt you brings consequences that makes it too costly for them to consider. It is the only way."

Martin looked up at his uncle, who seemed a hundred feet tall from where he stood. The older man's face was impassive, unsympathetic, with a hint of anger flashing in the depths of his chocolate eyes. The message conveyed was clear – Martin had disappointed him, and in his uncle's hierarchical world he'd brought shame to the family by allowing himself to be beaten like a dog. Martin had heard the stories about the *Don*, about his merciless rise to power and his reputation as a killer. How could he not, even if they were only whispered snatches that quickly died when the speakers saw Martin lurking within earshot?

"I…I don't want to go back."

Aranas nodded. "Of course you don't. But you have to. Take a few days to heal, and then you will return with your head held high, and you'll show these boys what you're made of. Do you understand?" Aranas's tone left nothing to be discussed.

Martin nodded. Aranas turned to the empty doorway and called out, "Ynez! Get this warrior cleaned up. He looks hungry. Call the doctor and have him look him over, stitch him up, whatever he needs."

Ynez scuttled back in, wringing her hands, worry written across her normally placid face. "Yes, *Don* Aranas. Of course."

Aranas gave Martin another hard stare and turned on his heel. His stride covered the Saltillo tile floor in three long steps and then he disappeared through the doorway, other business to attend to. Ynez moved to a rack for a fresh towel and waved Martin over. He shuffled toward her, his mind churning at his uncle's words, a core of fury searing in his stomach like a hot ember.

He would find a way to show them all.

He had no choice.

~ ~ ~

*Don* Aranas glanced up from his newspaper when Ynez approached. He set it down in his lap and eyed her, his coveted moment of evening relaxation disrupted.

"What did the doctor say?" he asked.

"Dr. Alioto put two stitches in one of the cuts and swabbed the rest with antiseptic. And he gave me some ointment. He said that the

4

bruising should go down in forty-eight hours. Nothing's broken, thank heaven."

"How's Martin holding up?"

"He's quiet. Doesn't want to talk."

Aranas nodded. "Then not much different than usual."

Martin was an odd boy, Aranas knew. He'd wound up living with Aranas after his father had been gunned down in a bitter territorial dispute in Tijuana. A loyal associate of Aranas, he'd been murdered within shouting distance of the border crossing by a split-off faction of the Sinaloa Cartel headed by a group of brothers as vicious as pit vipers. Martin had been calling Aranas 'uncle' since arriving three years earlier, and by now it was fact, regardless of what a blood test might say. Aranas had grown fond of the quirky child, who was easily startled by noises and avoided human interaction as much as possible – one of the reasons Aranas insisted that he go to a public school, so he could become better socialized.

Martin had proven brilliant with anything mechanical and, if allowed, would sit for entire days tinkering with some discarded piece of gear, making it serviceable again. Aranas had never seen anything like it, but figured that Providence made up for what it withheld in strange ways. At least the boy would always have a trade, if he didn't develop normally as he aged, and God knew that in Mexico there would always be broken items requiring a fix. Aranas liked to joke that it was a nation held together with sweat and bailing wire, where jury-rigging was the national pastime.

Not that if Aranas had any say, the boy would ever be relegated to a dirty shop somewhere in the barrio. But the future was uncertain, especially in Aranas's line of work, and to expect to be alive the following day was a conceit he couldn't afford.

He sighed and returned to his paper. "Thank you, Ynez. That is all."

"Of course, sir. Let me know if you need anything else."

~ ~ ~

The sun was high in the late spring sky, a blazing ball that scorched the town with unrelenting intensity. Three days after the incident in the schoolyard, four boys were splashing raucously in a backyard swimming pool, enjoying the relief from the heat. School would let out in another three weeks and then they'd have two months of slacking before returning to their studies – two months that at their age would seem endless at the start, pregnant with possibility, and yet far too short by the time it was over.

Paolo sprayed a sheet of water at his companions with a swipe of his hand. He laughed harshly when he caught them unawares, and they sputtered as they blinked away the drops and returned the favor. Soon it was an all-out water battle with the bully. Colorful insults were exchanged with the abandon of sailors on leave, the delight at using forbidden curses out of adult earshot heightening the delicious pleasure.

Paolo stopped mid-splash and stared at the doorway to his house, where a diminutive figure approached across the brownish grass. The others turned to follow his gaze, and watched in puzzled silence as Martin walked toward them.

"How did you get in here, retard?" Paolo demanded.

Martin didn't answer. Paolo looked down at the object in Martin's hands and back at his face, which was still discolored from the beating he'd received at Paolo's direction. "I asked you a question, dumbass. What are you doing here? How did you get in? And what are you going to do with that? Make us toast?"

Martin neared the raised cantera edge of the pool, hefted the toaster as if considering its weight, and then tossed it at Paolo with a shrug, the long extension cord that trailed behind it whipping through the grass like an infuriated snake. Martin watched with indifference as Paolo caught the appliance. Current shot through the water, electrocuting the boys in the pool; Martin had taken a few minutes to hardwire the fuse box to bypass the breaker that might have saved their lives. Martin's only reaction to the horror was to hold his hands over his ears, the dying boys' shrieking more troubling to him than the expressions of agony as they fried.

~ ~ ~

Ynez came running into the casita, where Aranas was meeting with his lieutenants. A thick cloud of cigar and cigarette smoke hung in the room, the overhead fan barely stirring the pungent pall, and the tabletop was littered with Tecate cans and empty shot glasses. She gasped when she saw whom she was interrupting, but Aranas held back on reprimanding her – he knew it had to be an emergency for her to dare the forbidden impertinence.

"What?" he snapped, the single syllable a whip crack.

"It's Martin. The…the police are coming for him," she blurted, one hand near her mouth.

Aranas pushed back from the table and stood. "Coming for him? For what? Where is he?"

"In his room. I asked him, but he won't talk. You know how he can get. As to why, they say…they say he killed four of his classmates." She glanced at the assembled cartel honchos and then gave Aranas a brief report on why the police wanted his nephew.

Ynez thought she saw the hint of a smile tug at the corner of Aranas's stern mouth before he turned to his men. He checked his watch and eyed a thug with a face like a boneless ham. "Jorge, take one of the trucks. I want him in Hermosillo by sundown."

Jorge nodded and rose. Aranas was already moving to the doorway.

"I need to talk to him," Aranas said. "Ynez, pack his things. I'll make a few phone calls so the police aren't looking too hard."

Her voice was barely more than a whisper. "They have a witness."

"He's a boy. It doesn't matter. But nobody in my family will ever get locked up if I have anything to say about it."

Aranas stalked from the casita, Ynez following close behind. His heels echoed like rifle shots in the courtyard as he made his way to the house.

# CHAPTER 2

*Two days ago, Mexico City, Mexico*

A line of men shambled along the clammy gray corridor. Their prison garb was muted, the coloring long ago washed out of it, leaving them looking like inhabitants of a monochromatic Neverland. The facility was one of three maximum-security prisons where Mexico's worst offenders were incarcerated – mass murderers, cartel hit men, and the gang bosses who operated the most powerful transnational drug-trafficking syndicates in the world. It was famous for having never had an escape, until the elusive assassin known as El Rey – the King of Swords – had vanished. The episode had been quickly covered up by the government, and as far as the public was concerned, the edifice was still the ultimate prison.

*Don* Aranas sat on his bunk and watched as his fellow inmates made their way past his cell. He always took care to keep the barred door closed and locked lest some overenthusiastic member of a rival cartel make a play for him. There were any number of high prices on his head, but his own influence in the prison was such that he could set his own hours and keep adequate security, so he was never in jeopardy.

He'd been arrested six months earlier in a bafflingly easy raid on an oceanfront hotel in Sinaloa, where he'd been taken without a fight. The papers had dined upon lurid accounts of the capture for months, but after the initial public fascination with the account had faded, other matters had filled their pages, particularly the bloody turf war being waged against the Sinaloa Cartel by a splinter group that had formed after Aranas had been taken into custody, led by his former second-in-command. Bodies were now found throughout the state on a daily basis, usually tortured and mutilated, as those loyal to Aranas battled their former colleagues for a business worth billions. The contagion had spread to Baja California and ultimately throughout the regions where Aranas had built networks, and the death toll continued to mount steadily as the police watched, powerless to slow it.

He rose, and with a glance at his watch, stepped to his sink and washed his face, taking care to smooth his dyed hair into place. His eyes absently swept the cell, which was filled with every comfort – flat-panel television, fully stocked bar, a pharmaceutical cabinet that would have been the envy of any addict, a chest containing weapons, and a microwave for late night snacks. He'd arranged for call girls to visit several times a week. All in all his time in prison would have been a nice life for any but the richest of his countrymen.

Aranas caught his reflection in the mirror and shook his head. Where had the time gone? Who was the aging man staring back at him? It seemed impossible that it was he, yet there was no denying that no matter how wealthy and privileged one was, time had its way with everyone, and the years of stress and abuse hadn't been kind.

"Better than the alternative, right?" he muttered to himself, and turned to eye the cell door once the corridor was empty. He checked the time again and resisted the urge to pace restlessly. It wouldn't be long now.

~ ~ ~

Officer Raphael Cifuentes walked along the cell block with ponderous steps. The decade he'd been working as a guard at the maximum-control facility weighed on him; although he was only forty, he felt more like sixty-five. But as he checked each cell and nodded to the prisoners, he reminded himself that he could have had it a lot worse. His cousins all worked in construction and hauled heavy cinderblocks up ladders in the hot sun ten hours a day. That was real work – whereas his job, which was in reality babysitting some of the most privileged criminals in the world, would have seemed like a vacation to them.

He reached one end of the wing and turned the corner, eyeing the convicts with familiarity. Most bore him no grudge. He was just going through the motions for a paycheck, and they understood that it wasn't his choice to keep them behind bars. Cifuentes was a small cog in this particular machine, and he made his daily rounds as bearable as possible, stopping occasionally to exchange a few words with a convict or to take a request for an illicit substance from an inmate who'd burned through his stash. As in prisons all over the world, if you had money, the time you did wasn't nearly as hard as that served by a broke lowlife. Money commanded respect, especially in a poor country renowned for its corruption. Everything was for sale, and in prison it was only a matter of price.

That any of these men was behind bars was the miracle, given their clout and the wealth they'd amassed. Most were believed to have gone to prison willingly, fatigued of the constant threat of death in the outside world after years operating as heads of their respective cartels. What families they had were well insulated from the violence that was their stock in trade, but they would never be safe from attack; no matter how elevated their rank, they could be killed at any time, if not by the army, by their rivals or even their own men. The stakes were high, and most had gotten to the top by using the same approach – striking when the right opportunity presented itself, eliminating their rivals or leaders.

"How's the back?" one of the prisoners asked as Cifuentes moved past his cell.

"Oh, you know. Some days are better than others."

"Don't try to lift anything heavy. That's a killer," the prisoner advised. This inmate was a lieutenant with the Knights Templar Cartel, rumored to have murdered hundreds with his own hands, but he was always courteous to the guards, Cifuentes included. Cifuentes had confided to him the prior day that his sciatica was flaring up, and the cartel killer had offered some advice on home remedies to alleviate the suffering. Cifuentes often carried requests for special tequilas or drug cocktails for him, so the inmate viewed him with the same benevolence he would have reserved for a trusted servant.

"The walking helps. But no fast moves," Cifuentes agreed.

The prisoner barked a harsh laugh. "Not many places to run to in here, are there?"

"True words, my friend," Cifuentes said with a wave, and continued on his round, anxious to return to his comfortable seat and portable radio.

When he reached the last cell on the wing he froze, open-mouthed.

It was empty.

Which was impossible.

He raised his handheld radio to his lips and whispered into it, not daring to raise his voice lest the other prisoners hear him. "Dispatch, I'm at C-121. Is the prisoner in the infirmary or something?"

The speaker crackled and a terse voice emanated from it. "Repeat."

"C-121 is empty. Where's the inmate?" Cifuentes didn't dare use the man's name, even in the security of the compound.

Static hissed from the radio, and he turned the volume down. It wouldn't do to have the cell block riled up, and there were few surer ways to do so than to introduce the unexpected. When the radio crackled back to life, it was a different voice, which Cifuentes immediately recognized as the shift supervisor.

"Prisoner is supposed to be in his cell."

The blood drained from Cifuentes's face and he swallowed hard as he raised the radio and murmured into it, "Negative. There's nobody here."

The pause seemed to last forever.

"Are you sure?"

Cifuentes's voice cracked when he spoke. "Positive."

He waited a few moments for instruction, and then the sirens klaxoned overhead and all hell broke loose.

The unthinkable had happened.

*Don* Aranas had escaped.

# CHAPTER 3

Guards waited outside Aranas's cell while the warden and a team of high-ranking officials stood in the enclosed space, studying every surface as they fumed. How were they supposed to announce that the most wanted man in Mexico had vanished into thin air? The political repercussions would be staggering, not to mention that most of their careers would be effectively over.

"I want this cell completely dismantled. He couldn't have gotten far. When did you sound the perimeter alarms?" the warden barked at his subordinate.

"Right after the report that he wasn't in his cell." Which wasn't completely true – before putting out the alert, the shift supervisor had double-checked to verify that the prisoner hadn't had an emergency medical problem and been transported to the infirmary. That had taken ten minutes, but there was no need to bore his boss with the extent of the lag – what was done was done.

"And when was he last seen?"

"Half an hour earlier. No more than forty minutes, on the outside. We're still checking."

"Damn it. We need to put out an APB and alert all law enforcement immediately," the warden griped. Any hope of containing the news had just evaporated. If the crime lord had managed to make it outside the prison, he could be just about anywhere in one of the world's most populated cities by now. "And the security cameras on the block?"

"They're being reviewed, but nobody saw anything, from early reports."

"Warden? Might want to look at this." One of the police officials was standing by the bathroom area, pointing at the shower stall.

Nobody mentioned the cabinets and other furnishings in the cell, nor that the prisoner's humble abode was essentially a private luxury suite. Some things were best not to belabor.

"What is it?"

"Looks like a seam to me."

The warden squinted at the area in question and then called over his shoulder to his assistant. "Bring a flashlight."

Five minutes later the men had dislodged a piece of flooring eighteen inches square and were peering down a dirt shaft, where a knotted rope dropped into the darkness. The warden reluctantly placed the call he'd been dreading, and the city's security force went to red alert as a squad of heavily armed police arrived to explore what was undoubtedly a tunnel.

A team of elite Federal Police arrived in full combat gear, and after taking in the situation, the leader ordered the room cleared and prepared his group to lower themselves into the void. They secured their lines and rappelled down the vertical shaft, their helmet lights illuminating the way, until the leader's boots thumped against the dirt tunnel floor forty feet below the prison. The rest arrived at the bottom moments later. The gunmen swept the darkness with their M-16 rifles, sensing nothing moving, but cautious nonetheless.

The leader used hand signals and two of the team switched on high-power LED lamps. The beams reflected off steel struts that supported wood beams overhead, and the leader murmured into his helmet mic.

"Christ. There's even an AC duct in here."

The group moved further into the tunnel, where fifteen feet from the descent shaft a set of railway tracks stretched into nothingness. The leader swept the area with one of the lamps and pointed into the gloom. The men nodded and began making their way along the subterranean passage.

An hour into the exploration they arrived at the far end, where a modified motorcycle lay abandoned, its drivetrain hooked to a makeshift railway car capable of accommodating at least three men. The lead officer glared at the chute leading upward and shook his head. He already knew what he'd find when they ascended to ground level: an abandoned building or construction site. There was no other explanation for how so much dirt could have been excavated without anyone noticing – either it had been hauled off or used as compaction for a new build, both of which would raise eyebrows unless it was an active construction project.

His worst fear was realized as he climbed the rungs of a well-traveled ladder that had been built into the shaft wall and surfaced in a gloomy cinderblock room, the walls unfinished gray, the ground dusty and filled with debris.

He radioed in his position, and within minutes dozens of similarly attired officers had taken over the site, a partially completed office complex that the building permit said had been started a month after *Don* Aranas had taken up residence in his cell.

When the warden heard the news, he looked shocked, as did the men gathered around him. Aranas had achieved the impossible right under his nose. Later, it would surface that the prisoner hadn't ever been moved from his cell, as protocol dictated in order to reduce tunneling risk; nor had it been considered to keep him on anything but the ground floor – both violations of basic prisoner handling that would cost everyone involved their jobs.

By the time the airports had been alerted, several hours had passed, which would cause further consternation when it was broadcast by an investigative reporter. With that sort of institutional incompetence, Aranas could have breezed around town, had a nice dinner, and taken in a few table dances before boarding the private plane that had no doubt spirited him away.

International outrage from countries where Aranas was also a wanted man had little effect, no more than did calls for everyone's head. In the end, the man who'd proved impossible to jail had shown his captors to be idiots, disgusting a population so jaded by political corruption that many were surprised that he'd ever seen the inside of a prison in the first place.

# CHAPTER 4

*Yesterday, Washington, D.C.*

A wall-mounted television blared CNN to an audience of six men seated around a mahogany conference table. A blonde with a trace of a New England accent, shellacked hair, and a vapid expression earnestly read the teleprompter with just the appropriate amount of outrage.

"Our investigation has determined that at least three of the most lucrative petroleum leases in Mexico were not awarded in what anyone could consider a fair or balanced matter. Charges of favoritism and bribery are widespread, although government officials in Mexico, who have launched their own investigation, assured our reporters that there was no evidence of impropriety."

The man at the head of the table exchanged a dark look with the attendee next to him, a graying official with a neatly trimmed beard. Nobody believed the Mexican investigation was anything but a whitewash operation, just as so many of their own country's tended to be. It was the way of the world, and this group was long over any illusion that governments did anything but mislead and lie. After all, that was their job, and they were specialists.

When the program segment drew to a close, the bearded man switched it off and a younger staffer with steel-rimmed square spectacles and an oil slick of hair combed over a premature bald spot hit the lights. The man at the head of the table sat back and took his time, looking at each of the assembly before clearing his throat.

"What the fine folks at the network don't know is that the usual story about paying for favorable influence is just the tip of the iceberg. Of course our companies attempted to do the same thing, through the usual channels, but they were stonewalled."

"Why?" the bespectacled staffer asked.

"We think there's something bigger in play here. When the usual suspects suddenly lose interest in feathering their nests, it flies in the face of experience. Especially down there. So we did our own nosing around, and what we discovered isn't good."

Radcliff Arlington was a senior official with a division of the U.S. clandestine apparatus that officially didn't exist. It didn't report to Congress, wasn't on the books anywhere, and had no formal budget. And yet it was one of the most powerful cabals in the capital, part think tank and part operational group that implemented the directives of its superiors without question. Today the managing council was turned to Mexico, but its interests were varied and global. Loosely, their function was to determine what risks and opportunities existed to further American interests. But those interests usually had little to do with the taxpayer and everything to do with what was best for the network of corporations that operated the government for their mutual enrichment.

"So who did the end run around our people?" asked the bearded man, Stanford Hope. "What happened? I thought we bought the bidding and had it locked up."

"Care to take the floor, Lawry?" Arlington inquired. The so-named analyst flipped a folder open and peered at it with a frown.

"One third of all the contracts have gone to front organizations we believe are ultimately controlled by the Chinese. It's a little more sophisticated than usual, but that's where our bets are placed. The shell corporations span the globe, of course, but the money's definitely from China, so whether they're domiciled in Slovenia or Macau is irrelevant.

"That spells trouble, obviously, gentlemen. The Chinese have been extremely active over the last few years funding infrastructure in Latin America – the new canal in Panama, bridge loans and highway projects in Argentina, dams in Central and South America. And they're doing the same thing in Africa. We believe this is a game changer – I don't need to remind anyone that Mexico's our backyard. If they can beat us there, it's over for our influence."

Heads nodded. It went without saying to the men around the table that whatever was best for the oil, pharmaceutical, and financial interests that helped fund the group's black budget was best for the world. The growth of Chinese and Russian influence in blocking American hegemony was considered the number one threat to the de facto American empire that had been carefully crafted post World War II, using a combination of military threat and central bank warfare. That the U.S. had military bases in ninety percent of the world's nations wasn't common knowledge – but that it used its various pet financial creatures, its development banks, to prey on other countries and convince their leadership to indebt themselves with dollars they could never hope to pay back, thus putting them under the American government's thumb, was even less well understood.

The men in the room were the second generation that orchestrated the machinations, who coordinated the strategy and tactics required to run the world their way, for lack of any other explanation. While democracy and freedom were touted as excuses for most of their campaigns, the truth was they only liked either idea if the countries involved did as they were told and sacrificed the well-being of their populations so U.S. companies could profit.

It was a simple approach, if unpalatable to the great unwashed. Arlington and his ilk didn't question the legitimacy of their actions or their presumed right to operate the planet like their personal fiefdoms, and a large part of their efforts went to convincing the public that not only did groups like theirs not exist, but that the constant military offensives and destabilizations around the world were anything but what they clearly were. Other nations weren't fooled, but that didn't matter – as long as Joe Public on Main Street believed, he would continue paying his taxes and slaving in a system that was working against him.

Hope leaned forward, his expression that of a man struggling with constipation. That was his usual demeanor, so nobody paid any attention. He was brilliant, if morose most of the time, and lived alone with seven cats, his life devoted to his work.

"We must take countermeasures, but we believe that the Mexican government is talking out of both sides of its mouth. More so than usual, I might add."

Arlington nodded. "The purpose of this meeting is to explore our options. Nothing's off the table: assassinations, false flags, even invasion, if necessary. But we cannot allow China to eat our lunch in Mexico, or we're their bitch. Do I make myself clear?"

The meeting lasted four more hours, at the end of which a rough plan had been crafted. It would need fine-tuning, but the foundation was sound. When the men went their separate ways, some to dinner with their spouses, others to their anonymous offices to crunch numbers, they at least had a direction, although final approval would need to come from their corporate masters.

Arlington was the last to leave the conference room, and before he did, he paused for a moment and shook his head, a bemused twinkle in his eye. Some said the devil's greatest feat was convincing the world that he didn't exist.

Satan had nothing on them.

He was an amateur.

# CHAPTER 5

*Today, Mexico City, Mexico*

Streaks of clouds marbled the early afternoon sky through the high-altitude city's infamous smog layer, which blanketed the metropolis in spite of the rigid emissions regulations in place to improve air quality. Living in Districto Federal, or DF, as the locals called it, had been compared by physicians to smoking a pack of cigarettes a day, and the life expectancy of its residents was a good decade below that of similar cities.

Carla Vega opened the door of her mineral white BMW 428 convertible and slipped from behind the wheel, the hard top locked in place. The neighborhood was one of many good ones located only a block from the ubiquitous slums into which police didn't dare venture. She was used to the paradox of so much wealth concentrated only meters from abject poverty – it was simply the way things were, and had been since before she'd been born. Like most Mexicans, she didn't expect circumstances to change and become fairer, because the politicians were all corrupt, and power resided in the hands of ruling families who'd been running the nation for generations. She was fortunate to be a member of the emerging middle class who could earn a king's ransom, but unlike the populations of other industrialized nations, she never took it for granted – there were too many reminders of how frail the social construct was.

She locked the door, activating the car alarm, and glanced at her watch. Her lunch date was in a few minutes, and she had plenty of time to make it – a rarity for her; she was usually ten to fifteen minutes late, as the local custom considered anything less than a half hour to be on time. Carla stretched her long, toned legs and began the walk to the restaurant on the ground level of a steel and glass high-rise.

The last months had been surreal. Her new relationship felt as unlikely as it was irresistible, the combination of the forbidden and the perilous potent fuel to an adrenaline junkie who thrived on constant stimulation. She was lost in her thoughts as she neared the corner and didn't register the three men who closed on her from a pair of doorways until it was too late.

Kidnapping or robbery was a constant threat, and she silently cursed her carelessness. She'd normally have been more aware of her surroundings, but a few seconds of distraction had been sufficient to court disaster, and she now found herself facing thugs whose desperation was written across their faces. Their clothes were shabby and worn, and their eyes darted with the manic energy of the meth-addicted.

The middle assailant pulled a .25-caliber handgun from his jacket pocket, held it close to his side, and growled, "Hand over your purse and your watch, hot pants. Scream or make a racket and you'll wish you'd never been born."

The man next to him grinned malevolently, revealing blackened gums and missing bottom teeth. "That's right. Now, bitch."

Carla slowly slid her purse strap from her shoulder and unclasped her watchband, her eyes never leaving the gunman's. She could always get a new iPhone or Tag Heuer; she was lucky they weren't going to force her to an ATM for an express kidnapping, where she'd be forced to withdraw money before they ran off with her belongings.

"Please, can I keep my phone? It has all my contacts in it," Carla pleaded.

The toothless man edged toward her and a switchblade flashed in the sunlight, its ugly blade gleaming. "How 'bout I cut off your nose instead?"

She gasped at his obvious intent as he neared — and then the gunman's eyes widened and his weapon flew from his hand. He pitched forward, stunned. His mouth worked silently as he fought for breath, the air knocked from his lungs, and she stepped back to avoid his bulk as he tumbled forward. Then the toothless knife wielder's look of surprise turned to one of pain. His switchblade made a slow balletic arc through the air as he went down with a strangled scream, clutching his forearm. The third mugger took off at a sprint, running as fast as his legs would carry him.

Carla was still in shock at how quickly everything had happened – in only seconds the attackers had been neutralized and disaster averted. Her eyes met her lunch date's as he stepped forward and scooped up the dropped gun.

"You okay?" El Rey asked, taking in the disabled attackers before his eyes drifted to her face.

"Y-yes. I'm just…I should have been more careful."

El Rey moved to the two injured thugs. "Two choices. Get out of here, or spend the rest of your miserable lives in wheelchairs. What's it going to be?"

The toothless man struggled to his feet and helped his partner up, and the pair limped off as El Rey watched them in disgust. Only once they were out of sight did he take Carla's hand and lead her wordlessly toward the restaurant. Carla inched closer and snuck a glance at his profile, as untroubled as a baby lamb's, no evidence that he'd just been in mortal combat, outnumbered three to one by armed lowlifes.

"Thank you," she whispered.

He shrugged. "I got here a little early and saw your car go around the block. I'm glad I was able to keep you out of trouble." The truth was more complex – the assassin's instincts were as sharp as when he'd been operational, and he routinely arrived anywhere he was to meet someone at least thirty minutes early so he could reconnoiter the area and spot any traps or surveillance. He didn't suspect Carla of any duplicity, but she wasn't a pro, and he had many powerful enemies, even though few would recognize him with his bleach-lightened modish haircut, sparse goatee, baseball cap, and sunglasses.

If anyone knew they were seeing each other, it could endanger him, and he left nothing to chance.

"Should we get my car in case they come back?"

He shook his head. "They won't. They saw easy pickings. They got broken ribs and a shattered radius for their trouble, and they lost their gun. But if it makes you feel better, when we're done with lunch, I'll get the car for you."

She smiled, still shaken but quickly recovering as the adrenaline seeped from her system. "My knight in shining armor."

He returned the smile. "Tarnished but serviceable."

Once they were seated at a quiet table at the rear of the restaurant, the assassin with his back to the wall out of habit, he leaned forward toward her and took one of her hands. "How's my favorite reporter?"

She took a sip of water. "Working hard on a few stories." She paused. "I missed you."

"Me too."

Carla had been out of town, chasing down a lead, and had just returned after a four-day absence. Her occasional dates with El Rey had intensified over the last month as they'd become intimate, and they now spent many of their nights together.

El Rey released her hand and sat back. "Any progress?"

"The sources are all terrified of being identified by the cartel, obviously. So lots of hearsay and supposition, but not a lot of concrete links."

"If it was easy, everyone would do it, right?"

She nodded. "That's always been my philosophy."

The waiter returned and they ordered. When he departed, Carla reported on the progress she'd made on her investigation into the rumored influence of the Los Zetas Cartel over several prominent national politicians. El Rey had proven helpful in his suggestions; his knowledge of the cartels was comprehensive, although he was always careful not to share anything that only he might know. The last thing either could afford was even a whiff that he was still alive, much less involved with her.

"Where do you think the trail will lead? Dead end or red-handed?" he asked.

"Hard to say. You know how these things go. Everyone's got an agenda – political rivals trying to smear each other, cartel mouthpieces posing as legitimate sources, trying to build support for their groups or mislead their enemies. The art's in sorting through all the chaff."

Their meals arrived and they ate quietly. Carla tried not to be annoyed by the way the assassin's eyes continuously roamed over the other diners, never settling on her for more than a few moments. She couldn't possibly grasp his background, the things that had made him the man he was, filled with contradictions and warring imperatives, and she saw no benefit to judging him. Yes, he was a stone-cold killer. Or had been. But he was also…

"Did you see that Aranas escaped?" he asked in his seductively soft voice.

"Of course. Biggest story in Mexico."

"Are you going to follow up on it?"

"What do you think?"

"Just be careful. My gut says there are wheels within wheels there. From what I know of the man, nothing is as it seems."

A single frown line creased her forehead. "What do you think happened?"

"All I'll say is that I was surprised when he was caught. The entire affair felt off to me," he said.

"Off, how?"

"One of the richest men in the world gets taken down over a series of rookie mistakes? Oh, I don't know. Let's just say my eyebrows rose when I read the coverage, which was identical across all the papers and appeared almost instantly – almost like they had the articles ready to go before he was arrested."

She studied him. "So suspicious for a young man."

"Maybe I'll go into the reporting game."

Carla laughed and toasted him with her mineral water. "I don't need any more competition. It's hard enough as it is."

"All I'm saying is that Aranas rarely does anything that isn't deliberate, and being too good at your job could carry more risk than being dumb and blind."

Her expression grew serious. "You really think it's dangerous to dig into?"

His eyes locked with hers. "I wouldn't go near it, and I don't scare."

The waiter arrived and cleared their plates. El Rey ordered coffee, leaving Carla to consider his words. A man who'd taken down three attackers without breaking a sweat was advising her to avoid a story. She wondered if he knew something she didn't, and tried to read his intelligent eyes to no avail. The same inscrutability she found fascinating was a double-edged sword – he'd advised her early on that there were some things he couldn't discuss, and part of their unspoken agreement was that she wouldn't press.

He seemed to sense her scrutiny and looked up. "Let someone else run point on this one, Carla. If for no other reason, because I'm asking you not to step into the line of fire."

"And you can't tell me any more than that? Just to ignore the biggest story of the year?"

"You already know the rest. Aranas is more powerful than many governments. He's got eyes and ears everywhere. And he'll stop at nothing if he thinks you're a threat. Trust me – you don't want that man as an enemy."

"You speaking from experience?" she asked.

He shook his head. "Maybe one day over cocktails I'll tell you more. Until then, let's keep you safe, shall we?"

"Are you sure there's nothing I can do to get it out of you sooner?"

He leaned across the table and whispered in her ear.

Carla could feel the blush from her hairline to her feet, and for an instant felt like she was thirteen again, kissed for the first time. This man, this assassin, was the only one who'd ever made her feel that way – and he did it effortlessly with only a few words.

She cleared her throat and ran her fingers through her hair. "Too bad you ordered coffee."

As if reading her mind, the waiter appeared with their cups and set them on the table before vanishing.

El Rey grinned. "I should have asked for the check."

She matched his expression. "Drink fast."

# CHAPTER 6

Captain Romero Cruz's intercom line buzzed as he sat at his office desk and morosely studied a pile of reports. He groaned under his breath as he reached over the stack and punched a glowing button on his phone.

"Yes?"

"*Capitan,* your presence has been requested at a meeting in the commissioner's office."

Cruz cringed. Meetings were the bane of his professional existence. Hours of infighting and political jockeying that normally accomplished nothing other than giving a bunch of functionaries with little else a way to while away their day. Cruz, on the other hand, as the head of the anti-cartel task force, was always overloaded, and since the new government had taken power, even more so. The arrest of many of the established cartel heads had created power vacuums that were being filled by ever more dangerous and reckless criminals, and the birth of a number of new cartels that were well equipped, motivated, and ruthless. The most visible, the Jalisco Nueva Generación Cartel in Guadalajara, had recently waged all-out war against the authorities, even bringing down military helicopters with surface-to-air missiles.

The Jalisco Cartel was the object of his attention these days, as the organization was making a big push in Mexico City to displace the Sinaloa Cartel and the tattered remnants of the Los Zetas, whose top leadership had been killed or captured in a series of daring raids that signaled a change of direction in the government's approach to criminal syndicates.

"Do I have to?" Cruz protested. "Can't you tell them I died or shot myself in the foot or something?"

His receptionist was silent. She had no sense of humor, Cruz knew, yet some part of him still tried to elicit a response even knowing it was in vain.

He sighed. "What time?"

"Five minutes."

"Of course, with no advance warning," Cruz griped, and hung up before he could say anything inappropriate. Just like the old days, when he'd be summoned whenever his supervisor had a whim, interrupting vital operations so the idiot could wax philosophical – or worse, propose lamebrained forays that would have resulted in countless law enforcement casualties. Since Cruz had declared his emancipation from the dolt, his life had been easier, reporting once a month to a group who largely rubber-stamped whatever approach he recommended. As the senior authority on cartels within the Federal Police, he was respected and deferred to, which was as it should be – he'd earned his stripes the hard way and had the bullet wounds and scars to prove it.

Cruz stood and moved to the door, where his uniform jacket hung from a hook. He pulled it on, glanced at his reflection in the glass covering one of the prints on his wall, and took a moment to straighten his tie. He had no idea why he was being called to the top floor, but whatever the reason, he'd project the authority of his office lest some new genius try to steamroller him.

The elevator ride was mercifully short, and when he arrived at the commissioner's office, the secretary nodded a wary greeting. "You're to go right in, *Capitan*."

Cruz found himself in a room with five suits, one of whom he recognized with loathing: Eduardo Godoy, his old supervisor, as big a waste of carbon and water as he'd ever encountered.

"*Capitan*, please, come and join us," the commissioner said. "Have a seat. We've been waiting for your arrival to begin." Cruz sat in the only empty chair, thankfully as far from Godoy as he could get in the confined space. The commissioner, another political appointee who'd taken the job after Godoy had been shifted sideways in the power structure, reviewed his notes with exaggerated formality before looking around the room. "I've called this meeting to announce a new emergency working group. The object is the investigation of *Don* Aranas's escape, with an emphasis on locating him and taking him back into custody at all costs. The group will have any and all support it needs, without restriction."

Everyone but Cruz nodded. It wasn't surprising to him that the official response to the public relations disaster was the formation of a crisis team, which would be ultimately blamed for lack of results. He'd seen the game played enough times that he was already framing his refusal when he was asked to chair it.

Cruz's mouth fell open as the commissioner continued, "To head the effort, I've appointed the best man for the job: Eduardo Godoy, whose expertise navigating complicated political waters and experience with police work should serve the group well."

Cruz said nothing. The plus side of the selection of Godoy was that he would be the sacrificial lamb when the administration needed a public face for the government's failure to recapture the crime lord. Godoy was too unseasoned to appreciate that he was being set up, which a part of Cruz delighted in even as he loathed the idea of working with the pompous imbecile.

Godoy stood, as though ready to address a class of junior students. "Gentlemen, a pleasure to see so many familiar faces. Together we'll get to the bottom of what happened, and we'll pick up the scent of Aranas and follow it wherever it leads. I've already commandeered working space for a strike team, and the president has given his personal assurance that we'll have anything we need."

"How?" Cruz asked, his voice mild. Godoy stared at him like Cruz had asked the question in Swahili.

"Pardon me?" Godoy sputtered.

"*How* will we achieve all this?"

Godoy waved a careless hand. "Through perseverance and tireless police work."

"I see. Such as?"

Godoy's eyes narrowed. *"Capitan* Cruz, may I remind you that this is a time of national emergency? It would be best to put aside personal differences and focus on the job, don't you think?"

"Couldn't agree more. How do we do that, exactly? Who's in charge of what, what are the first steps we should take, what approach should we use?"

The commissioner rescued Godoy from being forced to admit that he had no idea how to do anything he'd assured them they would accomplish. "The group is new. Your job is to figure out the best way to proceed. I want you all to hand off your current workload to subordinates, requisition whatever staff you need, and get to work on this. Godoy will act as a liaison between the group and the government, as well as manage the media. I need you to cooperate with each other," he finished, staring directly at Cruz.

Cruz looked away. "I understand, but honestly, I have a full docket of active investigations that require my personal attention. It is therefore with regret that I must respectfully decline the opportunity. But I'll be happy to recommend a worthy replacement."

The commissioner's expression hardened. "I'm afraid this isn't an invitation. We need our top people on this, Cruz. You're our best. We can't afford a substitution. I hope you understand."

Cruz was ready for the bulldozing. "My ongoing operations could potentially thwart conflicts involving hundreds of casualties. How could locating one man, who was no doubt running his cartel quite handily from inside the prison, be more important than stopping–"

Godoy cut him off. "We're not here to question why we've been chartered with this manhunt. Orders come from the highest levels." He stared Cruz down. "The highest. *Capitan,* I recognize that we've had our disagreements; however, I'm willing to put them behind us for the good of the mission. I ask you to do the same."

Cruz realized that for all his dismissal of Godoy as a fool, he'd been outflanked by the man. There was no way to refuse other than resigning, and if he did over disliking one of the members of the group, he'd have a hell of a time collecting his pension – nobody appreciated pettiness, even from a national hero, and he was sure

Godoy would lobby for some loophole to be found that delayed his payout indefinitely.

Cruz sighed. "Very well. But it will take some doing. I have a number of sensitive cases in play. To just drop them in someone's lap could cost police lives."

Godoy offered a patronizing smile. "Of course. We'll all do our best to accommodate you, *Capitan*."

When the meeting finally concluded, Cruz returned to his office lost in thought. There had to be some way to sidestep Godoy and foist his involvement off on someone else.

He just needed to figure out how.

But in the meantime, he had investigations to transition to his second-in-command, Lieutenant Fernando Briones. Cruz tapped his subordinate's extension into his phone and called him over. When Briones was seated, Cruz paced in front of his window as he explained the new situation.

"The most pressing operation is the child slavery ring. We're only hours from their next shipment from Guatemala, and if we're lucky, our informant knows where the girls are arriving," Cruz said. His group had been investigating the New Millennium Cartel's push into child prostitution in the capital, a widespread problem that had drawn the outrage of the media. Girls, barely adolescents, were kidnapped or sold by their parents to traffickers in impoverished Central American countries like Honduras, Guatemala, Nicaragua, and El Salvador, transported to Mexico City, and put to work as sex slaves while strung out on drugs. The average age of children in the ring they were investigating was twelve years old, but their informant had revealed that there were girls as young as ten routinely shipped north. Predators from the United States paid handsomely for sexual tourism where they could engage in illegal behavior with children, and the cartels were all too ready to capitalize on that market.

"I can run the interception. Shouldn't be anything but routine. The hard part's done – now we just need to keep surveillance in place and be prepared to move," Briones assured Cruz. The younger man eyed his superior. "You don't look happy with the new assignment."

"I'm not. It's bullshit and we both know it. They have a boob running it, and it's all for political theater purposes anyway. If they'd really wanted to stop Aranas from escaping, they'd have locked him in solitary on the second floor and checked his cell daily, rather than providing luxury accommodations and free access to anything he could think of. The whole thing's a bad joke for the papers. Waste of time."

"How long do you think it'll take before you can bow out?"

"Probably a week or two. After that, there will be some other crisis to occupy the public's attention – the president might get a new haircut, or some celeb might not wear panties to a nightclub."

Briones perked up at the idea. "I'm available to handle that investigation, *Capitan*."

Cruz smiled sadly. "Anything for the job, eh, Briones?"

"I'm a career man."

"I'll bear that in mind."

# CHAPTER 7

Dust motes swirled in a beam of light that streamed from the loft apartment's skylight. The area was silent except for the whir of a high-revolution power tool at a workbench at the far end of the expansive space. A hulking figure sat on a high-back barstool at a workbench, safety glasses in place, hunched over a project, his brow furrowed with concentration as he went about his chore. After a few more refinements, he held one end of the metal casing up to a lamp mounted to a shelf in front of him. He squinted at the furrow he'd made along the edge and inspected his work as he hummed atonally to himself.

He nodded in satisfaction and retrieved a package of orange foam earplugs. He tore the plastic open with his teeth and compressed the plugs before wedging them into his ears, and then activated a small vacuum, taking care to clean up the fine metal dust his labors had generated. He moved the nozzle in a geometric pattern, tracing squares, his movements as methodical as a robot's, cleaning until the work area was spotless.

When he was done, he toed the vacuum off, hung the nozzle back in place, and removed the plugs. Everything was going well. Perfectly, in fact.

A bell chimed, startling him, and he cried out involuntarily, his voice tense. He looked in disbelief at the digital clock blinking on the bench. He'd placed it there so he didn't lose track of his hours and work through the night, as had been his practice before his benefactor had suggested the simple preventive measure.

12:30 on the nose.

He gently set the casing he'd been grinding on a pad and laid the tool beside it, checking to ensure it was off even though it clearly

32

was. When he stood he was easily six feet – tall for a Mexican, pudgy from lack of exercise, but reasonably proportioned. He slid the safety glasses over his brow, placed them on a rolling tray by his side, and then moved to the intercom, which was equipped with a closed-circuit camera and screen. He activated the camera and peered at the black-and-white image of a young man waiting impatiently at the main door downstairs.

"Be there in a minute," he said into the speaker, his voice flat and toneless, and felt at the keys he kept on a lanyard around his neck. It wouldn't do to go out without them. He needed to lock up. Danger was everywhere.

He crossed the room to the kitchen, glanced up at the light from the overhead dome, and flipped a switch labeled "K-1." LED lamps blinked to life. He switched them off, muttering to himself.

"On. Off."

He repeated the process and the quiet words, and then moved to the next switch and performed the ritual until he'd flipped every switch in the room twice. When he arrived at his front door, he left the final lamp illuminated and twisted the top deadbolt with delicate fingers. A surgeon's hands, someone had once said, or a pianist's. The clank as the first lock sprang open caused him to wince, as did the sound of the second, and the third. Each time his shoulders shuddered as though gunshots were echoing through the room, but he continued until the door swung open.

Out in the hall he closed each lock with his keys, different shapes denoting which fit which deadbolt, the process as familiar as bathing or brushing his teeth – something he was guilty of doing obsessively, sometimes twenty times a day. After trying the pewter knob to confirm that the door was indeed secure, he walked to the stairs. Motion lights turned on as he approached the stairwell, which brightened as he neared.

At the street-level lobby below, he approached the front entrance, which at one point had been glass but which he'd long ago replaced with steel. Welded lateral bars reinforced the half-inch plate, outfitted with industrial hinges to support the heavy weight. He checked the intercom screen mounted by the side to verify the man waiting outside was the same one he'd seen when he was upstairs. It was. The man was watching something on the street, something outside of the security cam's field of view.

The occupant unclasped two bolts that secured a rectangular hatch mounted to the door at shoulder level and slid it to the side, wincing again at the sound the metal made as it moved. It was time to oil the groove, he reminded himself, and this time he wouldn't forget – as he had the last few times.

The man on the front porch looked up at the slot and held up a plastic bag. "Delivery. Pancho's. The usual. Just the way you ordered."

"Pass it through."

The delivery man did as asked, and after a long moment a tray slid out through the gap with a small wad of twenty-peso notes neatly wrapped with a rubber band. "The tip's included," the occupant's voice said from within the building, and then the tray retracted, closing the portal to the outside world and leaving the delivery man holding the cash.

He pocketed the money and retraced his steps to his motorcycle parked on the sidewalk and shook his head. Every day the exact same delivery, the exact same ritual, without variation, for the eight months he'd been working for the restaurant. Enough food to feed a family of four, always prepared the same way, the order sent online with detailed delivery instructions – as though someone might err and get it wrong, or forget that the customer wanted exactly three packets of salt and one of pepper, measured amounts of various salsas, and plastic utensils with an extra knife, just in case the first was dull.

Always the same.

The customer was a nutcase, obviously, he thought as he kick-started the ancient Kawasaki. But he tipped well, and that was all the delivery man cared about. Always twenty percent, whereas many of the cheapskates on his route gave him a measly five or ten like they were doing him a favor.

The occupant stood by the door until he heard the motorcycle rev and pull away, and then he checked and rechecked the bolts, feeling to ensure they were properly seated several times before turning and mounting the stairs. The building was empty save for his loft, but he still listened apprehensively for any sign of life when he arrived at the upstairs landing. You never knew. Not with complete certainty. Nothing in life was certain. One couldn't be too careful.

After a long pause he strode back to his door and unlocked the deadbolts, taking his time, humming. He was hungry, but the food would have to last until tomorrow's delivery. He could pace himself; the meals were individually wrapped so he couldn't mistakenly eat too much and be left starving tomorrow morning, a constant fear of his after he'd done so once, exactly nine hundred and seventeen days ago. That wouldn't do. He still remembered it vividly and hoped to never repeat it. Any trip outside his world required preparation, and that took time and planning. When he'd realized he had no food, he'd panicked, and it had taken the remainder of the day to recover from the anxiety he'd experienced walking the two blocks to the market.

No, that would never do at all.

Across the street, two men watched the delivery with boredom from the window of the apartment they'd occupied for four years. Both had prison tattoos that ran the length of their arms, and their faces were scarred from long-forgotten fights. The stouter of the pair grunted.

"El Maquino will dine well another day," he said.

His companion grinned. "The boss will be pleased to hear it."

AKM assault rifles leaned against the base of the window, spare magazines by their sides. They'd never been used. But that wasn't the point. The daily delivery was one of the risk points in their twenty-four-hour vigil. The men would be replaced by the evening crew in another eight hours, who would sit watching the screens that displayed images of the building from every angle, sent by infrared and night-vision-equipped cameras discreetly mounted for thorough coverage. Their instructions were simple and unvarying: protect at all costs the building's occupant, whom they knew only by his moniker, El Maquino. Protect him from what, they didn't have to ask.

Danger. Adversaries. Those who would do him harm.

Whether El Maquino knew they were there, watching the street and providing additional protection to the fortress-like building, they could never be sure. They simply knew their orders, which they followed to the letter. Failure to maintain vigilance would be greeted harshly, they'd been assured, and they believed it.

And so they watched and waited, passing the time telling each other stories and lying about conquests, never taking their eyes off the entrance. Another pair did the same at the rear of the building, monitoring the smaller alley and the array of motion detectors that lined the roof of the four-story structure. Two more sat in vehicles strategically positioned on the street, the drivers similarly armed and watching for anything suspicious.

"I wonder what he does in there all day. I mean, don't you? Tell me it isn't creepy."

"Mind your own business, and it'll be better for your health."

The first man nodded. Wise words from his elder.

Words to live by.

# CHAPTER 8

Carla took an appreciative final sip of coffee and beamed at El Rey.

"I have a surprise."

One of his eyebrows rose, and he sat forward. "I thought we already covered that. We're leaving."

She laughed. "No, I mean another one."

"Good or bad?"

"Good, I think. I just got a job offer. A big salary hike."

"Really? Congratulations."

"Thanks. The only problem is that it's in Spain. Madrid. Working for the network there."

"Do you want to take the job?"

She nodded. "Absolutely. But I want you to think about coming with me."

They sat wordlessly for a few moments. "To Spain," he repeated.

"There are worse places. And it's not like you're doing a lot here. You have no reason to stay."

"Only one," he agreed, and raised his cup to his lips.

Carla registered a tremor in his hand and shot him a look of concern. "What is it?"

"I'm due for my final shot. The antidote I told you about."

Her expression hardened. "Then get it."

"I've been trying. CISEN has been putting me off for a week."

"That's unacceptable. You kept your end of the bargain."

"Yes, although not completely unexpected. They're weasels. You have to be to take up that line of work. Nothing's ever as it seems."

"What are you saying?"

"That they don't seem to be in a big hurry to help me now that my usefulness is at an end."

She frowned. "Then you have to make them."

"Oh, I know. I'm way ahead of you. I always have at least one contingency plan."

"You think they're going to try to screw you? You have the president's word…"

It was his turn to frown. "A politician. A talking head who does what the ruling elite tell him to do. His word's worth about what any politician's promise is – which is not a hell of a lot."

"So what are you going to do? Are the symptoms getting worse?"

"They started six days ago. Just a few tics and a little muscle soreness. The shaking is new." His expression softened as he saw her obvious concern. "Don't worry. I'm not dead yet."

"I hate when you joke about it."

He shrugged. "We all go out the same way."

"Hopefully a long time from now."

El Rey nodded. "Hopefully. I'm thinking I'll pay an unexpected visit to CISEN today since I can't get anyone to return my calls. They always seem to enjoy it when I drop in unannounced."

"Aren't you worried?"

His face was unreadable. "I don't worry. I plan." He finally offered a small smile. "Weren't we talking about Madrid? That's way more cheerful than my situation."

"Once you get the shot, that's it, right? That's the final one?"

"Supposedly."

"You think that's a lie?"

"I treat everything as one until proven otherwise. In my former line of work, that was the prudent course."

She nodded. "You would make a great reporter, you know. Gorgeous, smart, charismatic…"

"I'll let you know if I need a day job. I hear you've got clout."

"Seriously, though. Will you think about Spain?"

"What's the timing?"

"I have to give them an answer by the end of the week." She shook her head. "The network here hasn't even made a new offer yet – that's how confident they are that they're the only game in town."

"One offer is no offer."

"Exactly."

"If they bettered the Spanish one, would you stay?"

She sighed and pushed her cup away. "I feel like it's time for a change. I've gone as far as I can here. Exposure to a major European market would make me far more valuable long term. Staying would be the wrong decision, at least for now. That's not to say I wouldn't ever return. But I feel like I've outgrown Mexico, you know?"

He studied her. "I do. It's an interesting proposition. Move to Spain to be the boy toy of a celebrity."

"The hours are good."

"I'll say." He caught the waiter's eye and signaled for the check. "Let me think about it."

"I won't take the job if you won't go."

He shook his head. "Yes, you will. You'll do what's smart and what's best for you. I just need to get used to the idea of leaving Mexico. I mean, I'm not married to it, and Spain is hardly the provinces…"

"It would be wonderful. We could start a new life." She didn't have to say *together.*

"You're very convincing."

The check arrived and she smiled again. "I plan to be more so."

# CHAPTER 9

*Zapopan, Jalisco, Mexico*

Steam rose off the parking lot of the Mariscos Sinaloa restaurant as the sun baked away the last of the moisture from one of the high-altitude morning showers that visited the Guadalajara area – the mountainous region drew flash storms like a magnet. Five SUVs were parked near the main building, which consisted of a massive concrete bunker topped by a three-story-high *palapa* roof. A set of brightly painted concrete stairs led to the entrance, which boasted a stylized image of a lobster and a shrimp wearing sombreros and shaking maracas. On the sidewalk in front, a row of placards had been set out by the service staff in anticipation of the restaurant opening for lunch, boasting the specials of the day prepared just like Mama used to make.

Four men with hard faces and hair trimmed close to their skulls in an unmistakably military style stood by the entrance. All wore baggy short-sleeved shirts that hung over their trousers, barely concealing the pistols in their belts.

Inside, a half-dozen figures sat drinking beer at a circular table near the kitchen. Three of them had cell phones clamped to their ears, and one was working on a laptop computer. An imposing dark-complexioned man with a mop of black curls atop a swarthy face checked his watch impatiently and sent a text message. From the four corners of the restaurant, flat-screen TVs blared the same banda video of sixteen men in identical yellow suits with purple shirts playing tubas, horns, guitar, and accordion, sidestepping rhythmically as a portly singer crooned about love gone wrong.

Hector Agundez had been, until recently, the number two man in the Sinaloa Cartel. But he'd split from that group and formed his own organization when the ever-present threat of *Don* Aranas was neutralized with its kingpin hauled off in chains. The new cartel, La Familia, had made rapid inroads into the Sinaloa Cartel's territory primarily because Agundez knew all the distribution routes and had developed relationships with most of the trafficking network as he laid the groundwork for his new gang. Sinaloa still held most of its home state, but Jalisco and points south were hotly contested, and he'd taken a lot of territory from the cartel in a short period.

Not that it had been easy. The remnants of the Knights Templar Cartel, the Jalisco Cartel, Los Zetas, and the Jalisco Nueva Generación were all fighting it out for dominance of Guadalajara, and not a day went by when there wasn't a pitched battle or a van filled with mutilated bodies abandoned in a prominent spot, accompanied by a message to rivals scrawled on a bedsheet that vowed more bloodshed to come.

*Don* Aranas's escape had sent a seismic shock through Agundez's group, and his key nucleus was busy strategizing how to best negotiate terms with Sinaloa; Aranas's reputation as invincible had been cemented by his miraculous prison break. Alliances were common between competitive groups in contested areas, and Agundez hoped Aranas wouldn't allow hard feelings to get in the way of good business. Until word of Aranas's newfound freedom hit, Agundez's plan had been to eradicate Sinaloa whenever there was a clash, but with Aranas on the loose, everything had changed. The man was a master tactician, and the Sinaloa troops would be revitalized with him at the helm again.

"Any word?" Agundez asked nobody in particular. The nearest man, Adolpho Gomez, shook his head as he continued speaking softly into his phone. Agundez scowled and rubbed a pudgy hand across his brow, the orbiting overhead fans doing little to dispel the growing muggy swelter.

A vendor in ratty clothing, his skin the color of roasted almonds from long years in the sun, was pushing an ancient icebox on wheels decorated with a hand-painted depiction of a polar bear enjoying a frozen ice pop. He made his way along the street toward the parking lot, every now and then ringing a little bell in the hopes of attracting customers, but judging by his demeanor, he wasn't having a productive time. The rickety conveyance bounced on worn rubber wheels as he neared the men by the stairs, and he rang the bell again to signal that he was open for business.

One of the guards reached into his pocket and retrieved a few ten-peso coins. He counted the change and took a few steps toward the vendor. "Got any coco?" he asked.

"Oh, certainly, sir."

The vendor opened the hinged lid of the cooler and reached inside. When his hand came out clutching a sound-suppressed semiautomatic pistol, the guard barely had time to register the weapon before it popped and a red dot appeared in the center of his head.

The coins hit the sidewalk as the dead man's knees buckled, drawing the attention of the others, but the vendor was already in motion, firing with steady deliberation as he neared. None had time to get their guns free, and all were dead before they hit the ground, the subsonic ammunition so silent the only sound was the snicking of the weapon's slide and the tinkle of spent shell casings bouncing against the pavement.

The vendor tapped his concealed earbud and muttered a few words, and then dropped the handgun back into the cooler and extracted a suppressed submachine gun. Three black SUVs rolled into the lot and pulled to a stop, and a dozen figures in full blue combat dress with Federales emblazoned across their backs leapt from the vehicles, weapons held at the ready as they ran to where the vendor waited for them, out of sight of the men in the restaurant.

The gathering of cartel thugs looked up in surprise when the armed contingent burst through the entrance. Two of the gangsters drew pistols and dove for cover as the police's automatic weapons opened up on them. The high-velocity rounds shredded through the wooden tabletops that the pair had knocked over to shield themselves, and within seconds both men were burbling their last breaths in a lake of blood.

The rest of Agundez's men stood frozen as the sound of gunfire died and the shooters approached, assault rifles trained on the survivors. Agundez's face twisted with anger as he slowly raised his hands, and the others followed suit.

"Have you lost your minds? I pay everyone for protection. Whoever is in charge of this operation—"

"Silence!" the leader of the squad barked. He glanced at the man to his right and then back at the cartel kingpins. "Which one of you is Agundez?"

Agundez's frown deepened. "I am. And who are you?"

The leader nodded and the police guns blazed. Agundez's men staggered backwards as rounds tore through them, the slugs churning their chests into hamburger.

When the gunmen stopped firing, Agundez was the only one left standing, stunned, his hands still held high. The leader walked toward him.

Agundez met his stare and hissed his question. "Who are you?"

The leader's gun butt caught Agundez on the side of the head, and he went down like a bag of rocks.

"Me?" the leader growled. "I'm your worst nightmare."

He turned to his men and nodded, and one of them moved to Agundez with a syringe. He popped its bright orange cap, holding the plastic nub between his teeth, and after finding a promising vein, emptied the contents into Agundez's arm as the wounded cartel boss moaned groggily. By the time he straightened, Agundez was out cold.

The leader tilted his head at the unconscious figure. "Get this sack of shit out of here. Take the men's weapons and belongings, and write a warning in their blood," he ordered, and then turned on his heel and made for the entrance.

Outside, the ice-cream vendor was on a cell phone, his eyes on the empty road. The leader grunted as he walked past him. "It's done."

The vendor spoke softly as the leader returned to his waiting SUV, the steam drifting skyward from the drying pavement a ghostly fog in the brightening sunlight.

# CHAPTER 10

*Mexico City, Mexico*

Cruz made his way down the hall of the condo to his front door and slid the key in the lock. He'd promised his wife, Dinah, that he would come home during the day at least twice a week rather than working his customary twelve-hour stints straight through, as had been his habit before they'd tied the knot.

He swung the door wide and stepped into the condo – the latest in a long string of temporary residences they'd been relegated to for their safety. As the number one law enforcement officer in the nation chartered with stopping the cartels, Cruz was in constant danger of one of them deciding to snuff him out.

"Dinah? I'm home," he called, setting his briefcase down in the foyer by the entrance.

"I'm in the kitchen," she said.

He made his way toward the sound of her voice and kissed the back of her neck. She smiled as he sniffed the mouthwatering aroma rising from the pan she was laboring over. "Wow. Smells delicious. What is it?"

"An Italian dish. I downloaded the recipe from the web. Chicken pizzaiola."

"I can't wait. How are you feeling?"

Dinah had been under the weather for the last week, every morning claiming she was vastly improved over the prior day, but by evening lethargic and moody. He'd been after her to see a doctor, but so far she'd resisted.

"So-so." She paused. "Lunch will be ready in five minutes."

"I'm not going to nag you, but…"

45

"I know, Romero. I already made an appointment to go in tomorrow morning." She watched him move into the dining room. "I don't suppose there's any way you could take a day off, is there?"

He laughed bitterly. "That'll be the day. They just stuck me on a task force to close the barn door after Aranas, who's probably halfway to Aruba by now."

"Well, you are the foremost expert on the man. I mean, you've even met him..."

"Which is why I know this is completely pointless. I mean, come on. Somehow the staff of our most secure prison missed that someone was excavating a tunnel almost a mile long directly under the facility, and I'm supposed to catch the mastermind who'd evaded arrest for twenty-something years? Ridiculous." Cruz sat down at the table. "But I haven't told you the best part."

"How hungry are you?"

"My stomach's growling, but I probably shouldn't eat too much."

Dinah entered the dining room with a heaping plate in her hand. "Starting first thing tomorrow." She set it down in front of him and pulled a chair free.

"What about you?" Cruz asked.

"I've been nibbling. Besides, I'm not hungry."

"Are you taking vitamins? You might be anemic."

"Every morning."

The extent of Cruz's knowledge of feminine disorders exhausted, he turned to the chicken, which tasted even better than it smelled. He cleaned his plate without speaking, and Dinah nodded when he put his fork and knife down and sighed.

"You were going to tell me the best part?"

He patted his stomach. "Guess who's heading up the task force?"

Her eyes narrowed. "Not you?"

"No. Why have an experienced authority on cartels direct things when you can call in the big guns?"

Dinah's voice softened. "That bad?"

He nodded. "Worse. Godoy," he said, his expression souring.

"I thought he was out of your hair permanently?"

46

"So did I. But the good news is that I think he's being set up to take the bullet when we fail."

"You're that sure you won't be able to track Aranas?"

"I've said all along that a guy like Aranas doesn't get caught unless he wants to. I haven't changed my opinion. The man's obscenely rich and wildly smart. We might as well put a fortune teller on staff, because he's as gone as you can get, and my bet is we never see him again."

"At least you're optimistic."

"It's a complete sham, but I got sucked into it, and now I have to hand off real investigations to Briones while I sit in meetings with a dolt who couldn't find his ass with both hands."

Dinah nodded sympathetically. "Can't you just have him killed or something?"

"Don't give me any ideas."

"Seriously, just refuse to work with him. They'll choose you over him."

"I tried. They're not taking no for an answer." He pushed back from the table and checked the time. "Besides, if I'm right, he's going to be the piñata who gets all the blame in the end, so I have mixed feelings about reporting to him. On the one hand I want to resign, but on the other I want to see him burn, publicly humiliated and gone once and for all. He's a menace. You should have heard him today. I'd forgotten how much I hate that cockroach."

"You want some dessert?" she asked. "I have flan."

"Not really on my diet, is it?"

"I think it's diet flan. You burn more calories digesting it than you take in," Dinah said with a straight face.

"Then I'd be a fool to refuse, wouldn't I?"

She smiled. "I'll be right back."

When she returned, she had a small portion for herself and a jumbo helping for Cruz, which she placed in front of him. He ate it with relish, and when he was done, grimaced. "I did it again. I ate too much." His gaze rose toward the ceiling. "Why, God, do you do this to me?"

"Somewhere there are starving children. Don't be an ingrate."

"If I didn't know how good the flan was for me, I'd feel worse." He grew serious. "I'm probably going to have to stay late tonight. I have to deal with my own workload as well as the Aranas thing. Briones can't handle it all himself, at least not at this stage."

"How late?"

"I wouldn't wait up."

She shook her head and exhaled in frustration. "You promised no more of these, Cruz."

"I know. But how could I have foreseen the Aranas thing?"

"Let Briones handle your other stuff. Mexico can do without you saving it for one night."

"I wish it was that easy." He told her about the child prostitution ring. When he finished, she closed her eyes resignedly.

"Okay. I understand. But I don't like it."

"I know. I swear once we do the raid, that will be it. He can deal with the rest. I'm sorry, Dinah. I really am."

She opened her eyes and reached for his plate, her face unreadable. But her shoulders were tight, her body language conveying her disappointment. When she responded, her voice was fatigued.

"So am I, Cruz. So am I."

# CHAPTER 11

El Rey pushed through the familiar bulletproof glass doors that served as CISEN's anonymous entrance, past a pair of burly security men in black suits, and strode to the reception desk, where an attractive young woman in an immaculate white silk blouse greeted him with a neutral smile.

"Yes?" she asked.

"I need to see Rodriguez."

Her brow lifted slightly. "The director? Do you have an appointment?"

His tone didn't change. "Tell him he has a visitor who's been calling his cell phone for a week, with no reply."

She looked over to the guards. "Sir, I'm afraid if you don't have an appointment—"

El Rey stepped closer. "Look, you seem like you're nice, so I'll spare you the unpleasantness. Just make the call. I've been in his office more than a few times – the director knows me well. So do as you're told, and it will go better for you." The cold menace in the assassin's voice must have gotten through to her, because rather than sounding the alarm, she pressed some buttons and whispered into her headset. El Rey moved to a beige leather couch and took a seat, clenching and unclenching his hands, which thankfully had stopped shaking earlier.

Ten minutes later, three men rounded the corner from the bowels of the building. El Rey recognized the one in the center as the new director of CISEN – the former assistant director, Rodriguez, who'd moved up the ladder since the assassin's last visit. El Rey stood as Rodriguez approached.

"Come into the conference room," Rodriguez said, and led him through a security area to one of the myriad rooms on the ground floor, followed by the pair of flunkies.

When everyone was seated, El Rey got to the point. "I've been calling. You haven't returned any of them. I need my final shot, so I thought I'd make my demand in person."

Rodriguez nodded. "I have to apologize. We've been under a lot of pressure, working double shifts. Bit of an emergency situation." He waved as though clearing the air. "But what counts is that you're here now."

"Right. So where's the antidote?"

"We anticipated your need. One of my assistants is retrieving it. If you'll wait for a few minutes, we'll have it right out."

El Rey studied Rodriguez, trying to decide whether he was lying or not. He was polished, seemed relaxed, and there were no obvious tells. Then again, you didn't get to the top of the intelligence heap by being an easy read.

Rodriguez returned his stare. "So, what will you do now that your service to your country is over?"

"I'm thinking of opening a strip club."

One of Rodriguez's bookend assistants coughed to cover his laugh.

Rodriguez nodded. "Dangerous work. I understand the ladies can take things personally."

"Probably worse than the cartels," El Rey agreed, glancing at his Panerai watch.

"Better you than me. Sounds like a young man's game."

Silence stretched uncomfortably as the banter died, and El Rey did nothing to break it. He thought he detected a faint whiff of nervousness from the men, but that was hardly surprising given his reputation. When a soft knock at the door sounded, the CISEN officials seemed relieved.

"Come in," Rodriguez called out, and another anonymous young man in a suit entered carrying a thermos. Rodriguez took it from him and passed it across the table to El Rey. "There. As always, everything you need."

El Rey opened the top and peered inside before standing. "Wish I could say it's been a pleasure. I know the way out."

Rodriguez watched as he departed. When the speaker on the center of the table beeped and the front office reported that the visitor had left the building, he looked at his associates.

"Think he bought it?"

The man on Rodriguez's left gave the ceiling a pensive stare. "He's suspicious, of course. Doesn't matter. We know which lab he uses to check it, and we've made arrangements for it to test as genuine. He'll believe it's the real thing, take it, and that's that."

"How long will it take to…finish him?" Rodriguez asked.

"Matter of an hour or two from time of injection."

"Then there's one problem over by day's end." Rodriguez tilted his head. "If only all my challenges were so easily resolved."

The other man sat forward. "Sir, we're doing the right thing. He's far too dangerous to have out there on the loose. We all know that. Our intelligence—"

"Yes, yes. No need to belabor it. His usefulness is at an end, and he's now a liability. Everyone understands," Rodriguez snapped. He rose and moved to the conference room door. "He's being tailed, of course?"

"We have a locater chip built into the thermos casing. He's too good for us to risk any physical surveillance. He'd spot it no matter how large a team we deployed or what techniques we used. Safer with the chip – it's undetectable."

Rodriguez looked dubious. "Right. Well, call me when it's over."

"Will do, sir."

# CHAPTER 12

Cruz and Briones sat in the audio-visual suite in a single row of theater seats, watching the security camera footage from the prison on a massive screen – a mind-numbingly tedious job due to the sheer number of cameras and angles. Everyone had assured Cruz that he didn't have to do it, that the footage didn't contain anything, but he'd stubbornly insisted, and a technician had arrived with the data right after Cruz had gotten back from lunch.

"There's no camera that was focused on his cell?" Briones asked for the third time since the man had begun showing them the grainy black-and-white sequences.

"No. As you can see, the primary concern is the public areas."

They'd been at it for over an hour when Cruz called out to the tech, "What are we watching now? Where is this?"

"The service entrance – number two, to be specific. There are three in the prison."

"Back it up and let's see it again, slower."

The technician complied, and they watched as a laborer in coveralls wearing a grimy baseball hat walked with a pair of guards from the exit. It could have been coincidence, or deliberate, but for whatever reason the worker's hat obstructed the camera's view of his face.

Cruz leaned into Briones. "Are you thinking what I'm thinking?"

"It's just one of the workers."

"Look at the time stamp.

"An hour before Aranas was reported missing."

"Which makes it at least noteworthy, don't you think?" Cruz craned his neck at where the technician sat in the gloom. "You have any other cameras on that sector?"

"The exterior there?"

"Yes."

"Should have. Let me see what we've got." The tech tapped at his keys as the grainy image froze on the wall.

Briones shook his head. "This is a dead end, sir. We know how he escaped – through the tunnel."

"That's certainly how it appears. But I've learned that with Aranas you can't take anything at face value. Let's just say I'm suspicious of everything and everyone on this one."

"You think he just walked out of the highest security prison in the country?"

"I haven't formed an opinion. I'm just following any loose threads. This is one of them."

"What's the difference, even if it is him? He's still gone."

"The difference is that if he had help on the inside and strolled out disguised as a laborer, then higher powers within the prison are involved, and we need to know so we don't waste time chasing down blind alleys."

"If that were true, why let us see this?"

"Because nobody else would even question it. As you said, he's gone, there's a tunnel, we're done, on to the next thing."

Realization dawned on Briones's face. "Ah. So the whole thing could be an act to protect his accomplices? Pretty elaborate, isn't it?"

"Not if your ass is on the line if it isn't convincing. And if you want to retire and spend the millions you earned getting Aranas out relaxing on a beach somewhere instead of rotting in the same prison you helped operate." Cruz's voice became almost inaudible. "Besides, I haven't seen this infamous tunnel with my own eyes. As far as I know, there might not even be one. I've requested time at the prison but have yet to hear back. I want to walk the tunnel – then I'll buy the story. Until then, like I said, everything's suspect. Everything."

"I understand."

The tech approached. "I have one camera that's only catching a little of that exit. Want to see it?"

"Yes."

The footage was of a security gate, but they could clearly make out the laborer walk toward a waiting vehicle and climb in. Cruz and Briones exchanged a dark look. Cruz turned to where the tech was sitting.

"Again."

When they'd finished watching it a second time, Cruz thanked the technician and led Briones from the room. As they stood in the elevator, Cruz's face was all angles.

"Don't see a lot of workers getting into Land Rovers, do you?" he asked the younger man.

"Too bad it was black and white. Hard to tell what color it was."

"And no license plate, only the top half of the car. Bad luck."

"I'm starting to believe luck didn't play a large part in this."

"Now you sound like me." The doors slid open and they stepped onto the task force floor. "I want you to pull any traffic cameras in the area and see whether we can pick up the Land Rover. Either get a plate or images of the occupants. There should be sufficient cams so one of them caught it."

"I'll get on it. As you know, it will probably take too long, but I'll tell everyone to rush it," Briones said.

"Good man," Cruz said. "When you're done, come to my office. I want to go over the prostitution raid. I'm still not convinced we aren't missing something."

Briones appeared surprised. "You handed all that off to me already. I've got it under control."

"I know. But I'm going to put in some extra hours, just in case I missed something critical before I gave it to you."

Briones nodded. "Another long one?"

"In an endless string. Needless to say, Dinah isn't delighted."

"I can only imagine."

Cruz left the lieutenant near his cubicle and continued on to his office. When he arrived, he found a message from Godoy requesting a status report. Cruz shook his head at the man's colossal ego and lack of appreciation for how police work actually took place. All they'd done was have a meeting. There was nothing to report, other than his suspicions about the footage, which at this point were indicative of exactly nothing.

Cruz sat at his desk and dialed Godoy's extension. His secretary answered and asked him to hold, and then he was forced to wait for a good five minutes before the great man came on the line.

"Yes, Cruz. Any progress?" he demanded.

"It's only been a few hours."

"I know what time it is. But we need to work fast. The man's on the run."

"Of course. I'm still going through the history for an idea of what happened. I have yet to be approved for visiting the tunnel, though. Can you help with that?"

"It's a tunnel. What's to see?" Godoy snapped.

Cruz bit back the response that threatened to burst from his lips. "There's a method to my madness, Godoy. I need to see it. Kindly put some pressure on whoever you need to so I can do so as soon as possible tomorrow."

"I'll add it to my list."

"I can also use some more bodies. I've had my lieutenant, Briones, helping, but he's handling my active cases, so I'm short-handed."

"Fine. I'll get to it as soon as I can. Is there anything else?"

"Just that for now."

"All right, then. I'll be out the rest of the afternoon, but I want to have a regular status meeting first thing every morning so we can all stay current. Nine o'clock in my office."

Cruz was going to point out that he typically got to work several hours earlier, but found himself listening to a dial tone. It took every ounce of self-control he possessed to not slam the handset down in the cradle, and he viewed it as a minor victory when he retained his composure and set it down softly.

He would not let Godoy get to him. It would be that pompous ass's funeral, not Cruz's, when the investigation revealed nothing. That was the payoff, and Cruz could wait for it.

Which didn't stop him from wishing Godoy a slow and painful death.

Cruz was comfortable with the fact that he wasn't a particularly good man some days.

This was definitely one of those days.

# CHAPTER 13

El Maquino jumped at the sound of the buzzer, which startled him even though he was expecting it. He stood, moved to the front door, and went through his on-off light ritual before unlocking and relocking the deadbolts and making his way down the stairs. When he arrived at the entrance, he activated the monitor and nodded to himself at the sight of his benefactor.

Two locks that would have been at home in a bank vault clanked open, and El Maquino pulled the heavy slab toward him. His visitor stepped inside and waited as he relocked them behind him, and then led him up the stairs.

"How have you been?" Aranas asked.

"Good," El Maquino said, the single word all the information he considered necessary.

"How is the project coming?"

"Almost ready."

They arrived at the condo door and Aranas waited patiently while his host unlocked the deadbolts. Once they were safely ensconced inside, he walked slowly around the living room, which had been converted into a large work area. El Maquino latched and twisted the locks to ensure they wouldn't be interrupted as Aranas took in his surroundings. To say it was Spartan would have been kind; the only furniture was that which was absolutely essential – a small dining room table with two chairs, a sofa that had seen better days, a single chair by the window, whose blackout curtains were pulled tightly closed, and a long workbench framed by bright red automotive toolboxes the height of a man. Aranas didn't comment on any of it. He was used to the man's peculiarities, and if this was how he chose to live his life, so be it.

Aranas turned to El Maquino, who was standing by the door as if uncertain what to do next. "Come, show me what you're working on."

El Maquino nodded and moved to the first of three metal boxes near the bench. "These are the devices. Or the casings." He continued with a long explanation of the system he'd devised, and as Aranas listened, he recognized that what the man was describing would have been impossible for most to understand, just as it was to Aranas. But he didn't need to grasp every nuance – he just needed them to work, and to be foolproof.

Aranas snuck a look at El Maquino's face as he went on with his monologue, his voice that odd, inflectionless tone he'd had since a child. The young boy had become a man, but clearly his inner dialogue and self-awareness was stuck somewhere in a past Aranas would never fully appreciate – a world only El Maquino could navigate.

When he was done, Aranas began asking pointed questions about operating the devices, which were amazingly simple, it turned out. Half an hour later he was satisfied that his charge would not only deliver what he needed on time, but that there was no way he could see for anyone to undo his work – which was critical to Aranas's plan.

"You have made me proud, my boy," Aranas said, and for an instant thought he saw a flicker of something in the man's eyes. He knew he might have been projecting the glimmer of emotion he so wanted to see, but he didn't care. At his age, he'd take it, even if it was crafted from futile hope.

El Maquino walked him through the minutiae of arming and disarming the systems, and then seemed to run out of words, like a clock winding down. He stood staring at the boxes like a statue until Aranas nodded in approval. "This is wonderful work. I knew I was right to put my faith in you. But now, I must go. Do you need anything? Want for anything? Say the word and I'll make it appear for you. You have but to ask."

The big man slowly shook his head at the idea. He had everything.

Aranas was surprised when El Maquino seemed to brighten.

"Want to see my birds?" he asked, his voice suddenly shy as he looked at a doorway on the far side of the room.

"I'd love to," Aranas responded with a surreptitious glance at his watch.

El Maquino led him to the doorway and flipped on the lights. The room was filled with drones of all sizes plugged into wall chargers, some of the aircraft only a few feet wide, others the size of a small bed. El Maquino moved into the space and pointed to the smaller ones. "These are armed with enough C-4 to knock out a tank." He gestured to several with elaborate apparatuses affixed to them. "Those have stabilized gun platforms I plan to mount small submachine guns on, because of the weight. That one and that one have cameras – video, infrared, thermal. And this last one will support a man – it's a hovercraft."

"Really? They'll carry that much weight?"

"Oh, yes. They're amazing. The only problem is battery life. But I could see where we could use them either offensively or defensively, like the American army. Or to carry merchandise, or cash, over borders."

Aranas nodded thoughtfully, trying to be polite. He was glad the odd boy had grown up and found something with which to occupy his time, but the drug lord had little interest in flying toys, even if they were lethal. The amount of product he transported across the border each week was measured in tons, not kilos, so they'd be of no use to him. None of which he told El Maquino, for fear of bruising his feelings.

They discussed the possibilities of remote flight for another couple of minutes and then Aranas excused himself – he had other matters that required his time.

The locking and unlocking and escorting Aranas back to the lobby door took five minutes, and then, after allowing a small hug he clearly felt uncomfortable receiving, El Maquino sealed himself back into his dwelling, exhausted from the energy the visit had required from him. He never had guests of any kind, and even if it was Aranas, the atmosphere of his loft felt like it was charged, disrupted at some fundamental level that might take a long time to dissipate. He shambled over to the light switch in the kitchen and tried to resist the impulse that came over him, an almost physical need to restore order and balance to his space. He considered going to brush his teeth, but even as he had the thought, his beefy fingers reached for the switch.

"On. Off. On. Off."

# CHAPTER 14

After navigating the busy streets of downtown Mexico City, El Rey jettisoned the thermos in a dumpster and ducked into a gym where he'd purchased a one-week trial membership that morning. After drawing some of the purported antidote for testing, he secreted the vial in one of the lockers, withdrew a light gray windbreaker and blue baseball hat and exchanged them for the black hat and jacket he had on, closed the padlock, and pocketed the sample. That the thermos had a tracking device was a given – he would have done the same, and he didn't even question that it was chipped.

Fifteen minutes later El Rey circled the block where the laboratory was located, and once satisfied that he wasn't being tailed, swiftly moved to the front door and pulled it wide. Inside was as he remembered, as though it had been only yesterday that he'd made his last visit and not six months earlier.

The front desk clerk was the same woman as on his prior trip, and he had a sense of déjà vu. He shrugged it off and continued to the counter, where he placed a small plastic vial of antidote and asked the clerk to run a spectrum analysis on it.

In his back pocket he had the results from the prior test, so he could quickly compare the two once the lab had performed its magic. His internal alarms had been clamoring ever since meeting with Rodriguez, and he'd taken special precautions this time around – the final shot that was supposed to fix everything was also the perfect opportunity for the ultimate betrayal.

He, more than most, knew the temptation there would be to renege on the deal. He was a student of human nature, and it would have actually surprised him if CISEN had behaved honorably.

The assassin took a seat in the waiting area while the woman carried his sample into the rear of the laboratory, where some faceless technician would analyze it and print out the chemical breakdown.

The woman returned and smiled. "Can I offer you anything while you wait? Water? A soda?"

"No, thanks. I'm good."

The last visit she hadn't offered anything. It was just a small detail. Probably inconsequential, he told himself, wanting badly to believe it even though his operational instincts argued that nothing was ever meaningless – everything contained information to a man whose job it was to correctly read the signs.

That was paranoid talk, he thought, one of the side effects of not receiving the shot in time. Like the tremors, it didn't mean anything beyond what it signaled – that he was overdue and in trouble.

The test took forty-five minutes, and he didn't bother looking at the results until he'd paid and gotten well clear of the building. He found a small taqueria that was teeming with a late afternoon crowd, took a seat in the back, and then carefully unfolded the old results and compared them to the new ones.

The antidote was genuine. The chemical composition matched.

El Rey glanced at his watch and moved to the back of the restaurant, where the bathrooms were located. He continued past the stalls to a wrought-iron rear gate and slipped through it into a reeking alley filled with refuse and noxious pools of suspect fluid. At the intersection he flagged down a taxi and gave the driver an address a few kilometers away, and then settled back into the seat to watch the city blur by.

The second lab was as modern as the first, and was one of several El Rey had located that could also run a spectrum analysis. He'd used the other laboratory too often, and he didn't trust CISEN to be so incompetent that they couldn't locate the place and jigger the results. But this one was virgin territory, and as such would serve as a reasonable confirmation stop before he gave himself the shot.

An hour later he emerged with a grim look of determination. His worst suspicions had been confirmed – what was in the second tiny vial he'd drawn was nothing like the antidote. The technician had warned him that injection would prove fatal, and he assured the young man that he understood that.

El Rey didn't particularly care whether the tech made a call to the authorities once he was gone. The damage was done — he was exhibiting symptoms and had nothing to cure them.

Which he'd prepared for.

The problem was that he'd narrowed down the original source for the CIA's neurotoxin, but not with complete certainty. He'd spent almost half a million dollars to ascertain that the agency contracted specialists with private firms to develop their potions, and he had a short list of seven of the likeliest suspects, all biochemists, all working for large military contractors who routinely did top-secret work for the government. Most were also linked with universities, where the scientists carried out research using generous federal grants to fund their activities, and he had no doubt that their cooperation with the clandestine apparatus was directly related to the government's reciprocal largess.

Seven names, but too little time.

He needed to narrow the field. And there was only one person who could help him do so.

Rodriguez.

Who was probably celebrating with his quislings that El Rey was no more.

That would work in the assassin's favor, of course. He'd made a career out of exploiting opportunities created when his adversaries underestimated him. This would be no different. If CISEN believed that he was dead, that meant they wouldn't be watching for him.

Which was all he needed.

The rest would be easy.

# CHAPTER 15

Carla finished dusting her dining room table and pursed her lips. The housekeeper never seemed to do as good a job as she did, and Carla typically went around her home after the woman's weekly visit and tidied up obsessively. She didn't mind, because with the number of things that typically weighed on her, the busywork helped her relax – something she especially needed now, with a major career decision to make as well as a turning point in her relationship.

Which stopped her. How had she gotten so far down that path? Without question, it was he who had made the first overture after their adventure together, their chemistry obvious from that brief time in each other's company, but from there she had pursued it.

She sighed. Something about the man fascinated her, drew her like a moth to the flame, and she found herself unable to resist him.

That the sex was incredible went without saying.

But it was something more. He was damaged goods, but she didn't think he was a sociopath, at least not in the sense of a serial killer who was unable to feel emotion. Even though he clearly was a repeat murderer, if she wanted to be accurate. But more in the way a sniper was – as part of a job, not because he delighted in snuffing out life.

She'd dared to ask him about it on their third night together, both of them naked and spent, and that was how he'd explained it. He was a craftsman, exactly like a special ops soldier who focused on those who needed killing. He felt no remorse over ending the lives of cartel thugs, and she didn't argue it – his targets routinely had the blood of many on their hands, so in a way he was doing the world a favor.

While getting rich, she reminded herself.

Her thoughts were interrupted by a soft scrape behind her, and she whirled around to find him standing by the doorway, watching her.

"God. You scared me," she said, clutching the dusting rag to her chest. She'd given him a key a month ago and had gotten used to his coming and going, but she hadn't been expecting him, and his sudden presence threw her. "How did it go with CISEN?"

His expression remained neutral. "Not well. They tried to poison me," he said in measured words, as though he was discussing a flat tire or an insect bite – an annoyance, nothing more.

Her face fell. "What? How?"

"They gave me a toxin that would have buried me within minutes." He shrugged. "I half expected it."

"But they can't do that! You need to go to the president…"

He shook his head. "No. The time for that is past. And for all I know, he ordered it. It doesn't matter. Now I'm racing the clock, so I have to move fast. I just wanted to tell you in person – I'm going to be gone for a while."

"Where are you going?"

"The agent was created in the U.S. for the CIA. So that's my first stop."

"What are you planning to do? It's not like you can just knock on Langley's door and ask for an injection."

"I know." He told her about the scientists. "I've done my homework. Find the one who made the poison, and I have the person who can make the antidote."

"How will you narrow it down?"

"I'll persuade someone to point me in the right direction."

She absorbed that, afraid to ask how he planned to do so. "You have the chemical composition, right? Why not just have someone else make it?"

"The analysis is at a relatively gross level. It's fine for verification, but I worry that there's something in the mix I don't know about that could kill me – some nuance or trace element that works in conjunction with the others in a critical way. I'm not a chemist, and I'm not going to leave it to chance." He paused thoughtfully. "And I don't have the time to have the antidote reverse engineered. I thought about it, believe me, but I need an actual sample, and until today I didn't have one. The prior shots might have been a different composition than the one required for the final one – I just don't know enough about how it works to give anyone instructions. Could be shot one is X amount of Y, shot two is Z amount of Y, and on and on."

Carla approached him and put a hand on his chest. "How do you feel?"

"Fine, for now. But that will change, I know from experience. I just didn't want you to worry when I wasn't around. I'll take care of this my own way."

She nodded as her eyes held his. "I'll come with you."

He pulled away and shook his head. "Absolutely not. Speed's key now, and with all due respect, I can't afford anything that will slow me down."

"You're making a lot of assumptions. I'm a journalist – my credentials get me into a lot of places you might not have access to. What if one of those places holds the key to saving you?"

Her voice was calm, reasoned, and El Rey held off on an automatic rejection of the idea. He considered her point – women often were treated with less suspicion than men, and were discounted as being harmless by certain types of males.

She stepped closer. "I swear I won't do anything to slow your progress. I'll just hang in the background. But if you need me, I'll be there; whereas if I'm still in Mexico City, I can't do a lot for you." Her gaze searched his face. "Please. I want to do this." An idea occurred to her. "It might be a lot easier to get into the U.S. if you're traveling as my cameraman."

"I was thinking more about a tunnel or a boat."

"If you have a Mexican passport, I can get you an expedited visa through my contact at the American Embassy. We can just fly directly to the U.S. tomorrow. Or even tonight, if he's willing to process it immediately."

"I have several."

"Then give me one, I'll make it happen, and we'll hop on the first flight north once we have the visa." She reached up and brushed a lock of hair from his brow. "Please. Let me help you."

He thought about it for several moments, and then nodded. "I can have the passport in your hands in an hour."

"I'll make a call. Any ETA on when you want to leave?"

"I have another errand I need to run before we go." He checked the time. "It shouldn't take too long. Let me check and see if I can get a private jet for this evening."

"I have a contact at the largest brokerage in DF. He can probably pull some strings. Say…eleven, assuming I can get the visa?"

A small smile tugged at the corners of his mouth. "I forgot how resourceful you are."

"Yes, before I had you to rely on, I even had to brush my own teeth."

His smile turned into a grin. "I'll be back."

She watched him leave and sighed heavily. "I hope you know what you're doing," she whispered. "Because I'll be damned if I do."

# CHAPTER 16

A rusting pickup truck bounced down a muddy road on the outskirts of Tlalpan, a suburb of Mexico City, swerving to avoid the worst of the muddy puddles that had accumulated in the ruts. An early evening cloudburst had transformed the dusty track into a treacherous game of slip and slide for the intrepid drivers forced to negotiate it as they got off work. The area was industrial, although a scattering of shanties ringed the district, which had neither water nor sewage, and which bootlegged their electricity – a common practice in impoverished areas of Mexico.

A platinum Escalade passed the truck, splattering it with brown froth as the Cadillac blasted down the road toward one of the nearby single-story warehouses. A heavy iron gate slid open as the SUV neared, the driver having alerted the watchman of the vehicle's arrival, and the big vehicle barely slowed as it swung into the high-walled compound and rolled toward the sprawling main building. It stopped in front of one of six roll-up loading dock doors, beside a pedestrian entrance flanked by two gunmen, smoking, their AK-47s hanging from shoulder slings.

*Don* Aranas stepped down from the Escalade and navigated carefully along the wet gravel, taking care to avoid soiling his beige linen slacks and Ferragamo shoes. The men stood as he neared and he nodded to them, pausing briefly to eye the five other vehicles parked alongside the building before twisting the door lever and entering the warehouse.

Claudio Trevi, the *Don*'s newly appointed second-in-command, emerged from one of the receiving area offices and approached. "He's conscious now," Trevi said, his voice gravelly.

"Good. Where do you have him?"

"Back by the forklifts. He just arrived two hours ago. There were several roadblocks on the way into Mexico City."

"Looking for me, I assume?" Aranas asked with a smile.

"They're always two steps behind, aren't they?"

"It's all just for show, anyway. They know they have no chance of catching me, but they have to appear to be doing something. Same as usual. Nothing changes."

Aranas had most of the police and army officers that mattered in his pocket and would receive ample advance warning were there any chance an operation to apprehend him was getting anywhere. Which was unlikely – it was in nobody's financial interests to incarcerate him again. Besides, the power vacuum created by the arrest or killing of several other top cartel bosses had done little to slow the rampant violence along the trafficking routes, demonstrating that a little evil you knew was preferable to even more aggressively violent new entrants scrambling for turf.

His media contacts had been making that observation for some time, lobbying subtly for his cartel to reassert its dominance, and positioning him in the minds of many Mexicans as a benign authority who kept the peace. Which was partially true: Aranas used violence judiciously, understanding that too much brought unwanted attention, whereas too soft a hand resulted in rivals becoming emboldened and making land grabs. His PR arm regularly uploaded videos to the Internet showing adversaries who'd been captured by Sinaloa, accusing them of kidnapping, extortion, and murdering innocents – all of which Aranas's cartel avoided, not because they weren't lucrative endeavors, but rather because the take from the trafficking business was so large it didn't make sense to chase what he viewed as table scraps, and he didn't need the attendant bad publicity.

That had resulted in Aranas assuming almost mythical proportions among the poor in his home state, as well as with the millions of disenfranchised peasants who lived in squalor and were routinely abused by any authority figure. One of the reasons crime statistics were so unreliable was that over ninety percent of crimes in Mexico went unreported, the victims fearing either reprisals from the police, who were often in on them, or inaction, which was the norm. A strong leader like Aranas with a reputation for not only having great wealth but being even-handed and reasonable was an appealing popular culture icon, and he played it up with the skill of a film star. Aranas was well known as a supporter of numerous charities and animal shelters, as well as the silent partner in a host of groups that lent small amounts to the poor so they could start small businesses, making him a national treasure to many.

But today he had serious business to attend to. His old second-in-command, Hector Agundez, had betrayed him, and Aranas understood that the rot might run deeper. Before his arrest, Aranas had suspected informants at a high level within his organization, and part of the benefit he saw being taken into custody was that everyone in his group was tempted and tested with the possibility of usurping his position.

Agundez had moved against him, aggressively and quickly. That explained much, such as how some of the competitive cartels Aranas had held at bay for years had been able to take territory from him in his final years at the helm. The answer was obvious: they had help.

"Chuco and Paco are here?" Aranas asked.

"Of course. As you ordered. They're keeping an eye on our boy."

Aranas exhaled and withdrew a Cuban cigar from his breast pocket. He snipped the end off and Trevi lit it for him, a common ritual for the pair. "Let's get this over with. Lead me to him."

"This way."

The two men walked past stacks of paint cans and construction materials to the rear of the cavernous space, and Trevi paused in front of a steel door. "In there."

Aranas nodded. There was a way he preferred to handle interrogations, and the fewer witnesses, the better. Trevi opened the door and Aranas leaned close to him. "Have Chuco and Paco stand by. I'll call for them."

"Will do."

Aranas stepped into the darkened room, which was thirty feet square. Dim light filtered through high windows caked with grime, and Aranas strolled over to where Agundez hung, his ankles and wrists bound and his arms above his head, suspended from a chain. Agundez sniffed at the air as Aranas walked toward him and nodded ruefully.

"I figured it had to be your doing," Agundez said, his voice thick.

"You more than earned it when you stabbed me in the back."

"You were in jail. Finished."

Aranas grunted. "The rumors of my demise were somewhat exaggerated. Which if you had half a brain, you would have known."

"I did what I had to do. You would have done the same."

"Perhaps. But that's not the case. Which leaves me with a problem: your fledgling cartel is a thorn in my side."

"Your distribution is in shambles. You need hard money to pay for new shipments – your credit's no longer good with the suppliers. Too much uncertainty, too many new groups challenging you. You need me. I can help, and you know it. I have relationships with everyone. I can make this right."

"You expect me to work with a traitor? Have you been using your own product?"

"I'm proposing that you partner with me in the areas where I have the most influence. What's done is done. It's a new landscape, and you need to adapt. Without me, you have nothing. Your partners in the U.S. have been negotiating with me, and we've struck a bargain. The Colombians have likewise reached an agreement. They view your cartel as a relic now. Past its prime. No insult to you, but that's the truth."

Aranas took a long pull on his cigar. "It's your truth. Not mine."

Agundez shook his head. "Don't do anything you'll regret."

That elicited a laugh from Aranas. "The only thing I regret is not suspecting you sooner. This? This is justice. You'll discover I don't forgive easily firsthand."

"Killing me will solve nothing. All your problems will remain."

"Maybe. But I'll get the satisfaction of roasting you alive – which at my age is a consideration. None of us knows how much more runway we have left, although I think you can safely assume you've run out of yours. So it's the simple pleasures I have to enjoy – especially in this business." Aranas cleared his throat. "Before I'm done, I'll know everything about what you've put into play and have planned. I will know who else in my organization is working against me. I'll know everything that you do, which means your value to me is nil." His voice softened. "You really called this one wrong."

"You're making a mistake."

Aranas turned and called out, "Paco? Chuco? Showtime."

Agundez's eyes widened at the names. He had been Aranas's right-hand man long enough to know what the men's specialty was. He struggled against his bindings and made another attempt to salvage the situation. "I won't tell them anything. I'll die in silence. And you'll be finished because you let your pride interfere with your business judgment."

"You make many assumptions. I'd have thought by now you'd know that I always have a plan. Within a few days, I'll have both the government's support and a renegotiated deal with our friends from the north. You, on the other hand, will be a smudge on the floor here and a lingering bad smell."

The steel door opened and two rough-looking thugs entered. Aranas nodded to them and dropped his cigar on the floor. "Nice seeing you again. Enjoy your stay in hell."

"Aranas! We can work this out," Agundez said, his voice cracking.

"Afraid not. If you want to treat me like one of your underage *putas*, you're going to get the reward you deserve: a gasoline bath once the boys here are done with you, which won't be for a while. Resist as much as you like, old friend. It makes their work more challenging."

Aranas marched to the door, never looking back, ignoring Agundez's frantic pleas. The man had feigned loyalty for a decade, and there could be only one price for betraying Aranas's trust.

Which he would pay in blood over the course of the night at Aranas's enforcers' capable hands.

# CHAPTER 17

Cruz looked up from his screen as Briones entered his office. The long hours had worn at him, dinner had been nothing more than a burrito off a cart eaten at his desk, and now his eyes were red and burning, with an endless amount of work still remaining. Briones pulled Cruz's door closed and placed the laptop he was carrying on the small circular table they used for their meetings. Cruz watched him and stood when Briones took a seat.

"What have you got for me?" Cruz asked as he moved to join Briones at the table.

"I pulled all the nearby traffic cam footage and just finished going through it. Of course what we were looking for was the last I got to."

Cruz pulled a chair closer to the younger man and sat heavily. "Isn't that always the way it works?"

"Anyway, we have several good images of the Land Rover as it goes through an intersection."

"Really? Plates?"

"I ran them. Stolen."

"Ah. So we have a worker being transported around in a stolen luxury vehicle. Not really common, would you say?"

"No, but I'm not sure how much good it does us."

"Let me see the footage."

"Of course." Briones tapped in an instruction and the computer screen blinked. A monochrome image came to life, and they watched as the target vehicle rolled through a yellow light. "Not much, as I said."

"That one does us no good at all."

"Here's the next." Another virtually identical few seconds of Land

Rover blurred across the screen. "Also a bust, other than to confirm that he isn't intimidated by traffic signals."

"Tell me this gets better."

"Last one." This footage was slightly clearer.

Cruz nodded. "Can you zoom in so I can see their faces?"

"Yes. But you can't make out the worker. Hat's in the way."

"Not really our lucky day, is it?"

Briones typed in a few more commands and then thumbed the cursor button until he'd magnified the image to four hundred percent. "That's as high as I can get before it starts breaking up. Not enough resolution on these cheap cameras. Plus the lenses are always filthy."

"Let's see it again."

They watched the same footage, and Cruz's eyes narrowed. "Can you freeze the frame where the driver is looking up?"

"I think so." More typing, and then Briones had the image as a still on the screen. Cruz squinted at it for a moment and then pushed back from the table. Briones glanced up at his superior. "What is it?"

"Pull everything on the car. When it was reported stolen, what district it came from, whether or not it's been found. If it has been, I want it dusted for prints by forensics. Every inch of it, am I clear? And I want the results on my desk the second they're done."

"Will do. It'll take a little while, though. Night shift." Briones closed the laptop. "But why the sudden interest? Beyond what we already have, which are only suspicions?"

Cruz stood at his window, staring out at the lights of Mexico City shimmering before him, considering how much to tell Briones. Several moments went by, and then he turned to the lieutenant with a clenched jaw.

"I know that face," Cruz said softly.

"You do?"

"I think so. He looks different, but some things never change."

"Who is it?"

"You wouldn't recognize the name," Cruz hedged.

"I can run it through the system."

"No need. Now go. Clock's ticking, and this is the only lead we have."

Briones nodded and strode from the room, obviously not happy about being kept in the dark about the driver's identity. He returned two hours later, his expression tense.

"I had the technicians follow the Land Rover on the traffic cameras, until it disappeared in the Pedregal district."

"Then we lost him?"

"I'm afraid so."

Cruz scowled at their bad luck. "Put out the word tonight to every informant we have. We're looking for a member of the Sinaloa Cartel – a driver thought to be in Aranas's inner circle. We know the man's here, or was. That's our only chance, I'm afraid." He moved to the window. "Put out an APB on the Land Rover."

Briones looked at his watch. "Very well, *Capitan*. I'll do so immediately. But don't expect miracles. We don't even have a name."

"True, but you know how these guys are. They talk. Brag. Someone has to know if he's still in town. Offer whatever reward you want. A quarter million pesos. I'll okay it."

Briones nodded and left with his marching orders, the night looking like it would be longer with the additional project.

Cruz returned to staring out his window, eyeing the familiar skyline like it held a precious secret. He paced as he did so, until he finally retraced his steps to his desk.

"You're out there, aren't you, you bastard? It was all a setup. Everyone else may have bought it, but not me," he whispered.

Cruz sat and looked at the pile of paperwork and the graph on his screen, and then threw a final stare at the city's glowing sprawl.

"You didn't fool me for a second."

# CHAPTER 18

The crowd at Cambalache in Mexico City's upscale Polanco district was boisterous now that the day's toil was over. The Argentine wine was flowing like water, and the aroma of thick steaks and expensive perfume drifted through the dining area. Godoy took a small sip of the wine the sommelier had recommended and nodded his approval. The young woman seated across from him, obviously less than half his age, pushed her glass toward the man just as he moved the bottle toward her, almost causing a spill. She tittered nervously, and Godoy winked at her as the sommelier poured her cup a third full, and then did the same for his.

Godoy raised his glass in a toast and she clinked hers against it. He watched her face as she took a taste of the crimson nectar, and savored the smile that spread across her features.

"Oh my. That's really good, isn't it?" she exclaimed.

"Yes. It's a Malbec from an excellent year. Very different from Mexican wine, more robust."

"I wish I knew more about it…like you."

"Stick with me, my dear, and you will."

She chanced another sip and then put her glass down so she could fidget with her sequined top – which, Godoy noted, she filled out more than amply. Her caramel skin glowed in its reflected light, and her bleached blonde hair lent her a cheap, unsophisticated quality that was like catnip to him. The polar opposite to his wife, who was as class conscious as a member of a royal court and who'd transformed from a svelte ingénue into…he preferred not to think about it.

Leticia was twenty-three and worked as a teller at Godoy's bank, and had caught his eye when he'd been making a deposit. He was always on the lookout for new talent, and after some small talk he'd invited her to cocktails after she got off work. One thing had led to another, and now he'd been seeing her for a month, during which time her fortunes had improved considerably, mainly due to his generosity in helping pay for her apartment and his showering her with gifts.

He ordered for her and tried to rein in his annoyance as she checked her phone every few minutes and texted. That was one of the things considered to be 'progress' that he viewed with dismay – the elevation of rudeness to acceptable social behavior. He'd have never considered bringing a television into a restaurant on a date, but many these days saw nothing wrong with abruptly interrupting their conversations to text or tweet or Facebook.

The steaks arrived, perfectly prepared, and by the time they were done with dinner, Godoy was ready to be rid of the restaurant, which had gotten increasingly crowded and noisy. He paid the bill, the wine's warm glow flushing both their faces, and he led Leticia to the exit, marveling at her long legs, made all the more remarkable by her impossibly high heels. Out on the sidewalk the valet waved a waiting taxi over. They slid into the rear seat, Leticia giggling as Godoy murmured lascivious suggestions in her ear.

Her apartment building was in a reasonable area of town, a working-class neighborhood that still remained affordable even as it was slowly gentrified by speculators eager to improve the scarce available land for the burgeoning middle class that had emerged in Mexico over the last two decades. He tossed the driver a few bills and Leticia spilled onto the sidewalk, the street devoid of traffic as the residents tucked in for the night.

She lived on the third floor. The elevator was out of service again, a state in which it seemed to spend the lion's share of its existence. Godoy was panting slightly as they reached her landing, but he still mustered the energy to grab her ample bottom.

"Oh, you! Can't you wait until we're inside?" she chided.

"I can't help myself. Hurry up or I'll make a spectacle of myself right here in the stairwell."

She stepped away from him and they hurried down the hall to her door. Godoy continued his fondling as she felt for the keys, and he was beginning to feel a familiar stirring by the time she got the door open.

They stepped into the dark hallway and Godoy pushed her roughly against the wall, his hands sliding her miniskirt up over her hips as he locked his mouth on hers. She was squirming free when he sensed motion behind him. He pulled away as a blow landed on his skull, and his vision starburst into a thousand points of light. His knees buckled and he moaned in pain, and then two strong hands gripped him beneath his arms as a black cloth bag slid over his head.

"Don't struggle or it'll be worse for you. And if you scream, I'll cut your balls off. Do you understand?" a voice asked from behind him.

Godoy managed a grunt in the affirmative and wondered why Leticia wasn't yelling. His confusion deepened when he heard a different voice addressing her. "Did you really think you'd be able to get away with this? Stupid bitch. Now he'll pay for your treachery."

"Please…" Godoy pleaded through the cloth. Some part of him hoped to convince his attackers to release him, although another understood that it wasn't going to happen. Kidnappings were a regular occurrence in Mexico City. Godoy had believed himself to be immune from the crime, given his station within the police department, but his throbbing skull convinced him otherwise.

"Shut up," his assailant growled. Another blow struck the side of Godoy's head and he gasped as he fell to the floor. He was spared the agony from a kick that landed on his ribs a moment later, his consciousness replaced by the comforting numbness of oblivion.

The kidnappers worked quickly and efficiently, two of them hoisting Godoy between them as the third placed a call on a cell phone. They manhandled him down the stairs, and after checking to ensure the sidewalk was still empty, waited till a dark brown van drew to a stop at the curb in front of the entrance.

Two minutes later the van was on one of the capital city's wide boulevards, Godoy stashed in the cargo area with a pair of captors for company. The third kidnapper sat in the passenger seat and lit a cigarette. The snatch had gone off without a hitch, and the prospect of a healthy payday was now a virtual certainty.

One of the men in the back tossed Godoy's wallet forward and the passenger caught it with ease. He rifled through the thick sheaf of cash and pocketed it, and then stopped when he came to Godoy's official credentials. His boss hadn't told them anything about whom they were grabbing – it was immaterial, given the sin he was guilty of – and the passenger's eyes widened at the photo ID with the Federal Police crest emblazoned across the top. He leaned toward the driver as he took a drag on his smoke.

"Looks like we've got a VIP aboard. A cop, no less."

"A cop? He's not armed, right?"

"No. We searched him. He's clean."

"What kind of cop doesn't carry a gun these days, even off duty?"

The passenger studied the identification, sounding out the words. His reading skills were rudimentary, limited to whatever he'd mastered when he'd quit school in fifth grade.

"Says he's some kind of associate commissioner. So a higher-up."

The driver turned onto another street and shrugged. "Well, he picked the wrong bimbo to bang – which he'll figure out the hard way. Hey, got another smoke?"

The passenger shook a cigarette free and handed it to the driver. "I guess it doesn't matter, does it?"

The driver grinned as he reached for the lighter. "Not to me. He could be the pope, for all I care. I just need to know that the boss wants him."

"Stupid bastard should have known better than to cross him."

The driver nodded grimly. "You got that right."

# CHAPTER 19

El Maquino stood over his boxes like a mother hen as he checked and rechecked the wall clock. He'd forced himself to stop switching his lights on and off, but his teeth were tingling from the constant brushing. He trembled with nervous energy at the thought of strangers soon to arrive in his abode, even though he knew it was necessary for them to be there. He couldn't carry the boxes downstairs by himself, or he would have. He'd tried but given up when his back had transmitted the reality of their weight now that they were fully assembled.

They weren't much to look at, he knew, but like many treasures, their inner beauty was what gave them their value. He'd been working on them for a month, first designing them, then machining all the parts required, and finally fitting them together with the precision of a Swiss watch. Now all his work was done, and the only thing that remained was to hand them off like a proud parent.

"Big surprise. Going to be a big surprise, all right," he said softly, reaching out to touch one of the smooth surfaces and then jerking his hand back like he'd touched a stove burner. "Oh. Got to clean it. Don't want any fingerprints. That would be bad. Very bad."

He moved to the workbench, spotless now that he was finished with his current project, and slid open a drawer. Inside was a package of bright yellow hand towels. He withdrew one and took a bottle of cleaner from the top shelf, and set to wiping the exterior of the box for the tenth time that day.

The door buzzer chimed. He shuddered and swung around, jarred from the comforting routine of the task. He looked at the clock approvingly.

"Right on time. That's good. Very good. Prompt. Time's

valuable," he said, repeating a saying he'd heard his entire life.

He resisted the desire to switch the lights on and off again and instead made for the door, leaving the room illuminated as though banishing the night with technology. "It's a big day. A very big day indeed. Right on time. Yes, sir. Good."

He unlocked the deadbolts and relocked them once in the hall, then rushed to the stairs, his anxiety building with each step. Strangers in his place. Unthinkable. But there was no other way. It was necessary, and they'd be gone soon enough.

At the front door, he eyed the four heavyset men in the dim light of the security screen before calling through the metal plate, "Yes?"

"We're here for a pickup. The *Don* sent us."

The *Don*. He'd almost forgotten that was how his benefactor's men always referred to him, so long had it been since he'd interacted with any of them.

"You have something for me?"

The man nearest the camera fished a photograph from his breast pocket and held it up so El Maquino could see it onscreen. It was a picture of a boy at eleven years old, his limbs gangly as he'd begun to grow, awkward as a colt even in the still. It was El Maquino as a child, after he'd been forced to leave Sinaloa to be raised by distant relatives of the *Don* in Mexico City.

"Okay. Just a minute."

He unlocked the door and pulled it open, the heavy steel barrier perfectly balanced on hinges that rarely got any use, a tribute to El Maquino's engineering talents. The men stepped through, two of them pushing heavy-duty hand trucks designed for moving refrigerators, and he closed it behind them and relocked all the deadbolts before nodding to them. "This way."

Once inside his loft, he approached the boxes and gave a long set of instructions on how to move them without damaging the contents. The men paid close attention, even as he repeated himself again, like a tape loop. On the third go-round, the leader of the group held up a hand to stop him from going through the entire process yet again.

"We understand. But we're on a schedule, so we need to get

moving. Thank you for all your help. We'll take good care of them, don't worry."

"Right. But remember they're delicate. Won't do to drop them or jostle them. Won't do at all. You need to be careful. Very careful. Otherwise it could all go wrong, and that would be bad. Very bad."

The leader nodded. "Of course. We'll be careful." He paused. "Too bad the elevator's out of commission."

"I don't like elevators. Better to get exercise. Stairs are good for you. Very good."

"Well, we have our work cut out for us. How much did you say they weigh?"

"Exactly one hundred sixty-two kilos apiece. No doubt about it. One sixty-two. I verified it."

"And it's okay to incline them some? We'll have to."

"Just don't drop them. Tilting them is fine until they're activated. Once they are, though…"

"I remember. The slightest movement. Got it." He turned to his men. "Let's get busy. Slide this first one onto the hand truck and we'll work it down the stairs." He gave El Maquino a look. "Gently, of course."

Half an hour later the boxes were gone, along with their transporters, and El Maquino was left in peace. His heavy boots clumped on the hardwood floor as he traced and retraced his steps as though trying to psychically expunge the damage the intruders had done to his home's aura. He wished he had more food, but wouldn't touch the breakfast portion of his delivery that was waiting in the nearly empty refrigerator. Instead he contented himself with chugging two liters of water to kill the hunger pangs.

"Everything will be okay. It will all be fine. They're gone now. All locked up," he muttered. "All locked up. Gone."

The project had engaged him more than most, and he would miss the technical challenge it had presented. But he still had his hobby, at which he was an expert: drones. The concept of remote-controlled flight had fired his imagination from an early age, and he'd used most of his spare financial resources buying components and designing and building ever more elaborate examples. His one frustration was battery life, and he'd been toying with innovations that, if successful, could revolutionize the remote flight industry.

Not that he cared. He just hated limitations, and batteries were inherently limited. He viewed inefficiency as his mortal enemy, offensive to his sensibility. True, he might only bathe once a week when immersed in a project, and cut his own hair with a vacuum attachment that left it looking like he'd fallen against a fan, but El Maquino had a highly refined sense of the elegance of order – which was why, outside his projects, he spent most of his time reading physics textbooks. He loved the concept of discovering the underlying organizational principles of the universe, and theoretical physics allowed his mind to roam free, unfettered by the boundaries of the Newtonian. Had he wished to engage with others, he could have amazed them with his insights, but interacting with humans was difficult for him, so he avoided doing so. He still remembered how he had been treated during his formative years, and he wasn't about to repeat that as an adult – although the concept of time, like aging, was foreign to him, not because he was oblivious but simply because each day was like the last, with no differentiation other than the end of one project and the beginning of another.

Two hours after beginning his pacing, he finally slowed and moved back to his workbench. He had things to do. His projects weren't going to build themselves, after all.

"Idle hands. No rest for the wicked. A busy man is a happy man," he whispered as he reached for a small motor bought for a steal online in need of rebuilding; its rotor shaft was beginning to wobble from worn bearings. "Got things to do. Yes, I do. Things to do," he repeated, and began to hum as he dismantled the hub with a set of tiny wrenches.

"Tell me that wasn't frigging weird," the largest mover said as the SUV they'd loaded the boxes into made its way through town. "He may be a genius or whatever, but that was a ten on the creepy scale."

The driver nodded. "He's absolutely out of his mind."

"Yes, he is." The large man craned his neck as he looked toward the rear of the big vehicle. "Let's just hope that he's as good as they say. Otherwise we're going to be in a world of hurt."

Nobody had a glib response for that. They knew the stakes. And they were now all relying on the handiwork of a character who belonged in a padded room.

"A world of hurt," the man repeated, and returned to watching the lights streak by as they traversed the still-teeming streets, the after-dinner crowd preparing for another long night of celebration in a city that never slept.

# CHAPTER 20

Rodriguez left headquarters late, as was his custom. His duties as the head of the Mexican clandestine agency were never-ending, and he'd had a particularly demanding day, a series of small crises building to a climax with a dinner meeting that went on for hours.

In other words, par for the course.

His predecessor had been a political appointee who'd suffered a massive stroke at home, and the medical examiner had said he'd died within seconds of the clot stopping bloodflow to his brain. The president had considered naming another empty suit as director of the agency – the appointment of allies or political supporters was a tradition in Mexico – but cooler heads had prevailed, and for the first time someone with actual experience had gotten the job. Rodriguez had spent his entire career with CISEN and had de facto run it for the last few years, so he'd been the natural successor.

But after a week like this one, he was having serious second thoughts about his good fortune.

He walked across the parking lot to his car, a nondescript government-issue Ford sedan, and placed his briefcase on the passenger seat as the engine warmed up. He checked the time and shook his head in frustration – his wife would be asleep, and he could expect to be chastised by her in the morning for working late into the night.

He waved to the security guard manning the gate, and the man pressed a button that slid the iron slab open. The lot was ringed with ten-foot-tall walls to prevent snoopers from identifying members of CISEN staff, although Rodriguez had pointed out to his assistant that anyone in one of the surrounding high-rises could easily photograph the lot, should they be so inclined.

The chances of that happening were slim, though. Unlike in Russia or the U.S., the role of the intelligence service was largely defensive; the agency lacked the resources to be much besides an enforcement arm for the president, and deliberately steered clear of the largest threat to the nation's stability: the cartels. Instead, CISEN ran security when diplomats or heads of state visited, engaged in surveillance on the embassies that dotted the Polanco district, and eavesdropped on the political rivals of the ruling party. Mexico didn't fight wars of aggression in foreign countries, so it didn't have any external threats to speak of – there were no angry mullahs calling for its destruction or foreign powers struggling to dominate it. Any that wished to have the nation dance for it simply had to bribe the right parties, which was how it was always done in Latin America.

He hit his turn signal and rolled onto the small street that led to the larger boulevard two blocks away. The headquarters building was completely anonymous, located on the fringe of a residential neighborhood with no signage marking it, and well-concealed, sophisticated countermeasures deployed on its roof ensured that nobody could eavesdrop on its operations.

Rodriguez switched on the stereo and began humming along to the music, one of his favorite singers who'd become a national emblem of pride with his oversized sombrero and a string of films in the sixties and seventies. He was coming up on the first intersection when the wheel twisted in his hands and a warning light flashed amber on his dashboard. The thumping of a flat tire greeted him as he braked and steered the vehicle to the curb, and he cursed his luck – the last thing he wanted to have to do at that hour was change a tire.

He killed the engine and set the parking brake before swinging the driver's door open and stepping out onto the dark street. A glance at the tire confirmed his worst fear: it was mangled, the sidewall shredded from the rim slicing through it.

Rodriguez popped the trunk and lifted the cargo liner in search of the jack. He was freeing the handle when a familiar voice spoke from behind him.

"I should shoot you in the base of the spine. Paralyze you for the rest of your life."

El Rey. Who Rodriguez had been assured was no longer of this world by now.

"Turn around slowly. Drop the jack handle," the assassin ordered, his soft words more menacing than if he'd screamed the instructions.

Rodriguez debated making a wild swing at the killer and dismissed it. He had zero chance of tackling him one-on-one, but he might be able to talk his way out of the situation. Once before the assassin had appeared like a ghost in his house, and Rodriguez had managed to survive. This time could prove no different, although he suspected it wouldn't be as easy.

He dropped the handle and slowly turned. "I gave you the antidote. What do you want?"

"To spend some quality time with you before I send you into the abyss."

"I don't know what you're talking about."

El Rey shrugged. "You will." The gun in his hand popped, the report almost silent, and Rodriguez winced as a tranquilizer dart imbedded itself in his neck. He reached up to pull it free, but his hand refused to obey his brain's commands, and all he managed was to paw at it. His heart rate slowed, and then his eyes glassed over and he slumped to the ground.

The assassin watched him drop and slid the air gun into his belt before hoisting Rodriguez with ease. Thirty seconds later he was pulling away in a Toyota Highlander he'd stolen earlier, Rodriguez sprawled in the backseat. The drug El Rey had used would reliably keep him unconscious for a good hour, if not longer.

Which was all the time he would need.

~ ~ ~

Rodriguez blinked awake, his lids heavy. His head was throbbing, the sensation not unlike the worst hangover in history, and his mouth was a desert. He was seated on a hard wooden chair, his ankles tied to the legs and his arms cinched behind him. His shoulders were sore from the strain of the odd position, but when he tried to shift, he found that his wrists were secured to the rear of the chair, keeping him upright.

El Rey stepped into his field of vision. His expression detached and calm, he took two steps toward Rodriguez and stopped. "Now we begin."

"Every cop in Mexico will be looking for you after this. We have your picture, your fingerprints…it's not like it used to be. You'll never be able to hide," Rodriguez said.

"I'm guessing that's your way of apologizing for trying to kill me? Your bedside manner could really use some work." El Rey gave him a humorless smile. "Remember that your organization believes I'm dead. From the poison you tried to trick me into injecting. I like my odds of not being hunted – even your crew of morons aren't stupid enough to be looking for a dead man."

"They'll figure it out."

"No, they'll find your tortured corpse burned to an unrecognizable crisp, along with a message from the Los Zetas Cartel stating that this is just the beginning. Of what, I'll leave to their imaginations." El Rey paused. "I'm curious, though. The president himself pardoned me and made the deal. I have his word. And yet that counted for nothing." The assassin's voice was velvet. "Did he authorize this?"

"What if he did? What are you going to do about it? All I can tell you is that it wasn't me. I was just following orders. Exactly as you have dozens of times, putting a bullet in some innocent."

El Rey's smile never faded. "I've never killed an innocent man. If someone was on my list, it was because they were scum."

"Oh, right. Like the ex-president?"

"He's responsible for tens of thousands of deaths, and we both know it. Most world leaders are. He was in bed with at least two cartels that I know of. The blood of their victims was on his hands."

Rodriguez gave him a look of disgust. "Tell yourself that if it makes you feel better."

"The only innocent men I've killed were on your orders, you piece of dung. Which makes *you* responsible, not me. You don't blame the car for killing hapless pedestrians, you blame the driver."

"A meaningless distinction."

El Rey shook his head. "While I appreciate the lesson in moral philosophy, I'm afraid that due to your treachery, I'm on a tight timeline. So I'm going to ask you some questions. They're easy questions, and if you answer them honestly, I'll ensure that your death is painless and your family doesn't pay for your sins. If you decide to play hero, you'll die in excruciating agony, and your wife and children will follow." He took another step toward Rodriguez. "If you doubt me, you're even stupider than you were for risking my wrath."

Rodriguez's eyes narrowed. "My family has nothing to do with it, and you know it."

"I know that you have the choice between them living long, full lives or being found mutilated in a drainage ditch. You hold that power in your hands."

The questions began, and Rodriguez answered as many of them as he could. Some, El Rey knew he didn't know anything about. Others, El Rey already knew the answers to. The only time he lied was when the assassin introduced the topic of who had developed the antidote.

"I told you. The CIA gave it to us. I have no idea who created it for them," Rodriguez insisted.

"See, I think that's not true. I think you know exactly who did, and you're holding out on me. Which is a real shame for your family – I'm sure when I'm flaying your wife's skin off and forcing her to eat pieces of your babies, they won't share your noteworthy sense of honor and duty."

"Please. I've told you everything."

El Rey began his interrogation session in earnest, starting with a pair of wire cutters before escalating to a rotary sander and a bottle of bleach.

Rodriguez lasted longer than most would have, even missing his eyes and much of his face. But he made one slip that was all the information El Rey would need to narrow his search. At one point, he'd referred to the chemist as *she*.

There were only three women on his list of candidates.

El Rey disposed of Rodriguez's body by burying it in a shallow ditch filled with quicklime he'd excavated below the foundation, and then poured a cement cap over it so the area appeared to be part of the floor slab. Rodriguez would have simply disappeared with no explanation, which he hoped would throw CISEN into a tailspin of misdirected activity. Nobody could be sure who had done what, so the agency's efforts would be futile and flailing.

Which would ensure nobody was hunting a dead assassin.

Rodriguez had given him everything he needed; now he just needed to get into the U.S. And while he had no intention of going after Rodriguez's family, he would snuff out the life of the man who'd given the order responsible for El Rey's attempted murder by lethal injection.

Once he returned.

But for now he didn't have the luxury of time to extract his revenge.

He hadn't argued the point with Carla any further, but there was no way he was going to put her in harm's way by allowing her to accompany him to the United States. He knew she was trying to be helpful, but she was an amateur, and he needed the flexibility that came with going it alone. He'd explain to her upon his return, and while he was sure she'd be furious and hurt, he'd have to be alive to see her reaction, and the odds of that would be reduced with her in tow. He'd already foreseen the need for a seamless entry into the U.S. weeks before and had a Canadian passport that would allow him to stroll past immigration without a second glance.

All that remained was to stop by his apartment, retrieve his go bag, and slip into Carla's home to leave a quick note of apology. Then he would board a private plane that awaited his arrival and fly to Ciudad Juarez for an early morning stroll into Texas, and from there, to his first destination.

# CHAPTER 21

The predawn sky glowed purple as the sun's first rays gilded the edges of the eastern mountains that ringed Mexico City. Early morning commuters battled their way toward the city center in a procession of steel and glass, their headlights bouncing over endless potholes.

An ancient panel van with the logo of one of the city's largest cleaning companies lurched to a stop at the rear entrance of the Museum of Anthropology, where a guard with a face darkened with two days' growth watched with boredom.

Three men exited the van and unloaded their supplies from the back, and then a pair of them lowered a ramp and eased a rectangular mini-dumpster onto the pavement. When they were finished, they closed the van up and locked it before moving to the building's rear maintenance exit.

"Hey, Julio. How's it going?" the janitor leading the way called to the guard. He'd been working at the museum for a month and a half, and routinely shared cigarettes and stories with the guard after his cleaning duties were done.

"You know. Same old. Coming loaded for bear today, are you?" the security man asked, eyeing Roberto's companions and their trash container.

"Yeah. I got bitched at yesterday, so I need to haul a bunch of garbage away. You can search it, as usual, when we're through."

"I look forward to it with every beat of my heart," the guard joked, and all the men laughed at the ridiculous notion. The guard would only do a cursory inspection, they knew, to ensure that they weren't making off with any relics, which had never happened in the facility's history. "Who's your crew? Haven't seen them before."

"Oh, sorry. My cousin Octavio, and his friend Cruz."

The pair of laborers waved, and the guard nodded as he unlocked the service entrance. "You know the drill. Stay away from the displays. Don't trigger any alarms. Be out within three hours."

"You got it."

Once inside, the men went about their business of cleaning, figuring that the guard was monitoring their movements from the security center. Toward the end of the shift they moved the rolling dumpster into a maintenance area, and the man using the fake name Roberto unlatched the side panel.

Ten minutes later the cleaning crew rolled the trash-filled dumpster out of the museum. The sleepy-looking guard did a quick look through of the waste they were carting away and nodded to Roberto. "Got any smokes?" he asked.

Roberto told his men to load up the van and shook two Marlboro reds loose from a well-fingered pack. "What time do you get off today?" he asked as he lit their cigarettes.

"The usual. Nine."

"Pretty easy duty, huh?"

The guard blew smoke at the morning sky. "Nothing ever happens here. Easiest job I've ever had. Staying awake's the hardest part about it."

Roberto dropped his partially smoked butt on the ground and ground it out. "Well, I've still got work to do. See you *mañana*."

"You got it."

Across town at one of the main federal buildings a similar scene played out, as a faux cleaning crew delivered its precious cargo into position, taking care to ensure that the messages stenciled on the sides of the box were plainly visible.

The same event took place at the main hospital, where the crew pushed several of the bins due to the large size of the facility. They were interrupted while removing their box from the dumpster by a male nurse who rounded a corner, surprising them.

"What's that?" the nurse asked, eyeing the box.

The nearest janitor smiled as he approached, his hands empty. At the last instant a switchblade materialized in the cleaner's hands, and he drove it without hesitation through the nurse's eye, deep into his brain.

When Roberto was back behind the wheel, he waited until he was through the museum gates and off the grounds before retrieving a cell phone and placing a call.

"Everything's in place. Armed and ready."

"Any complications?"

"No. Nobody suspects a thing."

*Don* Aranas's voice sounded alert in spite of the early hour.

"Good. You've done well." Aranas paused, and when he spoke again, his voice had an ugly edge to it. "Get well clear of there. Within an hour, the games begin. Ditch the vans and head out of town – it's only a matter of time before they have security footage of your faces. I want you back in Culiacán by then."

"We're on our way."

# CHAPTER 22

El Rey walked across the bridge spanning the Rio Grande and then stood in line at the U.S. border crossing as a beagle with a hangdog expression sniffed at his pant legs. An American immigration official, who looked more Hispanic than El Rey, asked him a few perfunctory questions and then stamped his Canadian passport and motioned to the next traveler.

He continued through the complex and out to where dozens of taxis waited. He took the first in line and slid into the back, placing his duffle beside him on the hot bench seat. The driver glanced at him in the rearview mirror and El Rey sat forward. "Airport."

The driver nodded and started the engine. The air conditioner was a relief and the trip to the Brownsville South Padre Island International Airport blessedly short. El Rey peeled off some bills from a fistful of dollars and paid the driver before exiting the cab.

He'd arranged for a charter flight to take him to New York, where the first of the three targets lived – a professor at NYU, who lived in an Upper East Side brownstone and also owned a home in the Hamptons. Recently divorced, she cut an impressive figure in the photographs and videos he'd found of her, mostly from academic conferences.

The jet was a Citation X, easily capable of the 1800-mile flight in a little over three hours, and El Rey recognized the plane's distinctive profile as he approached the private plane terminal. After a muted discussion with a clerk behind a reception desk, a waiting attendant – a stunning brunette with legs to her ears – led him across the tarmac and up the stairs into the fuselage.

The pilot introduced himself and his copilot, and El Rey stashed his bag behind his seat. Five minutes later the flight had been cleared for takeoff and the jet was racing down the runway, pressing the assassin into the comforting folds of the leather throne as the drab sameness of Brownsville blurred by his window in a rush.

The plane lifted into the air and soared effortlessly in a near vertical ascent, and then banked over the Gulf of Mexico's sparkling azure surface. El Rey took a sip of his water and set the crystal glass down on the polished walnut tray as he replayed the prior night in his mind. Carla had been asleep when he'd stolen into the house, and he'd felt a pang of remorse when he'd left his note and pressed a soft kiss to her face.

She'd be waking up about now, and he fully expected her to be enraged at his callous disregard for her wishes. He'd make amends when he returned. For now, he needed to focus on the task at hand, which was locating and interrogating the first of his subjects. He'd need to knock out the two in the U.S. quickly if he was to make it to Israel to find the third before his symptoms became so bad they interfered with his ability to carry out his mission. He hoped that trip wouldn't be necessary – that either the woman in New York or the one in Baltimore was the creator of the toxin – but he had to be prepared for the worst, which meant that he was already badly behind schedule.

The flight from Mexico City had been uneventful. The Lear 65 was comfortable enough, and there was nobody around in the private terminal to be interested in a single male in his early thirties embarking on a private domestic flight at two a.m. His bag hadn't been checked by the sleepy security worker; at his request there had been no attendant on the plane; and the pilots had studiously avoided interacting with him. He'd managed several hours of sleep on that flight and hoped to do the same on this one. Still, though, he couldn't help but notice the faint facial twitching that had arrived with dawn.

He knew the progression he could expect from prior bouts with the neurotoxin, and he hoped that the tics, like the tremors, would abate before returning with increased severity later. But by his reckoning, it was no more than forty-eight hours on the outside before his cognitive functioning became impaired – which was more alarming than the other symptoms, because his edge was his ability to reason faster than his adversaries. If that quit, he might as well pull the trigger of the gun that would end his ordeal himself.

The morose inner dialogue was also a symptom of the neurotoxin's insidious progress, he recognized, and he forced the negative thoughts away. The errand was straightforward: find the women, question them, and proceed as necessary.

He felt no remorse at the prospect of terminating the scientists. They were all engaged in research and development for the military industrial complex, crafting nightmare substances for their masters and fully aware of what those agents would be used for. That made them no different than soldiers, although extremely well-compensated ones – he knew from the background checks that all three were in the seven- to eight-figure net worth range, and it wasn't because they'd won the lottery. Being the lapdog of the clandestine agencies was lucrative, and part of that was hazard pay, as well as hush money so they would never discuss their work.

El Rey didn't judge them for their deeds – if it hadn't been them, it would have been others – nor did he bear the creator of the toxin any grudge. They did what they had to do, and he would do what he had to. It was a simple equation.

Whether his trip would be for naught was a different matter. His greatest fear was that the antidote was something that couldn't be easily manufactured, or that would take more time than he had, or that required specialized ingredients or equipment that he wouldn't be able to source.

He quieted his imagination. There were always obstacles; he'd tackle them as they arose. Worrying about the unknown served no constructive purpose, and he banished the doubts, at least partly attributable to the poison working its dark magic. He knew better than to allow his imagination to run away like this, especially once he was in play – all it would do was distract him and diminish his focus, which he couldn't afford.

The plane leveled off at forty-three thousand feet, and he pulled the shade down over the window. He took a final swig of water and replaced the glass on the tray, drew a deep breath, and willed himself to sleep. El Rey slowly drifted off to the lullaby of the muted roar of the twin turbines, and the last image in his psyche was Carla, hair spread across her pillow like an angel's halo, slumbering like the innocent she was.

# CHAPTER 23

*La Paz, Baja California Sur, Mexico*

Ernesto stood in the shade of a doorway and scanned the dusty street. A rooster crowed down the block in the barrio that framed the main highway that stretched north to the U.S. and meandered south to Los Cabos. The homes were all four hundred square feet and broiling in the 114 degree heat, their occupants accustomed to the oven-like conditions, doomed to a lifetime of suffering by poverty and lack of opportunity.

At twenty-six, Ernesto had lived in La Paz for four months, and detested every moment of it. He'd come over on the ferry along with dozens of others, from Topolobampo in Sinaloa. He'd grown up near Culiacán and cut his teeth when barely a teen as a street dealer for the Sinaloa Cartel. He was in Baja because he'd recently gotten a better offer from the new group Agundez had formed, which had raised his weekly take from three thousand pesos to four – or roughly two hundred and fifty dollars – and as much of the meth as he could trim from the gram baggies he sold twelve hours a day.

Ernesto spied a girl with a shapely figure several houses down and whistled at her. That was Maria, the daughter of a hotel worker, just turned fifteen, whom Ernesto had been plying with marijuana for several weeks as he enjoyed her considerable charms – in secret, of course, because her father would have gone ballistic if he'd suspected one of the neighborhood gangsters was tapping his delicate hothouse flower.

Maria waved at him and waggled her hips invitingly, her short shorts and yellow halter top offering scant concealment of her curves. He held up three fingers – he'd be off in three hours, his night shift complete, his position replaced by another just like him who ran the day crew.

La Paz, which meant "The Peace" in English, had been ravaged by a violent drug war as Sinaloa battled the upstart Agundez Cartel for territory that had previously been exclusively Sinaloa's. For twenty years Aranas had cut deals with the mayor and governor, paying for the plaza of La Paz and all points south, but he'd been betrayed once imprisoned. The rumor was that the mayor had sold the plaza twice, accepting money from Agundez as well as Aranas, and in the process bringing mainland-style bloodshed to a region that had boasted a lower homicide rate than most of the industrialized world.

It was rumored that the mayor's family had fled to San Diego, where he owned a vacation home on the water in La Jolla, and that he was now living on the army base, surrounded by military, fearful of being taken down by one of the angry cartels. Selling the plaza twice was a huge no-no, the penalty for which was death. That was well understood by every politician in Mexico, but the mayor had decided to risk it with Aranas incarcerated, at the direct expense of the population and any tourism the area enjoyed.

Ernesto didn't know how much of the rumor was true, and he didn't care. It changed nothing for him – his job was to sell the locals their drug of choice and to avoid drama. So far it had been hard to accomplish, because the barrio access road was the line of demarcation between the two cartels' territories, with Sinaloa claiming the west side and Agundez the east.

There had been sixteen shootings in the last two days as rolling gun battles ravaged the city. The weapon of choice was the "Cuerno de Chivo" – the "goat's horn," the slang term for the AK-47, due to its distinctive curved magazine. The cartel shooters were indiscriminate, as well as generous with their expenditures of ammo, and the average shooting involved at least thirty rounds – the entire capacity of a full magazine, usually emptied on full auto. The last killing had been at four in the morning, near the waterfront, where two of Ernesto's colleagues had been gunned down as they walked along the *malecon* after a hard night dealing in the clubs that fronted onto the bay.

Ernesto was already jittery from the meth that kept him alert through the night, and the escalation in violence had done nothing to calm his nerves, even though there had been no incursions into his barrio. But he knew that every minute on the street posed a risk, and he was keeping his eyes open; the old Beretta 9mm pistol stuffed into his waistband at the small of his back gave slim comfort.

Traffic had been dead for the last five hours. Nobody wanted to get caught in the crossfire of a drug war, and only the most desperate of addicts were willing to brave a trip for their fix. That would hit Ernesto in the wallet if it kept up. Standard operating procedure was to hold the street dealer accountable for any slowdown, even if due to circumstances outside his control, the assumption being that if the business lagged, it was because of something the dealer was doing – either diluting the drugs too much or robbing his customers or behaving abnormally. Ernesto knew the game, having grown up in it, and was already calculating what the lull would likely cost him if there was no pickup soon.

His burner cell phone vibrated in the front pocket of his below-the-knee shorts. He pulled it free, his eyes constantly surveying the dusty street as he raised it to his ear.

"Yeah?"

"How you doin'?" his friend Gerzain asked.

"Got nothin' happening. You?"

"Dead, man, dead. You hear about Lala and Gumbo?"

"Yeah. Shit's getting real now, homey. Watch yourself."

"I hear that. You seen anything your way?"

"*Nada*. Although I heard somebody pop a few caps maybe an hour ago."

"Oh. That was just some punkass. We set him straight." Occasionally one of the barrio youths tried to cut into the business, which was dealt with swiftly by whichever cartel ran the neighborhood. The penalty for trying to sell a baggie of rock was death. Even so, there was a regular move by the dimmer of the locals to make some easy money, and this year Ernesto's crew had snuffed out a dozen homeboys who'd missed the memo. All part of the game, he knew, as unremarkable as a flat tire or a spilled Pacifico.

The going price to kill a man in La Paz had dropped to two hundred dollars, a fraction of what it had been before the cartel clash. Ernesto had murdered three men since arriving in La Paz – welcome pocket money for him that subsidized his habit. They had all been strangers to him, who'd either offended the wrong person or were banging the wrong man's wife or whose business had interfered with someone else's. He never asked and didn't care. He just popped them and went home.

"So what's up, man?" Ernesto asked.

"Getting ugly, you know?" Gerzain said.

"Yeah, well–" Ernesto was cut off by the sound of an unmuffled motor as an old Nissan pickup truck swung down the dirt track and accelerated toward him. He froze for a half second and then reached for his weapon as he backed toward the door. He'd almost made it when the silence of the street was shattered by the rattle of a Kalashnikov.

The wall behind him exploded into chips of mortar as rounds slammed into the cinderblock dwelling, and then a spray of red fountained from his back as three slugs punched through his chest. His finger squeezed his pistol's trigger as he tumbled backward into the house, but the shots ricocheted harmlessly off the building across the street as the vehicle sped off.

Maria came running once the dirt road had fallen still. Ernesto labored for breath as his savaged lungs filled with blood. His deeply tanned skin was pale from shock. She screamed at the sight of him dying, and then his consciousness faded; the final sound of his short life was her strangled cry for someone to call an ambulance.

It took almost half an hour for the police to arrive, and when they did, it was two pickup trucks with municipal cops – experts in avoiding confronting any crime that might involve risk. They emptied out of the truck, and one of them placed a call to the hospital as he studied Ernesto's blood-soaked corpse, the street dealer's face now covered with bluebottle flies. His passing was unremarkable and unmourned except by a teenage girl down the way who would soon discover that she was two months pregnant with Ernesto's progeny, and who would have to run away from home and ultimately work in a strip bar to support herself and her infant son – another casualty in a war that was an ongoing part of the Mexican condition.

# CHAPTER 24

*Mexico City, Mexico*

Rafael Norteño tilted his head toward a member of the president's inner circle as he strode down a polished marble corridor that led to his office, a burgundy ostrich-skin briefcase in one hand and a cup of Starbucks coffee in the other. He wore his thick ebony hair slicked straight back, and his expensive blue suit had been immaculately pressed and tailored to his slight frame. He paused at the door and smiled to himself when he saw the plaque announcing him as the president's chief of staff. He'd replaced his predecessor six months earlier, and since then had made a point of arriving early most days and working well after the rest of the staffers had gone home.

Norteño was a man on the move, his rise to the lofty position unexpected for a man so young – he was only thirty-seven, and most of those who'd held his office had been in their fifties. His family's political connections had launched his career, but it was his ruthlessness and his willingness to work long hours that had taken him the rest of the way, and he'd earned the respect of the rest of the president's entourage after a somewhat rocky start. Envy and backstabbing had nearly brought him down, but he'd persevered, made alliances with his enemies, compromised with those he'd had to, and was now firmly enthroned in what many considered to be the penultimate position of influence in the Mexican government – second only to the president himself.

His secretary looked up from her desk when he pushed through the ornately carved mahogany door, a concerned look on her face. "There you are," she said. "I've been trying to call you."

"I'm sorry. I had my phone on silent. What's going on?"

"Number One wants to see you as soon as you get in," she said, her voice low. Number one was the staff's slang for the president.

Norteño's eyebrows rose. "Well, then, I better get over to his side of the building. Did he say why?"

"Only that it was extremely important. His assistant has called three times. First was half an hour ago. Then every ten minutes."

Norteño frowned. That was unusual. "Let me drop my briefcase in the office and I'll head over." He made his way to his door. "Call Numero Uno's assistant and let her know I'm on the way."

"Will do."

He parked his case on his desk, took a long pull on his coffee, and returned to his secretary's station as she was hanging up. "Anything else? Anyone call? Pressing emergencies I need to deal with?"

She shook her head. "No. She said they're expecting you."

"They?"

"The Security Council. Number One convened a meeting."

That was serious. Norteño didn't delay any longer. "Phone's now on ring. Only call if the world's ending."

He hurried to the executive wing and felt his stomach lurch when he saw the president's assistant's face, which could only be described as drawn. She stood and rounded her desk and, as she neared him, murmured quietly in passing, "I don't know the details, but judging by everyone's mood, it's ugly." Her hand brushed his, and then she was at the antechamber door. "Good luck."

"That bad?" he asked, trying out a small smile.

She didn't return it. "They're waiting."

Norteño stepped into the large sitting area and his unease increased when he saw the number of aides crammed into the space. It seemed like every top analyst and member of the military's upper ranks was waiting in the antechamber. He strode past, returning a few nods, and lightly knocked at the president's office door.

"Enter," the president's voice called.

The six members of the Security Council were seated with the president at an oval conference table, along with the heads of the army and navy. All eyes drilled into Norteño as he approached the only vacant chair, immediately to the president's right, and sat. "Sorry. Phone problems," he said.

The president waved the explanation away as he refocused his attention on the flat-screen monitor on the wall.

"Now that you're here, we'll watch this again," the president said, and nodded to his aide. The man tapped something on his computer and the screen blinked to life.

Norteño gasped when *Don* Aranas's face filled the screen. He stared straight at the assembly for two pregnant seconds, and when he began to speak, his voice sounded as smooth as a diplomat's.

"Gentlemen, I'm assuming the president is watching with you, or has already seen this, so I'll keep this short in the interests of time. This morning, while Mexico slept, three explosive devices were placed in critical locations around the city: the main hospital, the federal building by the cathedral, and the Museum of Anthropology."

"Louder," the president commanded, and his aide complied by boosting the volume.

"There are several things you should know. First, there is enough explosive in each bomb to destroy the targeted building. Second, the devices were designed by an expert who has engineered them so that any attempt to move or disable them will result in them detonating. Third, they will go off in forty-eight hours, at precisely eight a.m., unless my conditions are met. And finally, any attempt at duplicity on your part will result in me detonating all of them simultaneously." Aranas cleared his throat. "I trust I now have your attention."

"Bastard," the president whispered.

"Now for my demands. They are simple. I want a billion American dollars' worth of diamonds within forty-eight hours. Delivered to my men at a place of my choosing, with time to verify that the stones aren't fakes. I'll caution that I have experts waiting to pore over each diamond, and at the first sign of a dummy, the bombs go off." Aranas smirked. "You're probably thinking that you can pull a fast one, but that would be the worst mistake of your life, because I won't hesitate to blow all three buildings to kingdom come."

"He's insane," Norteño muttered. The president cut him off with a curt hand gesture.

"You are not to breathe a word of this transaction to anyone, or the bombs will be detonated. It will remain our little secret for all time. Failure to comply will result in the deaths of thousands – which would be on your heads." Aranas checked his watch and nodded. "So it begins. Nobody is to be allowed in or out of the buildings during that forty-eight hours. Any violation will result in detonation. You are responsible for containing the crowds inside. Use any explanation you like with the media and law enforcement, except the truth – I'd tell them it's terrorism, an always popular ruse thanks to our neighbors to the north. In any event, you should know from my reputation that I don't bluff, so do not make the mistake of testing me. One billion dollars' worth of untraceable diamonds – a paltry sum, you'll agree, but the amount I value my time at for the period you kept me behind bars." He smiled again. "There will be no negotiations. Comply, or you will be responsible for the death of countless innocents. Don't behave foolishly. I'd suggest you talk to the Americans about securing the stones, or perhaps contact DeBeers. Where they come from is of no concern to me, as long as they are delivered by my deadline."

Aranas looked to his left and then back to the camera. "Oh, and Mr. President? I'd advise you to discuss this with your advisors, because if you're thinking of behaving dishonestly, as you have so often in the past, hopefully they will talk you out of it. It would be disastrous for your political party, as well as for you personally, if it were to become known why I'm doing this. So it will remain between us: we had a deal, and you reneged once in power. You negotiated with the most wanted cartel leader in the world to become president, and then tried to wiggle out of your agreement. That will not be tolerated. If you force my hand, I will ensure that it's broadcast until it's common knowledge all over Mexico. I have our pre-election discussion on tape, so it will be irrefutable, and broadcasting it will destroy you as certainly as a gunshot to the head. Consider that carefully. You have forty-eight hours."

The screen went black.

The president sat back, his youthful face having aged ten years in as many minutes. "All right. How do we proceed?"

The next half hour was pandemonium, with the members of the council frantically trying to find an alternative to acceding to the drug lord's demands. Norteño remained silent throughout the deliberations, waiting for everyone to assert their positions and make recommendations. Eventually the president tired of the circular discussion and turned to Norteño, as Norteño knew he would, and sat forward. "What do you think, Rafael? What would you do?"

Norteño badly wished he'd drunk the rest of his coffee as he considered how best to frame his recommendation. His next words could either destroy his career or make him irreplaceable in the president's eyes. Every hour of effort had led him to this exact moment, and he needed to be both convincing and reasonable if his advice was to prevail.

Norteño sighed and stood. "Aranas has created a perfect trap. Any hint of his accusations about the president will destroy the party and his legacy, so he knows we must keep it secret. He knows that it doesn't matter whether there's any validity to it – such is the state of trust among the people that it's a convincing enough story to be taken as truth. It's virtually impossible to prove a negative, so he's painted us into a corner with that."

The president nodded slowly. "And?"

"The amount of money he's demanding seems large, but in reality it can be done without being discovered – we lose many times more than that each year to petroleum and energy theft, so we could easily hide the loss somewhere it will never be discovered. He chose an amount that, while large, is sufficiently bite-sized that we can do it without detection." Norteño paused. "I've heard a lot of good arguments for refusing to negotiate with this criminal, for standing on high moral principle, all of it is based on good instincts. The problem is that doing so would result in a lot of dead citizens, our administration in tatters, the party destroyed, and the public trust so badly damaged that it could well result in a revolution."

"That would never happen," one of the advisors argued. "We have all the guns."

"If by *we*, you mean the government, I'd argue we don't – the cartels are armed at least as well as our forces, if not better. And remember that the soldiers we would use to quell a rebellion are the sons of the very people we would be ordering them to put down. With all due respect, I think you're misjudging the political consequences." Norteño shook his head. "What I would advise is that the president consider what's best for Mexico, not what's best for some elusive ethical position. I can't see how having three buildings blown up, proving to everyone we're incapable of protecting our population, would be worth the cost, never mind the toll in human life. And we have to consider the international ramifications – if this is allowed to escalate, it will signal that the country is out of control. That will decimate investment, which would plunge us into a depression we aren't prepared to weather, and would likely result in the same sort of political unrest I've described."

"Then you're recommending we pay this…this criminal?" the head of the council sputtered. "Impossible. It would set us up to be blackmailed whenever he likes. Worse yet, by still others." The man leaned forward and fixed the president with a hard gaze. "We cannot reward extortion, regardless of the cost to us."

The president considered the man's words. "I need to take this all under advisement and mull it over. Gentlemen, let's reconvene in two hours. I'll have made my decision by then. In the meantime, not a word to anyone. Consider this a matter of national security. Anyone who breathes even a hint will be jailed for treason."

The men rose, and as they were filing out, the president cleared his throat and tapped Norteño on the arm. Norteño glanced over his shoulder and caught the president's look – he was to stay.

The door closed behind the last member of the council and the president moved to his desk and sat behind it, motioning for Norteño to take a seat. He rubbed a hand over his face and blinked twice. "Coffee?"

"That would be much appreciated, Mr. President. I have a feeling we're going to need it."

The president pressed a button on his handset and ordered a pot, and then focused his attention on Norteño. "I need a compromise position, Rafael. For the record, I completely agree with everything you said, but I need to give the council something, or they'll hang me. Put on your thinking cap, because I believe, like you, we need to deal with this in the manner that's best for Mexico, not best for our machismo, which is what a lot of that posturing seemed to be about."

"The only concession you can make is to either try to screw Aranas on the ransom, or try to disarm one of the devices. Both are disastrous ideas, Mr. President."

"I understand. But I have to at least try to do something, wouldn't you agree?"

"Do you think the people who die if the attempt fails will care much about your motivation for okaying it?" Norteño asked softly. "To risk disarming even one of the devices could cause him to detonate them all. To what end? To save a billion of public money? As I said, it's a billion that will never be missed. Or to salve some bruised Security Council feelings? It's the wrong decision, Mr. President."

Another aide entered with a silver service, set a china service before them, and poured the cups full with rich, dark brew before disappearing wordlessly.

"I know. But the reality is I need to try, even if it's ill advised. So I want you to figure out how we can recover from an attempt – and how we can explain it to Aranas, as well as the public, if the worst happens."

Norteño drank half his cup in two swallows and placed it on the desk. "The terrorism angle isn't bad. I'd suggest we go with that as the official explanation – and it is terrorism, make no mistake. We just don't identify who exactly the terrorist is or what the demand is – we only offer half the story. Madmen have placed bombs in prominent places. We're working around the clock to save the world. If one goes off, they're to blame, not us."

The president nodded. "And Aranas?"

"Figure out who you're going to hang that on. You have to claim that an attempt was made against your direct orders, by a rogue faction in law enforcement or the military. And you need to offer up a scapegoat."

"I can't do that."

"Of course you can. You suggest it as a condition of making the attempt. These geniuses want to press for disarming it? Then they have to be prepared to take the blame if it fails. No agreement to do so, no attempt." Norteño stared off into space. "You can always pardon them later. They can serve their time in their mansions, under house arrest. It will all be a show, nothing more."

"You think that will appease Aranas?"

"I think he wants a billion dollars in diamonds more than he wants to prove a point. Give him an out and he'll probably take it."

"And if you're wrong?"

Norteño swallowed the remainder of his coffee and frowned. "Then God help us all, because it will be Armageddon if all three buildings go up and we could have prevented it for a few pieces of silver."

"It's more than a few."

"It's a rounding error on the budget. They'll lynch you, Mr. President. Your adversaries will be able to put an exact price tag on what you weren't willing to pay for each Mexican life lost – never mind the damage to the city and to the country's integrity, which would be long lasting, as I outlined."

"Then you don't think we should even attempt it."

"If you do, pick the least crowded building. Probably the museum – it isn't open yet, so it will only be a few of the staff and some guards. The federal building will have thousands in it at this hour. Same for the hospital. So the museum's the only choice."

"God, I don't want to make this call," the president said. "I really don't. Even if it's only twenty people, if we're wrong…"

"You know where I stand on it – I think it's the wrong move. I'd tell the council you're going to give in and do the least damage possible under the circumstances."

The discussion lasted ten more minutes, after which the president asked to be alone until the council reconvened later. As Norteño was leaving, the president called to him. "Figure it will be the museum, even though there will be outrage at the loss of irreplaceable artifacts if it all goes wrong. But lives are more important than relics." The president sighed. "Issue orders barring anyone from leaving all three buildings, effective immediately. I'll sign them. We'll go with the terrorist threat, more to follow, and iron out the details with the council. Kill all cell service in those areas of the city, too. We can't take the chance of a stray signal detonating one of the devices."

Norteño nodded. "Yes, Mr. President. Good thinking. I'll get right on it."

He pulled the door closed behind him and eyed the full chamber without expression, and then made his way past the gathered staff. Whatever happened from this point on, he was the president's most trusted confidant.

Now they just needed to survive the next forty-eight hours without a blunder, and he'd be golden.

# CHAPTER 25

Dinah waited for the doctor to return with the results of the blood test. She'd been poked and prodded and was anxious to hear the verdict. The doctor had been typically tight-lipped, refusing to speculate about her symptoms, and had told her that the first results would be ready shortly – he'd put a rush on the order.

That had been almost two hours earlier, and still no word. She was getting frustrated with the shuffle, made worse because her damned phone wouldn't work in the building. She'd tried to get on the Internet to check her messages, and her cell had shown no service, no signal. Probably something to do with the construction of the massive edifice, she reasoned, and chalked it up to the way her luck was running.

A nurse emerged from the medical offices and called Dinah's name. She rose and dutifully followed her through the crowded waiting area back to the doctor's exam room.

Five more agonizing minutes went by, and then the doctor entered, several pages of test results clutched in his hand. He looked around the room, spotted a pen, walked over to it and made a notation, and then pulled up a stool and sat across from Dinah.

She swallowed, her mouth suddenly dry. "Doctor – what is it?"

"Your results show you're healthy as a horse, Dinah. White count fine, red good, everything within normal parameters."

"Then why do I feel so out of sorts?" she demanded, all the frustration of the long wait mingling with the relief that nothing material was wrong with her.

"You feel that way because you're pregnant, Dinah." He held up the test results. "My hunch is about seven weeks. Did you miss a period?"

"What? Pregnant?" She processed the question. "Sometimes I'm irregular. I have been my entire life. I didn't think anything…" Dinah locked eyes with him. "Are you a hundred percent sure?"

The doctor smiled for the first time. "It's hard to be just a little pregnant, Dinah. You either are or you aren't. The blood test is reliable. Sometimes the urine tests aren't, especially the home versions, but the blood test doesn't lie." He nodded. "Congratulations. This is your first, correct?"

"Yes," she answered numbly.

"I'll make an appointment for you with one of my colleagues – the best ob-gyn in Mexico City, if you don't have a preference for your own."

"Oh, mine's pretty good, but if yours is better…"

"She's considered the top pick in town, Dinah. It's who my wife sees."

Two minutes of small talk and several stammered questions later, Dinah found herself standing outside in the waiting room with a slip of paper in her hand. She looked up as an older woman accompanied by two security guards, their expressions serious, came through the door and demanded everyone's attention. The patients quieted and the stern woman scanned the room.

"We have a breaking emergency in the hospital. I'm afraid nobody can leave – police orders. That's all I know right now, and I ask for everyone's patience and cooperation in a difficult situation. If anyone needs care urgently, you'll be prioritized." The woman paused. "No cell use, either. They've apparently shut down the towers." She looked around the waiting area with a glare that could have peeled paint. "I'll return when I have more information. Are there any questions?"

The room exploded into bedlam as fifty people all clamored to be heard. It took fifteen minutes of the woman reassuring everyone that everything was for their own safety, as well as reiterating that the exits were barred by the police and the military, to quiet the crowd. Dinah finally got to ask the question that had been burning in her throat. "Is there something contagious they're trying to quarantine?"

She hated even voicing the possibility, but this was a hospital, and not allowing anyone to leave was beyond draconian.

The woman shook her head. "Not that I know of. But I would definitely stay in this area. We haven't been told enough to be completely sure, but I didn't get that impression. And I believe I would have been told. This seems more like something criminal or a security threat. Maybe they're looking for someone in the facility. Again, I'm sorry," she said, holding up her hands at a new round of shouted questions. "I have to go see other floors. These two gentlemen will be guarding the doors to ensure you aren't disturbed. Thanks for your cooperation."

"Then we're prisoners?" Dinah exclaimed.

"Not any more than I am," the woman countered. "I'm not allowed to leave either. Please. Let me do my job. I promise I'll be back as soon as I have more information."

"You come in here, announce the building's locked down and we're all forbidden to leave, and we're supposed to just smile and thank you?" Dinah countered, biting back an insult at the last second.

"Señora, I'm afraid none of us has any choice, so whether you like it or not doesn't change anything. Now I have a difficult job to do, and several hundred more patients to break the news to, so you'll have to excuse me. I'm not the one who's keeping you here – it's the police and the army. If you have a problem with that, take it up with them."

"And how am I supposed to do that with my cell not working?" Dinah spun and faced the reception desk. "Can I make a call on a landline?"

The woman's veneer cracked and for an instant her humanity leaked through the severe façade. She obviously hadn't received instructions on whether or not to allow patients to use the hospital phones.

"I…I need to check."

"That's not going to wash. My husband is the head of one of the city's Federal Police task forces. I want to call him. Right now. He needs to know what's going on."

The woman's countenance hardened. "I said I'd check. That's the best I can do."

"And I'm saying that's not good enough." Dinah's voice softened. "Look. I just found out I'm pregnant. My husband doesn't know. Give me a break here. I want to tell him. Please."

"I can't. But I'll be back shortly with an answer."

"By what legal authority do you deny me the right to communicate with my husband?" Dinah asked. "That's kidnapping. I haven't done anything wrong. I've committed no crime."

"Look, lady, I sympathize, but I'm not a lawyer. I said I'd ask, and I will. But you don't have a right to use hospital phones. Let's just get very clear on that, all right? We own those, not you, so just settle down, be patient, and I'll be back."

Dinah shook her head. "What kind of automaton are you? By what right do you keep us locked up like criminals?"

"It's not me. I'm just following orders."

The nameless woman turned and marched out the door, leaving the stunned room to stare down the guards, who responded to the frightened and outraged looks by fingering their batons nervously, clearly as unsure of their role in the unfolding drama as anyone.

Dinah and three other women pushed to the picture window at the far end of the waiting room and peered down at the street, where fire trucks, army personnel carriers, and police vehicles blocked the boulevard as emergency workers set up barricades. A shadow drifted across their faces and they looked up to see a military helicopter hovering nearby, and further away, a brightly painted network helo keeping a safe distance.

The woman next to Dinah shook her head as she took in the spectacle. "What the hell is going on? They've closed the whole street…"

Dinah moved back from the window as a trickle of sweat worked its way down her spine. Whatever it was, she needed to remain calm and not become overwrought.

Because now it was about more than her.

She had a life inside of her.

A baby. Unexpected, but not unwelcome.

Which gave her pause. She wasn't sure how she felt in the wake of everything that had happened, but her overwhelming emotion was joy at the idea that she was going to be a mother. But what about Cruz? She'd come to grips with the idea that he was married to the job – his career, "the other woman" in their shared existence – but how would he react to the fact that he was about to become a father for the second time in his life?

She knew his history, the atrocities that had been committed to his family.

Could he put that behind him and look to the future?

Would he be happy or shocked?

Dinah felt her phone in her pocket and choked back the frustration she felt at not being able to tell him the news. It wasn't fair. The biggest thing to happen in their relationship, and she was muzzled by circumstance.

She took several deep breaths and stared out at the street again.

Whatever was going on, it wasn't good. She'd spent enough time around her husband to know that when the entire apparatus mobilized, it had to be big. And big, in law enforcement terms, was never, ever a positive.

# CHAPTER 26

Static buzzed in Briones's earbud as he peered around the rear of the undercover van, eyeing the building where the delivery of the underage girls destined for short lives of drug-addicted prostitution was to occur at any moment. So far there were only a few vehicles parked at the curb, which a run of the license plates had told him belonged to anonymous corporations – no doubt fronts through which the cartel laundered money and bought assets.

He'd long ago understood that when the scale of illegal revenues was so large that it dwarfed many other aspects of the legitimate economy, many seemingly honest businesses would be tainted by the dirty money, especially in Mexico, where the cartels had been earning hundreds of billions of dollars for decades. He grasped that just about any investigation of apparently legit enterprises would sooner or later reveal a cartel connection, just as they would in the U.S., which shared its neighbor to the south's plethora of hotels that thrived even when there were never any guests, automobile dealerships that never seemed to sell cars, and real estate developers who always had ready access to cash even in the most doubtful of environments.

It was just the way of the world, and he'd have had to been blind not to see it.

Of course, the entire bureaucracy was devoted to not spotting what was plainly before its eyes, and there was no man so blind as one whose self-interest depended upon a lack of vision. The intersection of politics and organized crime was so obvious that it was assumed in any election that all the candidates were in the pockets of one cartel or another. Mexicans were pragmatic about human weakness and failings, and in a nation where two-thirds lived in abject poverty, it was naïve to believe that those fortunate enough to get rich by being able to run for office weren't doing so in order to advance the interests of the criminal elite who operated the country for their enrichment.

If Briones had been predisposed to alcoholism, the reality of his job and its ultimate futility would have been more than enough pretense for him to drown himself in the bottle. The only thing that kept him from doing so was the knowledge that his actions did matter to the victims he saved – and today, he was the defender of children destined for unimaginable degradation at the hands of human animals.

The drop-off location was an industrial building next door to a strip club, and their informer had told them that interested patrons of the latter establishment, once vetted as discreet, could take a locked passage between the two structures to where the children were kept. The thought made Briones's skin crawl, but he forced himself to remain calm – allowing his fury at the wanton destruction of young lives to dominate his thoughts would do nobody any good. He needed to stay impartial and dispassionate until the operation was over. As hard a part of the job as any, but a necessary one.

His earbud crackled and a voice spoke over the comm channel. "Truck just rounded the corner. Should be on your street within fifteen seconds."

Briones nodded and tapped his microphone active. "They're here. Let's do this by the book. No shooting unless fired upon, exactly as discussed."

"Roger that."

The laboring sound of a diesel engine reached him just before a senile split-axle bobtail truck with a faded red moving company logo lumbered around the corner and headed his way. Briones ducked back, out of sight, and waited until the squeal of brakes told him the truck was pulling to a stop in front of the building. He waited as the motor idled, and then heard voices. The driver shut the engine off just as Briones peeked back around the side of the van in time to see a group of figures emerge from the doorway and move to the truck's cargo door.

Another voice, that of a sniper on an adjacent roof, came over the comm line. "I make eight people, five with assault rifles."

Briones answered, "I see them. Target the guy in the red hoodie. He looks the most capable."

"Got him."

Briones watched as two of the figures reached up and unlatched the door. It slid up and disappeared, and the two climbed into the truck and dropped a loading ramp before sliding a stack of cartons out of the way. Briones saw a false wall with another door halfway down the truck's length, and waited as the driver climbed aboard and moved to it with a key in his hand. He unlocked the padlock and flung the door wide, and Briones's eyes narrowed at the sight of the first of the unfortunates emerging from the pitch black, her clothes soaked through with sweat from the long trip in what was apparently an unventilated compartment.

"I have a child sighted. Let's move in. Remember, only engage if there's resistance." Briones reached down and lifted a bullhorn, took a breath, and then depressed the speaker button. "Federal Police. Drop your weapons. You're surrounded. Drop your weapons – now."

His announcement was greeted by a hail of gunfire. Slugs thumped into the side of the van as the cartel gunmen shot in the direction of the warning. Answering fire rattled from the rooftop and the surrounding vehicles, where twenty of his men were concealed.

The exchange was over in moments, with all of the cartel slavers wounded or dead on the pavement except the two who'd been in the truck and the unarmed driver. The pair in the cargo hold tossed out their pistols and stepped into the morning sunlight with their hands raised, the sight of their dead companions freezing them in place as Briones's men closed on the truck, weapons trained on them.

Briones ran toward the vehicle, barking orders into his earbud. "Fuentes, take a dozen men and secure the building. There could be more in there."

"Roger."

A short sergeant shaped like a fireplug gestured to his contingent of men and led them into the warehouse as Briones neared the truck. His eyes met the little girl's, and he felt a surge of rage course through him that it took every bit of his willpower to fight down. She was emaciated, her eyes huge, her gaze the thousand-yard stare of a death-row prisoner.

Briones pointed his pistol at the three men still in the cargo hold. "How many in the building?"

"Only two."

A volley of gunfire from inside confirmed that Fuentes had found those gunmen. Briones motioned with his pistol. "One by one – get down on the ground. Keep your hands where we can see them at all times or you're dead. You," he called out to the driver. "You first."

The prospect of any last minute resistance faded in the face of eight M16s trained on the cartel thugs from close range, and the gunmen did as ordered. When they were all cuffed, Briones climbed aboard the truck and moved to the doorway through which the little girl had retreated as she watched the arrest from a safe distance.

"It's okay. We're the police. You're free. Tell the others to come out," Briones said, taking soft steps toward her. The fear on her face was obvious, but she turned halfway toward the doorway and called out in a tiny voice.

More faces peered into the sunlight and Briones almost choked at the nauseating odor that drifted from the hold. The girls came out, one by one, their bare feet tentative on the metal truck bed, all of them soaked through with perspiration and waste. When the last one moved to the edge of the truck, Briones helped them to the ground, and two personnel carriers arrived, trailed by four ambulances.

The first little girl pointed at the hold. "Two are really sick. They're still in there," she said, and then the ambulances were pulling to a halt and the paramedics were rushing to the girls.

Briones approached the door of the hidden compartment and withdrew a flashlight from his belt. He held his breath as he shined the beam into the darkness, and the light bounced off two forms on the floor, curled into fetal positions, tiny in the gloom. He forced himself forward to the first and knelt down to feel her neck for a pulse. Neither body had one, and he cursed as he moved back into the light streaming through the doorway.

"Two bodies. Probably died from dehydration or the heat," he reported to the watching paramedics, his voice tight.

"Lieutenant?" one of Briones's men called from where he was turning over the dead cartel shooters.

"On my way."

When he arrived, he stared down at the pair of miscreants on the pavement and shook his head. "Women. They must have been the madams. Good riddance," the officer said, and Briones managed a nod.

Fuentes waved to him from the building entrance. "There are about thirty more girls in here. And two hostile casualties. They fired first."

Briones relayed the information through his earbud in a wooden tone, dizziness hitting with the force of a blow as the rush from the assault faded and left nothing but a creeping sense of horror at the depths to which his fellow man could sink. He switched to the headquarters channel and radioed Cruz, who'd worked until the wee hours and only gone home to snatch what sleep he could before coming in early.

Cruz's voice sounded fatigued. "How did it go?"

"About what we expected." He filled the captain in.

"Good work. Get back here as soon as possible – leave Fuentes to clean up and make the reports. I need you to track down that Land Rover."

"I'm on my way, _Capitan._"

"Good man." Cruz paused. "Are you all right?"

"Yes. I...it's just hard to imagine why they'd lock these children in an unventilated hot box for a drive from the Guatemalan border. We lost two of them." Briones shook his head and sighed.

"You saved them, Lieutenant. The rest are alive and will have completely different lives because of you. I'd count that as a win."

"I know. It just gets to me sometimes."

"You wouldn't be human if it didn't." Cruz matched the younger man's sigh. "Now get in here so we can put Aranas back behind bars, where he belongs."

"Yes, sir."

# CHAPTER 27

*Mexico City, Mexico*

*Don* Aranas, his Gucci loafers soundless on the imported Iranian travertine floor, led his guest through the massive great room at one of the many mansions he owned through a string of untraceable companies. His companion was one of his top capos, the man who ran DF for the Sinaloa Cartel: Sancho Ramirez, more commonly known by his nickname "El Gordo" – The Fat One.

Ramirez tipped the scales at over three hundred deadly pounds and had been heavy since a child, hence his moniker. He was good-natured about it and even reveled in the name. His colorful silk shirts were the size of small tents and his trousers custom-made to accommodate his girth.

The men moved into a smaller chamber whose wood-paneled walls held at least a hundred backlit display cases. Aranas smiled as the big man walked slowly around the room, his eyes devouring the artifacts in the cases – pre-Columbian relics Aranas had spent decades accumulating on the black market, most of which weren't known to even exist.

"It's an amazing collection," El Gordo whispered.

"Yes. I'm fortunate I was able to find a safe home for them all in Mexico. It would have been tragic if they'd gone elsewhere. They are, after all, part of our heritage."

"Aren't you concerned about theft?"

Aranas laughed. "Who would be foolish enough to attempt to steal from me?" He shook his head. "No, I have a special alarm system with redundant backups, and armed men patrol the grounds.

This is the last home in Polanco that any thief would target – it would be certain death."

El Gordo moved closer to a relic in a prominent case on the far wall. "What's this?"

"Ah. You have a good eye. It's Toltec. I've themed the collection, you see. This section's Toltec, that one Mayan, that Aztec, and that Inca. I have other rooms devoted to some of the more obscure pieces and civilizations."

"How many pieces in all?"

"Oh, at least two hundred. Probably more by now. It's an engaging pastime, and I get somewhat obsessive when I'm on the hunt for a new acquisition. You probably know how that goes with your cars." El Gordo had dozens of American muscle cars from the sixties that he restored and housed in a warehouse in Toluca.

"Oh, sure. It's good to have a hobby to take your mind off the business. And you can only chase so many women and drink so much tequila."

"Exactly."

They basked appreciatively in the glow of the displays, Aranas pointing out singularities or telling short stories about the history of this piece or that, along with an occasional account of the trouble he'd gone to in order to acquire it. When they'd seen all the treasures, El Gordo shook his head in wonder.

"This must be priceless. Truly priceless."

"Well, whatever it's worth, it will be a lot more when the archeology museum blows. That will eradicate a huge trove of similar works, and scarcity tends to boost value."

El Gordo nodded. "They aren't making any more of them." He paused. "But you said *when* it blows. Are you certain they're going to make an attempt to disarm that one?"

Aranas contemplated a nearby statuette. "Did I? Slip of the tongue. No, I meant *if*. But either way, it's of no concern to me what the value of my collection is at any given time. I'm not a seller, so even if it increased in value by a factor of ten, it is still without any meaning to me."

"Of course. You only care about the price when you're selling."

"Or buying. I want to pay as little as possible. But as you can see, I have quite a bit already. I've been blessed."

"Any further word on how the president is going to respond?"

"No, but I didn't leave him much room to maneuver. I bet he'll go along with it, maybe make a try for one of the bombs. If that happens, it will be the museum. There are far too many people at the other locations, whereas the museum wasn't open when I sent the video. It's a simple equation."

"And how will you react?"

"Oh, I think outrage would be in order, don't you? They have to believe I'm on the hairy edge of losing it completely. A madman with his finger on the trigger. That's how I'll play it."

El Gordo smiled. "Few could pull this off."

Aranas returned the grin. "Well, it's not over yet, but I'd say that we've never been closer. I don't see how it can fail. They just might require a little convincing. That's why I put the bomb in the museum — it's a site that's acceptable collateral damage if I need to prove the point. They'll believe I hadn't accounted for there being nobody inside at that hour of the morning, and I won't argue it." He reached out and flicked a piece of lint from the glass of the display case in front of him. "In all battles, the most important thing is to always allow your adversary a clear way out. Why? Simple: cornered rats fight harder. And the point to any confrontation is to win."

They spent another twenty minutes discussing logistics, and then El Gordo departed, leaving Aranas to himself except for the housekeeping staff and the small army of virtually invisible guards. Aranas lit one of his Cuban cigars and climbed the stairs to the third floor, where he'd lowered the hatch that led to the attic in preparation for his forty-eight-hour vigil.

He ascended the ladder and edged to a small table he'd set up. On it sat a rectangular box with three glowing lights, below which were three buttons. A cable led from the back of the box to a power amplifier and antenna. El Maquino had explained how it operated, as though Aranas couldn't figure out three buttons, each marked with the location they would trigger. All Aranas would need to do in order to detonate one, or all, of the devices was flip up the safety cover and press the button.

His hand brushed the box in an almost loving gesture. "You were always a bright boy, my son. But this time I believe you've outdone yourself," he said, and took a puff on his cigar. It didn't bother him that the entire mansion stank of his habit – one of the benefits of having endless money was that you could behave as you liked and not care what anyone else thought.

The next two days would change the balance of power in Mexico – not only for his cartel but for the government. The idea that a youth from humble Sinaloa peasant stock could grow up to determine the fate of his country seemed like an impossibility to him, yet here he was, doing exactly that.

He was engaged in the game of kings, playing chess against worthy adversaries, with the prize ultimate power over all he surveyed. If he was successful, he'd own the president and his entire administration, pocket an easy billion, and have renegotiated essential relationships while annihilating his enemies.

If it got any better than that, Aranas couldn't think how.

"Now all I have to do is be patient. The rest will fall into place," he murmured, and then lowered himself from the attic, taking care to leave no trace of his visit in the highly unlikely event the house was raided. He didn't think it would be – the only ones who knew he was there were loyal to him and above suspicion – but he always had a contingency plan, and this time was no different.

"Let them look for me all they like. The die is cast," he said to the walls, and then retraced his steps to the ornate stairway that led back to the main living areas for a third, and probably unwise, cup of coffee with the remainder of his cigar.

# CHAPTER 28

Cruz was finishing up a phone call when Briones entered his office, carrying a folder. Cruz pointed to the conference table and waved him over to it before continuing.

"I've also gotten reports of the deployments. As soon as you have a straight answer, get back to me. If there's a big operation in play, it might overlap mine, so I need to know," Cruz snapped, obviously annoyed. He listened for several seconds. "Fine. That's all I can ask. *Gracias.*"

He hung up and fixed the lieutenant with a hard stare. "Tell me you have something substantial for me."

"I do. One of the informants said the driver has been spotted a number of times in a different car – a silver Durango. Apparently he sits in the thing for hours."

"Sits in it? Where?"

Briones gave him an address.

"Any idea what he's doing there?" Cruz inquired.

"No. But if you find him, maybe you can ask."

Cruz smiled and nodded. "I might just do that." He glanced around the office. "I told Godoy's secretary to call me whenever he arrives so we can have our daily status meeting, but apparently he isn't in yet, so I have nothing to do. The warden's also not in his office. Seems like this morning we're the only ones working." Cruz thought for a moment. "I'll take a few men over and see if I can locate the driver. If Godoy wants to meet, he can call me."

Briones bit his lip and considered his next question. "You've heard the reports about some of downtown being closed?"

"Of course. But nobody's talking."

"I have a buddy who's on the ground at the federal building. He said that the army officers are saying it's a terrorist threat."

Cruz frowned. "Terrorists? We don't have any terrorists. Are you sure?"

"That's what he said he'd heard."

Cruz frowned. "You know how the rumor mill works. I'd discount that until we hear an official explanation. They can't seal off large areas of the capital and not provide one. I've got my feelers out, too." He shifted in his chair. "At any rate, it's not cartel related, or we would have been notified, so it's none of our business. Have you been able to ID all the shooters from your operation this morning?"

"Yes. The Millennium Cartel, relatively low level, and the local gang that operated the brothel. The club owner is nowhere to be found, but we're checking, and it appears that he's in debt up to his eyeballs on it, so he'll probably vanish and stick the banks with the mortgage."

"Fairly sophisticated for them, you have to admit. They operate illegally, no doubt laundering millions, and all the real risk of loss is with whoever loaned them the money – which might be a cartel-affiliated bank, for all we know." Cruz sighed. "At least the girls won't be living in hell any longer. That's your good deed for the day. How are the other investigations going?"

Briones gave him a rundown and at the end offered to accompany him.

Cruz shook his head. "No, I already saddled you with my twelve-hour-a-day workload. Until Godoy pokes his head in or the warden calls me back, I've got nothing on my plate."

Cruz rose and moved to where his uniform jacket hung from his door hook. "I'll be on my cell if you need anything."

Briones stood and paused. "Oh. That's the other thing I heard. There's no phone coverage in large areas of the metro area. Part of this mystery operation."

"Great. Okay, then I'll be on the radio. I'll round up a few of the lads and go for a drive." Cruz gave Briones a small smile. "Good work on tracking down the driver. That's twice I've had to congratulate you today, and it's not quite eleven o'clock yet."

"You know where to reach me if you have any questions," Briones said, uncomfortable with the praise. "Good luck, *Capitan.*"

"Thanks. You too."

Briones left and Cruz slid his desk drawer open to retrieve a radio. His landline rang as he was closing it. He answered it on the third ring, puzzled by the caller ID.

"Cruz," he said.

"Romero? Thank God you're there." It was Dinah.

"Where else would I be?" he asked, and stopped, registering her tone. "What is it? What's wrong?"

"I'm at the doctor's, remember?"

*That's right.* He'd totally forgotten, fatigued as he was. "Are you all right?"

"Hardly. Haven't you heard the news? The government just held a press conference. We listened to it on the radio. Apparently there's a terrorist threat to the building I'm in. At the main hospital."

"What? No, I haven't heard anything. Listen, you need to get out of there, Dinah. If there's any kind of danger, don't wait for the doctor, just leave. Now."

"I wish I could. They won't let anyone go. We're being held against our will. We're basically prisoners."

Cruz digested the impossible information and a rush of anxiety bile burned the back of his throat. "They can't do that. They have no right."

"Apparently they do."

"Did they say why?"

"No. Maybe they think the terrorists are in the hospital or the other buildings?"

"Others?"

"The Federal building and the anthropology museum."

Cruz's mind worked furiously as he set the radio onto his desk and sat heavily in his chair. "What phone are you using?"

"The hospital's landline. Cell phones don't work in here."

"Give me the number. I'll see what can be done to get you out of there."

Dinah gave him the information, and then her voice softened. "Romero, are you sitting down?"

"Why? I mean, yes, I am, but what is it? Is it the doctor? What did he tell you?" Cruz demanded, his words tripping over themselves in his haste to get them out. He tried to keep his tone calm, but he sounded agitated to his ear.

"You're going to be a daddy, Romero. I'm pregnant."

Cruz's pulse pounded in his ears like a kettle drum, and he shook his head as though trying to clear it. "Pregnant – are you serious?"

Dinah's voice was flat. "Do I sound like I'm joking?"

"God…I mean, how did that happen?" Cruz blurted, and immediately regretted it.

"I thought you knew how that worked. There's a stork…"

"No…I'm sorry, *amor*. I'm not firing on all cylinders today. Pregnant! That explains a lot, right? The dizziness, the fatigue, the mood swings, the tenderness…do they know if it's a boy or a girl?"

"Not yet. It's too soon." Dinah hesitated. "How do you feel about that, Romero? About us having a baby?"

"Feel? I feel…I feel excited. And amazed. And proud, and happy, and fifty different kinds of joyful, Dinah. But I'm also worried. I mean, you tell me you're having a baby, but you're being held prisoner, and we have no idea—"

Dinah cut him off. "I know."

He took her hint. "Dinah, I love you more than anything, and I'll love our child just as much. This is amazing. It's just so unexpected, and with the other news…"

"I know you'll do whatever you can to get me out of here, Romero. Get *us* out of here," she corrected. "I need to get used to thinking of me as two, not just one. It'll take a little time."

"Don't worry, Dinah. I'll make some calls right now. I'll fix this."

A voice in the background said something, and Dinah covered the phone as she spoke, and then returned to Cruz. "I have to get off the line. It was an act of war just to use the phone."

"Okay. Let me get to work," Cruz said, but he was talking to a dial tone. "Damn," he exploded, slamming down the handset. He sat back and glowered at the phone like it had bitten him, and then lifted it back to his ear and dialed Godoy's extension. His assistant answered and told Cruz that he still hadn't arrived.

"That's not good enough. I need to talk to him. Now. What's his cell number?"

The woman gave it to Cruz. "I haven't heard from him yet today, *Capitan*, or I'd have passed your earlier message on," she said, her voice uncertain.

"I'll try his cell," Cruz said, and hung up. He dialed the number, which went straight to voice mail. "Godoy, this is Cruz. We need to talk immediately. My wife is being held at the general hospital against her will, and I need you to intercede. It's part of some terrorist thing – I don't have all the details. But we need to get her out."

Cruz disconnected and began calling everyone else he could think of.

He was going to be a father.

But what kind of father couldn't help his wife and unborn child in an emergency?

Memories of his last family flooded his mind as he listened to the phone ring, and he closed his eyes at the recollection of the last time he had been powerless to help his loved ones. His throat tightened, and he stabbed the line off as he fought to get control over himself. He'd be of no use to anyone if he was lashing out blindly, and remembering his wife and daughter's heads showing up at his office in boxes wasn't going to do anything to help Dinah.

Or his baby.

He inhaled deeply and gritted his teeth. No matter what happened, he wasn't going to fail his family again.

He'd die before that happened.

# CHAPTER 29

*Manhattan, New York*

Horns honked from Park Avenue, the nearly constant tooting providing an arrhythmic backdrop of unlikely musicality as El Rey walked the final blocks toward FDR Drive and the nearby brownstone that was his target. It was a blustery late New York morning, the wind warm and humid off the Harlem River. The women around him were long-legged and pretty in their late summer skirts and too-serious looks – the tough expressions of city girls warning admirers not to mess with them.

He slowed at a corner where an old man was selling roasted chestnuts and bought a bag, curious as to why anyone might want to eat them. He tried a bite and was surprised by the steaming soft texture. Even though he'd only been on the island for a half hour, he already felt like he blended in, the other pedestrians a cosmopolitan smorgasbord of ethnicities. In just the last block he'd heard English, Spanish, French, Russian, and Arabic spoken, and any fear he'd had that his accent might set him apart quickly faded.

The city was teeming and reminded him of Mexico City or Buenos Aires – large, highly concentrated metropolises with the haves and have-nots living in close proximity. Only in New York, poverty took on a whole different meaning from the Latin American variety, and most of the shambling homeless people he spotted appeared to be either mentally ill or substance abusers, rather than down-on-their-luck lower classes like in his home country.

He'd heard that even the poor wore hundred-dollar shoes and had iPhones in America, and he hadn't believed it until he'd seen it firsthand. The prosperity was unimaginable to him – the entire city was comprised of endless rows of monolithic skyscrapers, and the sense of harried wealth was palpable, especially here on the Upper East Side.

The assassin crossed the street, one of the few pedestrians who waited for the light to change, and was happy to see that as he neared the river the crowds on the sidewalks thinned out until he was one of only two or three others on the block. The neighborhood was quiet, reeking of genteel old money. The line of brownstones stood like senile sentries, vestiges of the past in a time that had long since passed them by. He'd been worried by the number of doormen only a couple of blocks back, but this section was devoid of the towering apartments that clogged the area by the main artery.

He munched on another chestnut as he ambled past the brownstone, noting from behind his sunglasses that the curtains were drawn. He continued to the end of the block and rounded the corner, calculating the best way to get into the building without being observed. He quickly appreciated the challenge he faced when he saw that there were no back alleys he could skulk along, only more dwellings crowded together.

That left the roof or the front door.

El Rey would have dearly loved to wait until nightfall for his incursion, but he was running on borrowed time. So it would be the worst kind of operation: a daytime sojourn in a highly populated area he hadn't had the time to reconnoiter. He'd worked under worse circumstances, but that scenario was close to the top of his list of undesirable ones.

He studied the manholes as he took his time circling the block, looking for easier adjacent targets where he could get onto the roof and make his way to the brownstone. But his perusal of the homes quickly convinced him that he'd have to take the most direct route and walk up to the front door and ring the bell.

An hour later he returned wearing a different windbreaker, his other tied around his waist, his baseball cap on backwards and a courier service envelope in his hand, with the address slip made out to Dr. Helen Garland. He waited until the sidewalk was empty and then hurried up the steps to the front door and pressed the bell, fidgeting as he imagined a messenger in a rush might. When there was no answer, he knocked loudly and waited, his ears straining for any sound from inside.

A window scraped open on the second floor of the house next door and an old woman's voice called out, "She's not here."

"Oh. Well, I have a package here for her. Any idea where I can find her?"

"I think she's at her place on Long Island. You got that address?"

El Rey smiled. "I'm sure they do. I'm just the hired help."

"Well, don't waste your energy here. Nobody's home."

El Rey gave the old woman a jaunty salute and a wave. "Thanks."

"Don't mention it."

The old neighbor woman had seen him, but it was a stretch to believe that she'd remember him in any detail by the time the doctor's body was discovered, much less make the connection between a failed package delivery and a murder many miles away, so he decided to risk letting her live. Besides, he had to work fast, and silencing her would take time he didn't have.

The walk back to Park Avenue went by quickly as he calculated how long it would take to get to the Hamptons for his meeting with destiny. Probably the better part of the afternoon, given his knowledge of the geography. He pulled up a website on his new cell phone and checked for the shortest route, and decided that a combination of the subway and taxis would get him there fastest, if the traffic was anywhere near as bad as it had been coming in from the airport. He glanced at his Panerai and turned onto Park Avenue, and then made for the nearest subway station, anxious to get on with his search before the neurotoxin made the odyssey a moot point.

# CHAPTER 30

*Mexico City, Mexico*

Norteño sat at a different conference table on the main level, in a much larger room than the president's office. The meeting with the Security Council was over and the course of action decided. The president had ordered an attempt to defuse the museum bomb against his recommendation, and extracted a promise from two of the strongest advocates of that approach that if the device detonated, they'd take the fall. It had been a tense meeting, but he'd gotten what he was after, and now Norteño and the others were briefing key members of the Federal Police and the army on the situation.

Both had been mobilized and had cordoned off the buildings, but there had been no details given other than that there was an emergency and that the president's office would be directing the response. That had been sufficient to get boots on the ground, but now the top brass wanted answers. After forcing everyone in the room to sign national security clearances swearing them to silence, Norteño had given a fifteen-minute presentation on the nature of the threat, using the terrorism explanation everyone had agreed upon.

The head of the Federal Police was scowling during the questions that followed, and allowed his subordinates to ask most of the questions before cutting them off with a dark look.

"So let me get this straight. Thousands of people are being held hostage by terrorists who intend to kill them if their demands aren't met? Within forty-four hours, approximately?"

"That's correct."

"And they want a billion to call it off."

"Also correct," Norteño agreed.

"And the plan is to play along while we try to disarm one of the devices."

"Yes. Which is why we need your cooperation." Norteño tilted his head and dropped the other shoe. "We've already contacted the U.S. State Department to see if they can help – they have a lot more experience with counterterrorism than we do."

The Security Council had recommended that they reach out to the U.S. government, over Norteño's objections, and the president had agreed, at least hesitantly, to put out feelers without making any firm requests or agreeing to anything specific. He wanted to understand his options and didn't want his reaction in retrospect to have excluded anything that might have saved innocent Mexican lives.

"So we're going to have to work around the *gringos*, in addition to the rest of this?" the Federal Police chief sputtered.

"Not necessarily. We'll see what they propose. But if they have some experts they can put on a plane, the president sees no reason not to invite them here. As I said, they have more experience than we do at this."

"That didn't do them much good, did it?" the chief countered.

Norteño had anticipated the turf concerns. "Look, nothing's cast in stone. We're exploring all our options. I've been asked to request that you and our esteemed military counterparts here assemble a strike force that can go in and disarm the bombs. If any foreign involvement takes place, it will be under our direction. So don't worry – we're not inviting the American military to invade." Norteño turned to the general to his right. "What's the status of the quarantined areas, General?"

"We've done as asked and sealed them off. We're working with the Federales on crowd control. Nobody can get in or out without us knowing, although we have to expect that unrest will set in as time passes, and a certain percentage of those in lockdown will want out. Our people see that as the biggest hurdle, followed by containing protests by family members who want their loved ones safe."

"And you're equipped to do that?" Norteño asked, obviously in charge of the meeting even though he was technically outranked by most in the room. He would savor the delicious power later. For now, he needed to be assertive without being abrasive, and get the various factions to pull on the same oar.

"Of course. We've devoted all resources necessary."

"What about your bomb experts? Who are your best men?"

"We're flying in two instructors from our special forces program. These are seasoned men with forty years of experience between the pair."

"Excellent. What about the Federales? Who have you got?"

"Nobody at that level, I'm afraid. This is relatively new to us," the chief admitted.

"Then perhaps we might want some American eyes as well," Norteño said, voicing the conclusion he'd been reluctant to arrive at.

"No," the general countered. "It's not like more people will make a better cake. Let our experts handle it. The likelihood that these devices are too sophisticated for them to defuse is about nil. Terrorists are usually amateurs; these are professionals. They literally wrote the book."

Everyone agreed to devote manpower to a task force that would work around the clock to manage the crisis, as well as to enforce a system ensuring there were no information leaks. Everything would be tightly compartmentalized, and each member would be required to sign the secrecy agreement before being briefed. A sleeping area would be set up, along with food delivery, so the members of the team wouldn't have to leave the building, and there would be no communication with the outside world other than through monitored channels, with no exceptions.

The rest of the meeting was spent agreeing on a short list of candidates for the team, which proved smaller than they'd imagined, largely because nobody had any relevant experience. The armed forces got six seats, the Federal Police four, with the option of adding more if necessary, and of course, Norteño leading the effort. Two of the Security Council members were on the military side, so there were really only eight additional faces to add, making the process expedient.

Norteño watched the somber men leave the room with their marching orders, and rose to deliver a report to the president, who wanted to be updated hourly. The thrill of being so close to the epicenter of power was intoxicating, even after six months as chief of staff – this was the first time he had actually been in charge of anything material, and the president had made it clear that he had twenty-four-hour access, no matter what the time.

In a world where access was everything, Norteño was now at the top of the heap, and he would do whatever it took to remain there. This crisis would resolve one way or another, but he would be remembered by everyone as a man of action who had stepped up when leadership had been required.

He was effectively in charge of the most critical operation in the country's history.

Now he just had to live up to the responsibility.

# CHAPTER 31

*Mexico City, Mexico*

Godoy shivered as he came to on the cold cement floor of a darkened room. His head swam as he sat up, and his body felt like he'd been thrown down a flight of stairs. The last thing he remembered was being grabbed at Leticia's apartment, and the rest was a haze. He reached to his right arm and felt a sore spot, and then squinted at where a small trickle of blood had dried on his dress shirt. He rolled up the sleeve and spotted the culprit: a dot where he'd been injected with something.

He tried to stand but only succeeded in slipping back to the floor, his legs refusing to obey his mind's commands, and kicked an empty metal pail by his legs in the process. He winced at the noise, everything amplified, no doubt from the after-effects of the drugs his assailants had shot him up with.

The only door in the room opened and three men entered. Two of them hoisted Godoy onto a chair as the third sauntered behind them, his body language that of a man in no hurry. The third man stood in front of Godoy, staring down at him, and then turned to one of the pair.

"Turn on the lights," he ordered, and the man on Godoy's right rushed to comply.

The room illuminated, and Godoy grimaced and closed his eyes. The pain the light caused was excruciating, but the agony from the hard backhanded slap that came next eclipsed it.

"Open your eyes," the third man said.

Godoy forced himself to comply, his eyes slits. The man's face came into focus, and Godoy's heart skipped a beat. He knew that face. The man was a cartel boss – but which one eluded him.

"I see you recognize me," the man said. "Which tells me that you're a greater fool than I would have guessed. You knew she's my girlfriend, and you still did it. I should grind you into hamburger and feed you to the dogs."

A name sprang to mind: Luis Hierro, the Mexico City head of the Gulf Cartel, now dissolved after a brutal territory war with Los Zetas.

"I...I don't know what you're talking about," Godoy protested, his stomach twisting in a knot at the sudden revelation.

"Leticia didn't tell you?" Hierro barked, and then laughed. "Then the joke's on you. She's my main squeeze. And you've been dishonoring me by screwing her, you shit grub."

"I...had no...idea..."

"That figures. She may be gorgeous, but she's got the morals of an alley cat, and she's greedy. Let me guess – you been paying for it?"

Godoy tried to shake his head, but the pain from the effort was too much. "Just gifts. And help with the rent."

Another laugh. "That's funny, considering I own the apartment and she stays for free. How much did she clip you for?"

"Ten thousand pesos a month."

Hierro grinned, and the effect was chilling. "That's not bad for tagging one that looks like her. Especially for a troll like you. Of course, now it's going to get a lot more expensive."

"Anything," Godoy managed.

"I'm glad you feel that way. I need your wife's contact information."

Godoy's eyes widened. "No. Don't tell her."

Hierro's face darkened and he took a menacing step forward. "Let's try this the hard way, then. Give me her info or I'll cut your balls off and film you eating them for YouTube."

Fifteen minutes later, Godoy slipped back into unconsciousness after Hierro had entertained himself by using him for a punching bag. The cartel honcho stared down at his bleeding form and shook his head.

"I almost feel bad for him. Nothing could have been worth this."

One of the two henchmen shrugged. "Seemed more worried about his wife than anything."

Hierro laughed as he rubbed his knuckles. "There's a lesson in that."

# CHAPTER 32

After an hour of fruitless calls to get someone to extract Dinah from the hospital, Cruz contacted his conduit in the government, who told him in no uncertain terms that there could be no exceptions to the lockdown on the buildings. He swore Cruz to secrecy and switched to a landline when he called Cruz back.

"They're afraid there's a bomb. Or bombs. That's all I know. But apparently the terrorists' conditions are that if anyone leaves, they detonate the devices when someone sets foot outside the building."

"This is my wife we're talking about, damn it. She's pregnant. There has to be a way. Underground, maybe?"

"I'll do what I can, Cruz, but it will take some time. I'll call your office when I have something for you."

"Please. I'm losing my mind here. You have to do something."

"Let me talk to some people. That's all I can promise."

Cruz spent precious time pacing in front of his window, and finally decided to keep busy while he waited for word. Everyone he'd talked to had repeated the official story, which was long on prohibitions but short on specifics. According to the press, there was a terrorist threat that involved explosives, and areas of the city were being sequestered for everyone's safety. And of course, that the public was not to panic.

The last being the most worrisome thing the administration could have said.

Other than that, there was a complete news blackout, which was typical when the government clamped down on the media. Unlike some countries, there was no assumption of a free press, and it was well understood that the networks and papers danced to the government's tune, or didn't, as the situation warranted. Just as there was no mention of the massive cartel war being waged in Baja, lest it scare tourists away, there was also no mention of anything else the government deemed too sensitive for public consumption.

Cruz had already spoken with one of his favorite sergeants, Lorenzo Torres, and ordered him to round up a half dozen of his best men and be ready within fifteen minutes. He knew it was a long shot that they'd find the driver, but sometimes long shots paid off, and he felt the need to do something, anything, while he waited for a solution to Dinah's predicament.

Torres was waiting out on the task force floor when Cruz strode from his office. Cruz noted that the sergeant, and all his men, were equipped with the latest H&K MP7 submachine guns with sound and flash suppression. A deadly little gun, it was compact and could put a round through a car door and still penetrate a bulletproof vest – and the shooter wearing it – at two hundred yards.

"Gentlemen, I should have told you – I want you in plainclothes. We're looking for a silver Dodge Caravan, driven by the man who helped Aranas escape. We need to take him alive if at all possible. Dead, he is of no value, whereas alive, we can convince him to cooperate." The driver might not know where Aranas was now, but if he could shed light on who at the prison had helped him escape, at least that was something. And if they won the lottery…he'd lead them to the drug lord. "We'll do a drive through of the neighborhood and see if we can spot him. If we do, depending on the layout, we can either box him in or approach on foot."

Torres and his men changed into street clothes, their compact weapons concealed by loose windbreakers. The outfits wouldn't withstand a close inspection, but from a distance the deception might work. Cruz wished he could devote more resources to the search, but with the city on emergency footing, he was reluctant to pull more men from their duties. He still hadn't gotten the green light from Godoy to commandeer staff, and anyone he took out of the pool would be officers Briones would need if he was to make progress on his file full of cases.

The group signed out three unmarked cars and drove to the

district where the driver's vehicle had been spotted, Cruz in the lead, Torres and his men in the other two vehicles. Once near the neighborhood, they divided up the area and performed a methodical grid search, communicating on their earbuds.

As Cruz rounded a corner, Torres's voice crackled in his ear. "I can make out a silver Dodge Caravan parked in front of an apartment complex. I'll be past it in ten seconds."

"Don't do anything to tip him off, if he's in the vehicle. Don't slow, just keep going. Where exactly are you?" Cruz asked.

Torres rattled off the street and address while keeping his speed constant. He avoided glancing at the van, preferring to wait to sneak a look in his rearview mirror, his sunglasses masking the direction of his gaze. He was so occupied he missed the second vehicle on his left, also a van, this one green, whose driver studied him with suspicion.

"There's a man in the Caravan. Repeat. In the driver's seat," Torres reported as he rolled down the block. "Can't see whether he's armed."

"Did he make you?" Cruz asked.

"Negative."

"How do you want to play this?" Cruz inquired, deferring to Torres's field expertise.

"Four men from behind him on foot, I box him in with my car so he can't drive away, and we bag him. Street's pretty calm. Should be a piece of cake," Torres said.

"Sounds good. Where do you want to meet?"

"Around the corner. I'll stay in my car with Carlos. The others can park and then we'll do this." Torres hesitated. "*Capitan*, no offense, but hang back until we're clear."

"Sergeant, I appreciate your concern, but I can handle myself."

"Oh, I'm not questioning that, sir. I just want the situation to keep from getting confused with more bodies than we need to do the job."

Cruz grudgingly conceded Torres's point. It was his plan and his ass in the line of fire, so it was up to him to make it work. "Fine. But remember – hold your fire unless he shoots first. We want him unharmed."

"Of course."

A thought occurred to Cruz. "What does it look like he's doing there?"

"Watching the street, best as I can tell."

Cruz's pulse quickened. Perhaps Aranas was closer than he'd guessed. He debated calling in backup but decided against it. A small group might get in and out without triggering any alarms. In an impromptu mission like this, bringing in fifty men to search the surroundings would be noticed before they'd disembarked from the personnel carrier.

Torres's group was ready to move on the van three minutes later. His men were rounding the block, and they agreed that he would wait until they were nearly at the van before Torres would pull alongside the driver from the opposite side of the street, Carlos's gun leveled at the driver's head. Even the most hardened cartel toughs would think twice about the business end of an H&K pointed at them at close range, presenting their best odds of taking him before he had a chance to decide to shoot it out.

The four walkers in their civilian garb made their way unhurriedly toward the van, talking among themselves, to untrained eyes just workers on a break. Cruz watched from the corner as they closed on the van, and then he spotted Torres's car crawling down the street from the far side.

"Five seconds and we have him," Torres said over the comm line, and Cruz held his breath as his men neared the rear of the van. Torres's car was about to cut across the lane when the street exploded with automatic rifle fire. Before they had a chance to react, the four plainclothes officers were cut down by a hail of rounds from the windows of the apartment down the block. "Shit–" Torres cried out. Carlos opened up with his weapon from the passenger window, returning fire at the apartment complex as Torres swerved.

Shots rang out from the green van Torres had missed, and his windshield starburst as slugs sprayed across it. Cruz floored the gas and withdrew his pistol from his belt holster, and was closing on Torres's car when it collided with the Caravan. The driver fired point blank into the police car and the rear windshield went red with splatter. Cruz realized as he was almost at Torres's sedan that all his men were down and he was seriously outgunned; their stealth approach had suddenly turned into a deadly crossfire from unknown shooters. He slowed as he took his cell from his pocket and speed-dialed dispatch, and then sped up again when chunks of asphalt flew from the street beside him.

Cruz slalomed in a zigzag to the end of the street, his foot floored, and careened around the corner. His tires screeched as rounds ricocheted off the pavement. He ducked down instinctively as several bullets struck the trunk of his car, and then he was clear, heart trip-hammering in his chest as he swore at his phone and the nonexistent signal on it. He hadn't realized he was close enough to the federal building to not have coverage, and he tossed the cell to the side and switched channels on his radio to issue an emergency call – officers down, hostiles at large.

Up the street from the van, a figure stood at a darkened second-story window with a parabolic antenna in his hand pointed at the departing car. El Maquino's face was expressionless as he recorded the driver's Bluetooth signal – the man was no doubt the leader behind the failed attack, his shooters sprawled dead on the sidewalk below.

He turned from the window once the car disappeared from view and moved to a laptop computer. El Maquino didn't know why the attack had been launched, but figured it had to be because of the boxes. The timing was too close.

The thought of having to leave his workshop, his living space, his beloved drones, induced panic in him, and anger – or more accurately, a desire to make someone pay for the disruption to his peaceful existence. He didn't want to flee, but he'd always been ready, at Aranas's urging. In addition to the arrays of cameras and motion detectors and electrified fencing on the roof, he'd long ago rigged the loft so that in the event someone came for him, it could be vaporized, leaving no trace of his work. He kept a dash bag in his bedroom with important documents, several changes of clothes, money and bank tokens, and a handful of specialty tools.

He tapped in a command and waited as the information on the Bluetooth signal converted, and then saved it to a dongle. He looked up at the wall clock and grunted, and then moved to the drone room, whispering to himself, "Time to fly. We'll see how they like that, won't we?"

# CHAPTER 33

*Westhampton, Long Island, New York*

Dr. Helen Garland's neighborhood looked expensive to El Rey as he walked along the quiet tree-lined lane, the sort of place that CEOs and bankers and white-shoe attorneys fancied away from the madding crowds – the homes not so large or lavish as to be vulgar, but of substantial enough size to convey quiet authority in an area of the world where the population was stacked one atop the other.

He'd had the taxi drop him four blocks from her address and had hoofed it the remainder of the way, partially to get a feel for the surroundings as well as to avoid any connection between the cab's fare and the doctor's unfortunate passing.

Her house was atypical in that it was two stories – most of the surrounding homes were one level – and obviously old although carefully maintained, he could see from the gleaming white paint and the emerald green storm shutters that framed the windows. Thankful the lot was large and verdant enough that he had some room to work, he edged onto the property, there being no point in delaying the inevitable. His plane was sitting on the runway, awaiting his return, which would take at least four hours based on his ride from the city.

He crept along a hedge, his senses hyperalert, his footsteps silent on the freshly trimmed grass. The sound of a television drifted from an open window, confirming that the doctor was in – whether alone or not didn't matter to El Rey, not when he was racing the clock. He made it to the rear of the house and spotted the back entrance – the door was open, a screen closed over the gap to keep insects out.

Getting in was childishly easy, and he paused at the kitchen to select a bread knife with a serrated blade before creeping along the wood floor of the hallway toward the living room with the blaring television.

Helen Garland was a handsome woman in her early fifties with a no-nonsense haircut, her skin bronzed from days outdoors – gardening, by the looks of her clothes, he thought as he inched into the room. She took longer than normal to look up and gasp. El Rey took in the bottle of Scotch on the coffee table and the tumbler beside it containing two fingers of amber liquid and understood instantly – the woman was drunk, or at least somewhat inebriated, drinking alone in the late afternoon to CNN's vapid blather with only her cats for company.

"Who – who are you? How did you get in here?" she demanded, a slight slur to her speech.

"Don't be alarmed. I won't hurt you unless I have to. I just need to ask you some questions."

"I don't keep much money in the house. No jewelry. But I'll give you what I have," she said, eyeing the knife in El Rey's hand with fear.

"As I said, I have some questions. I don't want your money. I need information, and I'm afraid I'm in a hurry."

Her eyes conveyed incomprehension. "Information? What are you talking about?"

El Rey motioned to her cocktail. "Drink that and we'll have a chat. Good Scotch is a conversational lubricant, is it not?"

She frowned at him in puzzlement. He set the knife on the table and took a seat facing her, smiling as he did so. "There. See? Nice and civilized. Now drink, and then we'll begin."

Helen seemed sufficiently unfocused that another jolt of alcohol to her system might make her careless about how she answered, which would save him time. He held her gaze and she nodded and sat forward, reaching for the glass with a delicate hand.

El Rey was surprised when she flung the heavy tumbler at his head and bolted from the sofa toward the kitchen. His reaction time was so compromised from sleeplessness and the effects of the neurotoxin that he barely dodged it as he leapt to his feet. She was halfway to the kitchen when he tackled her, and they both went down hard. Her ribs cracked as his weight on top of her knocked the wind from her, and then he had his hand over her mouth to muffle the scream.

She was no match for his strength, and after a brief struggle, he whispered into her ear, "I'll cut your tongue out if you keep trying to scream. I mean it." She stopped struggling. "Here's how this is going to work. We're going into your basement, and we're going to have a civilized discussion. You're not going to try anything more, or you're going to get badly hurt. I don't like to harm women, but I'll do what I have to in order to get answers, do you understand? Nod if you do."

Helen nodded, and he relaxed his grip on her. "I'm going to help you stand. I know your ribs must hurt, so I'll be gentle. Try anything and I'll beat you bloody, though. That's your only warning. Do you hear me?"

Another nod. He rose and pulled her to her feet, a grimace of pain flushing her as she faced him. "Who are you?" she hissed.

"I'm a man who's short on choices, doing what he has to in order to survive. Now let's go downstairs."

"I don't want to. There's nothing down there."

His stare hardened. "If you don't start walking, I'm going to go get your knife, and we'll start with you eating your nose and ears."

She gulped and her mouth worked, but no sound came out. He gave her a moment and then took a step toward her. "Move."

The basement was clammy even in the moist heat of the afternoon. She flicked on a light switch and a single incandescent bulb illuminated overhead. Once they were down the wooden stairs, he made short work of binding her hands, mostly for show – she needed to grasp that she was a captive whose survival depended on her cooperation, and tying someone was an effective way to drill that message home.

"All right. Sit there, against the wall. Here are the ground rules. We can do this the easy way or the hard way. I will ask you questions. You will answer them honestly and completely. If I don't think you have, I'll be forced to do things to you that you don't want to think about. I'll start by breaking your fingers, and then your hands, then your feet, until you're crippled for life. I am not exaggerating, and I will not threaten or warn you again. You should know something about me: I do this for a living. So don't make the mistake of thinking I am bluffing. I do. Not. Bluff. Do you understand?"

She nodded, her eyes now wide with fright.

"Good. First question. What do you do for Brightlabs? Specifically?"

She appeared confused by the question, and then awareness dawned on her and her eyes darted to her left for an instant, signaling to El Rey that she was about to lie. He held up a hand. "Remember that if you don't tell the truth, the agony you will experience is your doing." He held her gaze with eyes as dead as a shark's. "I should tell you I already know the answer to many of the questions I'm going to ask, so I wouldn't risk it, Doctor."

That got her attention, and she swallowed hard. "I'm in the product development division."

"Good. See? That wasn't so hard. What do you do in that division?"

"Mostly administrate."

"I can see that. How about your work developing bioweapons? Let's focus on that, shall we?"

"I...that's top-secret work. It's all classified. I can't discuss it."

"Yes, I know. But you have to, and you will. I assure you I won't tell another soul. This is for my consumption only."

She shook her head and El Rey sighed. He'd have to give her a demonstration.

An hour later, he closed the basement door behind him and wiped the perspiration from his face with the back of his arm as he considered how to terminate her. She hadn't known anything about his neurotoxin, but he couldn't take the chance of leaving her alive.

He moved to the kitchen sink and splashed cold water on his face, and dried it while he thought about how best to do it. In the end there was no need to make it painful – after a few digits had been broken, the good doctor had been entirely forthcoming, and he believed she was telling the truth as she'd described her work.

A sound from below drew his attention, and he rushed to the basement door. He threw it open and took the stairs three at a time, just as Helen's torso disappeared through a hatchway on the far wall near the ceiling. He cursed under his breath – he'd missed it in the gloom – and threw himself at her legs as she squirmed, trying to escape. She'd almost made it when he pulled her back down, slamming her against the ground like a rag doll from the momentum.

Her neck snapped like a dry twig and she spasmed beneath him, her appendages twitching from nerve damage. He didn't pause to think but grabbed her head in both hands and twisted, ending her life with a single swift motion.

His chest heaved from the exertion of the sudden sprint as he stood and stared down at the doctor's body, and then he headed back up the stairs to begin cleaning away all traces of his presence. With any luck, she wouldn't be discovered for some time; at least long enough for him to have concluded his business and be thousands of miles away. He glanced at his watch and did a quick calculation – if traffic was light into the city, he could make it to the airport by nightfall and be in Baltimore in time for a late night visit with the next on his list: Dr. Margaret Hunt.

# CHAPTER 34

*Baltimore, Maryland*

El Rey sat in a rental car, eyeing the underground parking area of the VA Medical Center, where his target was working a night shift. He'd called her office to confirm her whereabouts after breaking into her condo and finding only her eleven-year-old daughter, whom he'd bound and left with two liters of water – potential leverage on her mother, who he suspected might be reluctant to cooperate.

The terrified girl had informed him that her mother was at the hospital, supervising a clinical trial while making her rounds. He had no idea whether working late into the night was a regular occurrence for a physician who also created doomsday potions for military contractors, but regardless, it meant that his original plan – lying in wait for her at the condo – wouldn't work with his time constraint.

He studied the dossier that a private investigator he'd hired through a cutout had assembled for him. An intelligent woman with light brown hair and piercing blue eyes framed by soft laugh lines stared back at him from a photograph. That was from a lecture she'd given a year earlier regarding a breakthrough thermal approach to attacking malignant cells with a combination of rare metals. Her specialty wasn't oncology, but one of her employers was pioneering the technology, and she appeared to be on the cutting edge of a promising new approach to cancer treatment.

Margaret Hunt was forty-four years old, widowed after her husband died in a skiing accident a decade earlier, and lived with her daughter, Courtney. One car, a white BMW 428 coupe. She lived relatively modestly in spite of the income from her consulting work, and seemed to be genuinely decent, continuing to see patients and run trials even now that there was no financial reason not to delegate the work to underlings.

He tried to reconcile the description with someone who could create a toxin that would cause such lingering agony in its victims, and couldn't. But it didn't matter. What did was that he would soon know whether she'd authored the agent, and if so, what would be involved in obtaining the antidote.

He looked over at the BMW parked across the aisle in a staff slot and compared the license number to the one in the file for the third time. It was her car. He'd already been in the mammoth facility to look around and had verified that the security was laughable, consisting of a few guards who acted as though they were serving life sentences rather than protecting anything. Not once had he been stopped or asked why he was roaming the halls, but that didn't surprise him – he'd long ago learned that if he maintained a certain bearing, an innate authority to his stride, few would question him, assuming he knew where he was going and thus belonged there.

The assassin hadn't seen Dr. Hunt, but he'd quickly realized that it would be problematic taking her while she was in the hospital. Knocking her out wouldn't be an issue – he knew dozens of ways to do so swiftly and silently – but transporting her from the facility would be a risky obstacle. The security might have been a joke, but even the worst guards might want to know where he was going with someone on a gurney.

He'd decided to wait for her to end her shift and return to her vehicle, but was now getting impatient as his muscles twitched reminders of the toxin's insidious progress. With another glance at her car, he opened his door and got out, intent on hastening her arrival.

"Dr. Hunt?"

"Yes?" Hunt gave the approaching nurse a weary smile.

"We got a call from the parking garage. There's something wrong with your car."

Hunt's brow furrowed. "Wrong? What does that mean, wrong?"

"I don't know. The attendant just said that your alarm was going off."

Hunt made a notation on her clipboard and nodded. "Damn. Isn't that always how it goes? Just when you're making progress…"

"What do you want to do?"

Hunt sighed. "I think I better see what the fuss is about. Somebody might have hit it. Tell Sydney what happened and that I'll be back shortly." Dr. Sydney Grundwald was the director of clinical trials Hunt was partnering with.

"Will do, Dr. Hunt," the nurse said, hovering nearby as Hunt set her clipboard and pen on a rolling metal table near the ward window, beyond which lay a row of slumbering patients hooked to identical IV drips. Hunt shrugged out of her white physician's garb and moved to the bank of ancient elevators, and waited patiently until one of the oversized steel slabs slid open with a chime. This section of the facility was deserted at the late hour, admissions having ended earlier along with visitations, and any urgent cases were being seen in the emergency room. She wasn't surprised when the elevator had only one other passenger, an older staffer who nodded to her as he stepped out and disappeared around a corner.

Hunt pressed the button for the parking level and eyed her watch. Still three more hours to go. She'd already been on for eight, but that's what this kind of clinical trial demanded, and nobody was holding a gun to her head. She could have easily foisted her duties off on an underling and been at home watching a movie with her daughter, curled up with a good Chianti and some Chinese food, but she'd elected to run point, and the insane workload was the cost of her choice.

The elevator creaked downward and she tapped her foot impatiently. She hated leaving Courtney on her own, but the critical phase of the trial was only for two days, and she'd grown up with Mom having to be at the hospital for long hours occasionally. It was easier now that her daughter was old enough to not need a babysitter, but Hunt still felt guilty about leaving her baby alone.

The door opened and she stepped out, listening. Her alarm must have turned off by itself, which she supposed was good, because if something had damaged her vehicle, it would have still been howling. She moved to the car, her long legs covering the ground quickly. When she drew near, her stomach sank at the glitter of broken glass by the rear driver's side tire. Someone had broken her back window.

Hunt swore softly and was pulling her cell phone from her pocket when she sensed movement behind her. She tried to turn, but a hand like a vise clamped onto her neck, and a stab of pain shrieked up her spine before everything went black.

El Rey caught the doctor as she dropped, the pressure point a sure bet from behind, and dragged her to his trunk. He popped it open with the remote and lowered her body into its confines, and after glancing around the deserted subterranean area, closed it and slid behind the wheel.

At the street level, the attendant took his ticket and demanded five dollars, which the assassin was more than happy to pay. He pulled up the drive and turned onto the road, which was empty except for a utility truck parked on the right with its emergency lights flashing, and drove at a moderate pace, confident that the doctor would be out for at least fifteen minutes – five more than he'd need to get her to the garage he'd rented the prior week in anticipation of CISEN betraying him.

When he arrived, he raised the roll-up door and drove inside, taking care to lower and lock it behind him. He hoisted the doctor from the trunk and sat her on a chair that had been the only furnishing to come with the monthly workspace, and quickly bound her wrists and ankles so when she came to, she'd understand the situation.

He didn't have to wait long. Her eyes fluttered open and she took in the dark, bare brick walls and the exposed pipes running along the high ceiling before her gaze settled on him. She struggled against her bindings, but stopped when she saw his expression.

"What is this?" she demanded, her voice surprisingly strong given the circumstances.

"This is my way of introducing myself and getting information I need as expediently as possible, Dr. Hunt."

"Information," she repeated. "I see. And who are you?"

"A seeker of truth. That's all you need to know. Now we'll switch to me asking the questions, and you answering them." He went through his description of what he would do if she was less than forthright, and she listened in silence until he was through.

"Why are you doing this? What have I ever done to you?"

"That remains to be seen. But the short answer is that I have limited time, and I require answers you may be reluctant to give." He moved closer until he was standing in front of her. "Let's begin with your work for Bloomington Industries. Specifically your classified projects."

"If you know about that, you know I'm not allowed to tell you anything." Her eyes narrowed. "Is this some sort of misguided security vetting?"

"I can assure you this is exactly what it seems. If you don't answer my questions, I should also warn you that I am holding your beautiful daughter captive, and your willingness to cooperate will have a direct impact on her life expectancy."

Hunt's eyes flashed fear and fire at him. "Oh, God...no. Tell me that's a lie."

"Don't worry. She hasn't been hurt. She's comfortable and safe, for the time being, but I can arrange for that to change if you aren't completely honest with me. Do you understand?"

Her voice caught as she spoke. "What kind of monster are you?"

"The kind who needs answers. And whose patience is running exceedingly thin about now."

She exhaled disgustedly. "Fine. What do you want to know?"

"You were designing special projects there, correct?"

"If you know that, why ask?"

"I'll take that as a yes. Tell me about them."

"I was working with custom-designed agents tailored to the specifications of the client."

"The client. I see. Describe these agents."

"There were a number of them. Most acted on the central nervous system."

"Neurotoxins?"

"Yes. Or rather, all sorts of agents. But if you're after detail, I don't carry around specifics in my head, like recipes. So if that's what you're shooting for, you're wasting your time."

"Your clients were the government, were they not?"

She nodded and winced at the lingering discomfort from his assault on the pressure point at the side of her neck. "You seem to know an awful lot about it. Why don't you just cut to the chase? Ask me what you are really after."

"Dr. Hunt, you seem like a brave, intelligent woman, so before we continue, I'll explain something to you, and perhaps you'll understand why I've gone to these lengths. I was injected with a neurotoxin by the Mexican intelligence agency. That neurotoxin came from the CIA – one of your employer's esteemed clients. Since then, every six months I've had to inject an antidote, but I was assured that after a full course I'd be fine. I never received the final dose. So I have nothing to lose, and while I'm not in the business of kidnapping children – or their parents, for that matter – this is a matter of life or death for me. So be very careful with your answer: does that sound like something you might have crafted for…your client?"

Her face changed as realization spread through her. Hunt's mouth made a silent O and she closed her eyes. "I…it could be. I was responsible for a team that developed a particularly ugly one that I signed on to take through the animal trial phase, but after I thought through its only possible use, I quit the project and refused to do any further work on it." Her eyes opened and she fixed him with a pitying stare. "I'm so sorry if it got deployed."

"Describe how yours performed if no antidote was administered," El Rey ordered.

"It wasn't mine, it was the group's. But as I recall, there were a progression of symptoms, culminating in respiratory failure. Muscle spasms, twitching, dementia, fatigue, disorientation… and in the final stages, the victim would drown in their own fluids," she said.

"And what was the antidote course to clear the system?"

"I...I can't be sure, in a human. But the way it worked in the trial I participated in, there was a total of six injections, six months apart."

"Sounds like the same thing."

She shook her head. "But I don't understand. Why wouldn't they give you the final shot if they've given you all the rest?"

"My usefulness is over. They'd been blackmailing me into performing assassinations for them, holding the injections over my head. So I did what I had to. But now they don't want me walking around any longer. So no final shot, the problem goes away – drowns in my own fluids, as you know."

Her face changed as she grasped what he was after. "This is all about the final injection."

El Rey nodded. "Of course. What will you need to make the antidote?"

She frowned. "That's not how it works. It takes weeks, even if I could remember the composition exactly, which I can't. You'd be long dead." She hesitated. "But if they took it through development and deployed it, there would have to be a supply. And there's only one place Bloomington keeps all their active projects."

"Where?"

"In their pharma labs in Northern Virginia – at least that's how it worked when I left them six years ago. It probably hasn't changed. I haven't heard about them expanding."

"How would I go about finding the antidote in a facility like that?"

"The best way would be through their computer system – in their inventory management area. Assuming you could get inside, that would direct you to its location, if you understood their numbering and classification system." She sighed. "You don't stand a chance unless I help you get in. That's not a trick of some kind on my part – it's a statement of fact. The plant is guarded, but even if you somehow snuck by security, that's not the biggest problem. It's a huge facility, and you wouldn't know where to look. I wouldn't even be sure without accessing their database, assuming they're still calling it by its working name."

"Which is?"

"Doesn't matter what the trial name was. It might be just a string of letters and numbers now that it's a finished product – I'd have to see the list in order to narrow it down."

He edged nearer, a scowl creasing his face. She held his stare without flinching.

"Look," she continued, "you'd have to understand how their system functions to know where it's stored, and if you haven't worked with it, you'd never stand a chance. I'm not inventing this. I could guess, throw out a list of possible names, but it would be just that – a guess, which might do you no good." She hesitated, and when she spoke again, her voice was stronger. "So that leaves us at an impasse. You need me alive and cooperating if you're to survive, and your little interrogation won't achieve what you require."

"Is that so? What if I think you're lying?"

"Right. I'm willing to risk my daughter's life to…to what? Protect the secrets of a company I don't work for anymore?" She gave him a withering stare. "I want to live. I want my daughter to live. Which means I'll have to help you – I get that part. Without me, you won't find it."

"Let's say I believe you. I'd have to get into the plant, with you, correct? And you'd have to locate it in their system. How would you envision that working, exactly?"

"I don't know. But there's no way I'll help you unless you set Courtney free immediately. You can keep me prisoner, but my daughter walks."

El Rey shook his head. "That's not going to happen. What I might be willing to do is let you both go once I have my shot. At that point I'd have no reason not to."

"No. You could kill us both once you have what you're after."

"Why would I do that? What's the logic?"

"You kidnapped my daughter. There's no logic that applies to the kind of man who would do that."

"Dr. Hunt, you're smart. Think it through. I did what I needed to get your attention. I have it. If you'll help me get the antidote, there's zero reason I wouldn't release you."

"What if I went to the police?"

"Assuming I cared, which I don't, you'd have to start with how you committed an act of treason, purportedly under duress, and got an enemy agent into a top-secret area. How do you think that would sit? Because I guarantee you that's how they'll view it. I'd be willing to bet they'd more interested in hanging you at that point than chasing me." He shrugged. "Besides which, I'll have vanished, so you'll be the only one left to take down. Would you risk that? Maybe, but you'd be the one who'd have to be insane at that point."

"Why should I trust you?" she asked softly.

"You don't have any choice, do you?"

She studied him. "Your eye is twitching. If you're going to have a running chance, you better untie me, because you don't have a lot of time. Have you been cramping?"

"Some."

"Trembling?"

"Yes."

"Dizziness?"

"Comes and goes. Getting more frequent," he admitted.

"Confusion? Paranoia?"

"That's next."

"Then there's only one option, and we both know it – release my daughter, and I'll help."

He shook his head. "Out of the question. Help, and I'll give my word you won't be harmed. Neither one of you. That's the best I can do. Now do you want to save yourself and Courtney, or do you want to play poker?"

Hunt closed her eyes and El Rey watched a complex array of emotions play across her face. He could understand what she was going through – she wanted to save her daughter and herself, but she'd be committing a felony doing so, and would have to believe that the man who'd taken them hostage would release them once he had what he'd come for.

Assuming they were even successful.

"What if we can't find it?" she asked.

"Then we both lose."

"No. I need a guarantee you'll still release me."

"Dr. Hunt, we're wasting time I don't have. I came into this prepared to do whatever it takes to get the antidote. I want you willing to do the same. If you want to see your daughter again, if you want her to have a shot at a long, happy life, you'll stop trying to negotiate something and start trying to figure out how we're going to pull this off. You've already heard my best offer."

"And if I refuse?"

El Rey sighed. "Then I wind up cutting pieces off you until I've gotten at whatever's in your head and I take my chances, because you'll have left me with no choice. Your daughter will die in indescribable agony, and you will have made the decision to allow it. You could have saved both of you from a horrific fate, but chose not to." He looked at his watch. "I'm done talking. What's it going to be, Dr. Hunt?"

# CHAPTER 35

*Four hours earlier, Mexico City, Mexico*

El Maquino spun at the sound of the intercom's chime, alarmed at the intrusion. He thought rapidly and set down the drone he was carrying to move to the screen. He thumbed the camera to life and saw the faces of three of Aranas's men, who he knew guarded his building and who'd successfully fended off the attack only minutes before.

"Yes?"

"Let us in. We need to get you out of here. Boss's orders."

El Maquino nodded and shut the intercom off. He'd known what was coming when he'd seen the gun battle.

Resisting the urge to go through his ritual with the light switches, he hurried downstairs and unlocked the door. The men pushed through and the leader gave him a hard look. "We're running on borrowed time. The police will be here any moment. You need to leave."

"I'm almost ready," El Maquino said, turning and making for the stairs.

"You don't understand. If they catch you—"

"I have the building rigged with explosives. I need to finish arming them or the police will find everything. That can't happen."

The leader and his men exchanged a look as the big man ascended the steps.

"You have one minute. No more," he called after El Maquino.

Back in the loft, El Maquino worked quickly. He moved to his window and slid it open, and then returned to where he'd set down the drone and carried it to the aperture. He flipped a switch to

163

activate it and smiled slightly when the motors engaged, and then it was off, flying away from the building.

The other two drones took only moments to put into action, and then they too were following the invisible signal he'd programed them to target. Satisfied that he'd done all he could, he walked to his bedroom, grabbed his go bag, and crossed the floor to the intercom again. He flipped up a small panel, revealing a keypad, and pressed in a four-digit code. Craning his neck, he nodded to himself when a hiss sounded from the kitchen – gas had begun to flood the rooms, and when the mechanism he'd designed sensed sufficient density of the explosive fumes, his loft would cease to exist.

He closed the door behind him and, after a rueful look at the deadbolts he didn't have time to lock, rushed down the stairs to where the men waited. "I'm ready," he said, and followed them out into the street to where a green van idled at the curb, its side cargo door open.

"Get in," his escort said.

El Maquino placed his bag inside and climbed in, followed by the three men. The last slid the panel closed, and the driver gave the van gas. "Hang on," he warned them, and took off down the street.

Sirens echoed in the distance as emergency vehicles headed toward the building, and the driver leaned forward as he drove, scanning the sky.

"No helicopters yet," he said over his shoulder.

"They won't be long. Let's ditch this thing and get out of town," the leader growled. "I don't understand how they found him."

"Neither do I," the driver agreed. "But it doesn't matter now, does it? Six dead cops will have all hell breaking loose. Roadblocks, searches, the whole nine yards."

"You're sure they were police?"

"Who else would it be? I'm just surprised they came in so light."

"Is it possible they didn't know what they were walking into?"

"I'd say that's pretty obvious, wouldn't you?" the driver sneered. "Either that, or we were lucky enough to be hit by the most incompetent squad in the city."

"Where are we going?" El Maquino interrupted.

"Our priority is to get you clear. We'll take care of ourselves. We're taking you to a safe house. The boss will figure out what to do from there."

The leader glanced at him. "What took you so long?"

"I told you. I was arming the building."

"That's all?"

"And finishing up a project. It's not good to leave projects unfinished."

The leader stared at him like he was mad. El Maquino leaned his head against the van wall and closed his eyes, his interest in any further discussion nil. His uncle would know what to do.

He always did.

# CHAPTER 36

Cruz circled the district in his car, waiting for the cavalry to come over the hill. It was taking forever for backup to arrive, and he cursed Mexico City's congestion, which added to the delay. He slammed his hand against the wheel in frustration. They'd made a major miscalculation on the operation, which had resulted in everyone but Cruz being slain – a fact that would weigh heavily on him at the men's funerals, he was sure, even though he hadn't made the operational assessment that had led to their deaths. But as the ultimate field authority, he bore full responsibility for the botched raid. Those men would have still been alive were it not for his idea to grab the driver without a substantial contingent of support troops.

Then again, there was no way he could have known that the surrounding buildings were hiding multiple gunmen. And he still didn't know the answer to the key question: what had the driver been watching, day after day? Was it possible that Aranas was holed up in one of the apartments on that block? Earlier it hadn't seemed likely, but now Cruz wasn't so sure.

His radio crackled, and dispatch informed him that units were en route and would be at the shooting scene in a few minutes. Cruz acknowledged the communication and reported that he would return shortly to oversee the search of the area. That Aranas had been so close was frustrating, but it was a huge city, and the drug lord could have been anywhere, including in the car next to him. That was part of the logistics that worked against the police and benefitted the criminals, and it would do no good to rail against what he was powerless to change.

Sirens wailed through his open window and he made a U-turn. He was accelerating back in the direction he'd come when an explosion behind him blew chunks of asphalt through his back window, shattering it. He swerved, floored the gas, and zigzagged halfway down the block before stomping on his brakes and sliding to a screeching stop.

Cruz threw open his car door, pistol in hand, and scanned the street. Had someone thrown a grenade? Fired an RPG at him? The cartels had more than their share of both, pilfered from army bases or purchased from arms dealers who were more than happy to accept their money. But how had they pegged him? Had he been followed? Was he so shaken by the shooting that he wouldn't have noticed?

He heard an odd whirring from above and squinted at the evening sky. Something was hovering no more than thirty yards over his head. He blinked and tried to make it out, and then took off at a run when he saw that it was dropping straight toward him.

Cruz ducked into a doorway and peered around the corner just in time to see the drone pause, hovering, and then accelerate straight toward him. He fired six times, and three of his rounds hit the aircraft, disabling it. The drone wobbled in the air twenty yards above the street and then pitched down and dropped like a rock until it crashed next to the sidewalk.

Cruz's ears rang from the sharp report of his pistol. He pushed himself from the cover of the doorway as windows opened overhead, the explosion and gunfire having drawn the neighborhood's attention. Cruz holstered his Glock and walked toward the drone, but froze when he heard the whir of multiple rotors overhead.

He sprinted away, moving as fast as he could, but a glance over his shoulder told him that the drone had locked onto him and was following at the same speed. It was tracking him. *But how?*

He rounded the corner to test his theory and bolted down the street; sure enough, the drone made the turn behind him, accelerating. Cruz felt for his phone – it had to be his cell the thing was locked onto. How, he didn't know, but that was the only item he was carrying other than his gun. He stopped by an abandoned lot half filled with trash and hurled his phone deep into the lot, and continued running a swerving course, just in case he was wrong.

The drone performed a balletic arc and dove straight at the middle of the lot. The explosion shook Cruz's fillings and he heard screams from several of the open windows. He paused and drew his weapon, scanning the sky for more airborne threats. After a tense minute, he lowered his gun and walked back to the lot, where there was a crater ten feet wide and at least five deep. Smoke drifted from it and the surrounding debris like the aftermath of a bombing run – which he supposed it was.

He returned to his sedan as curious residents spilled from the doorways, and stopped by the car hood to make a short announcement. "I'm Captain Cruz, with the Federal Police. This street is now a crime scene. Don't touch anything, and stay indoors until we clean it up. Do you understand?"

Heads nodded and fearful glances took in his gun. The population was accustomed to being ordered around by the police and the military, and nobody wanted to incur the ire of a Federale captain to satisfy their curiosity. The handful of spectators returned to their buildings as he stared at them with a face that could have cut glass.

Satisfied that he'd done what he could, he used the car radio to alert headquarters about the drone attack and settled in to wait for a field team to arrive, along with the bomb squad. His hope was that they could disarm the downed drone and identify something that would lead to its operator. He would have to forego directing the tactical team at the shooting site until backup arrived here, and he called in the change of plans before ordering the dispatcher to patch him through to Briones.

The lieutenant's voice came over the radio a moment later, and Cruz switched to his earbud.

"Lieutenant, we found the driver, but we were attacked when we tried to grab him. Nobody survived. There were shooters everywhere in the buildings around here. Nobody on our team stood a chance. There's backup on its way, but I want you to get to the site and oversee a search. I'm stuck a few blocks away." Cruz told him about the explosions, and when he finished, Briones sounded shocked.

"Drones? Like they use in combat?"

"Exactly. Armed with bombs of some sort. They were homing in on my phone. I don't know how, but it got compromised."

"You're okay?"

"Yes, but I'm waiting to ensure nobody tries to make off with any evidence." Cruz paused. "Any calls from Dinah or Godoy?"

"Not that I know of. Give me a second and I'll check with your secretary."

"Thanks."

Briones returned two minutes later. "Nothing from either of them, but *Capitan*? You probably better get back here. Godoy's wife is in your office – she says it's an emergency and she needs to talk to you."

Cruz shook his head. "His wife?"

"Yes. I asked her what was wrong, but she said she'd wait to tell you. Only you. She stressed that."

"I'm going to be a while," he growled.

"She seems distraught. Barely holding it together."

"Damn. I don't have time for this."

"Yes, sir."

Cruz sighed. "Fine. When the bomb squad gets here, I'll come in. How soon can you get to the shooting scene? There's a strong possibility that Aranas was there. The chances that he still is are nonexistent, but nevertheless I want a building-to-building search, and I want the neighborhood cordoned off so nobody can get past police lines. Probably way too late, but we need to do something in case any of the shooters are in the area and try to slip by."

Briones hesitated. "That will require a lot of manpower."

"Then requisition it. It needs to happen."

"Will do, sir."

"Any further news on the buildings they've sealed off?"

"Not yet. All I can get is the official line: that it's a terrorist threat and there could be a bomb. If anyone knows anything else, they aren't talking."

"Damn." Cruz looked back at the coils of smoke winding into the air from the crater. "I'll need a cell phone. Mine's history."

"We have a ton of spares. I'll leave one in your office."

A huge explosion rocked the car, and Cruz stared off in its direction as a fireball lit the sky.

"What was that?" Briones demanded.

"I don't know. It sounded like a bomb. From where the shoot-out took place." Cruz frowned. "I have no idea what the hell's going on, Lieutenant, but whatever it is, I want you to be extremely careful. We're flying blind in this, and that's a good way to get killed."

"I will. I'll be on the comm line if you need anything."

# CHAPTER 37

The task force floor was quiet when Cruz returned, only a skeleton crew working the night shift. A janitor was mopping the ceramic tile floor as Cruz stepped through the doors and made his way across the expanse to his office in the far corner, furious at how the day had gone by in a whirl with no progress made on freeing his wife or Godoy's ridiculous task force, and their only lead on Aranas having turned into a bloodbath with nothing but dead officers to show for it.

He opened his door and found Mrs. Godoy sitting at his conference table, her face drawn. Cruz had never met the woman and was taken aback by how attractive she was. He'd always assumed that a cockroach like Godoy would be married to something equivalently odious, but even though she was in her fifties, the considerable beauty that must have been her youthful joy was still very much in evidence.

She stood as he approached and offered a delicate hand. Cruz shook it and took the seat opposite her.

"Mrs. Godoy, I'm afraid I have very little time. This is highly irregular, and I'm in the middle of several crises…"

"*Capitan* Cruz, I know you and my husband don't always get along, but he's mentioned your name a number of times as the most competent officer on the force."

"I appreciate the praise, but–"

Her voice dropped to a hush. "My husband's been kidnapped."

Cruz sat forward, his shock obvious. "What? When?"

"Last night. I got the call this morning. He was taken at his mistress's apartment. That's all I know."

Cruz looked away at the pained expression on the woman's face.

It was clear to Cruz that she hadn't known about her husband's dalliances until the call.

"Did you report the ransom call to the police?" he asked.

She snorted. "Are you kidding? The kidnappers just grabbed one of the senior police officials in the country. You think they're afraid of the cops? We both know the DF force is a joke – there are more kidnappings in this city than almost anywhere in the world. And how many wind up being solved by the police? I know the numbers, *Capitan*. Almost none."

Cruz couldn't dispute her reasoning. It was the ugly truth. Most didn't bother reporting kidnappings, preferring to pay in order to safeguard their loved ones rather than allow the local police to blunder through, which usually resulted in the victim's death.

His voice softened. "But you're telling me."

"Yes. Because you're not like the rest. You may actually be able to do something."

He considered her words. Here he was, almost nine hours after his wife had called to announce she was being held captive against her will, and he'd achieved absolutely nothing to free her.

Cruz shook his head. "Your faith in me isn't justified, Mrs. Godoy. I don't handle kidnappings. I have no real experience investigating them – that's not what I do."

"You're honest, which is a good start. And you know everybody. You run a large organization. You must have informants. All I'm asking you to do is try. I don't expect miracles."

"What are the terms of the ransom?"

"They want a million U.S. dollars."

Cruz's eyebrows lifted. "I see. And do you have that kind of money?"

It was her turn to look away. "I can probably get it. But it would make things very difficult."

Of course it would. Especially since she was probably planning to divorce Godoy once he was freed, if she didn't kill him first. That was *her* million the kidnappers would have walked away with, her piece of the marriage wealth she'd have claim to in divorce proceedings. Cruz could understand her reluctance to pay it in order to free a cheating spouse – especially an objectionable piece of excrement like her husband.

His face showed nothing. "How much time did they give you?"

"They want the money by tomorrow. I told them that was impossible, and that I'd need at least a couple of days. They didn't like it, but they agreed."

"So we have…thirty-six hours?"

She nodded. "About that."

"Have they called back?"

"No."

Cruz stood. He needed this like he needed a hole in his head. He was formulating his refusal when she began crying, as though she sensed his coming rejection.

"I…I'm sorry, *Capitan*," she sobbed. "I just don't know who else to turn to. He always told me that if he was ever in real trouble, you'd be the one he'd want on the case. And now…now he's in trouble. I hope he wasn't wrong about you. He said you are an honorable man."

Cruz moved to his desk and fished out a box of tissues he kept for his allergies. He handed her one and sat again. He'd never been good with crying women and felt his heart go out to her, even though he despised her husband.

"Can you think of anyone who might be connected with this?" Cruz asked. "Anyone who holds a grudge against him?"

She shook her head. "No. I've spent the whole day wondering about that, but there's nobody. Then again, it seems I don't really know anything about my husband, do I? I had to hear about this…this other woman, from his kidnappers."

"Did they mention her name?"

"No."

"And you have no idea where he was snatched?"

"None."

Cruz felt himself getting sucked into the situation and made a decision. "I'll do what I can, which isn't much. We can pull your phone records and see where the call originated, but that's likely a dead end. Most kidnappers know enough to place their ransom calls with untraceable or stolen cell phones. And we can look at your husband's credit card bills and see whether there were any charges yesterday that might indicate where he last was, as well as check his bank records to see whether he's made any suspicious payments."

Mrs. Godoy looked puzzled. Cruz clarified. "Often, if a married man is seeing another woman, money changes hands – perhaps some help with bills or a loan to help a sick relative…assuming it's not a more…commercial transaction."

"I didn't even think about that."

Cruz couldn't grasp how a good-looking woman could see her repellant husband as anything but a paying customer, but there was no point in belaboring it. "I'll need your signature on some forms to do all this."

Relief flooded her features. "Thank you. Thank you so much, *Capitan*. Of course I'll sign whatever you wish."

Cruz nodded and rose again. "Mrs. Godoy, I have to warn you that you'd be best off preparing to pay the ransom. You know how slim the likelihood is that we can locate him in time. These kidnapping rings are usually organized and experienced, and they rarely make mistakes large enough for us to track them down. I'm not going to lie to you. My efforts will probably do no good." He wanted to add that she should refuse to pay the ransom, and instead take the money and spend the season in Paris or Barcelona, but held his tongue.

She stood and dabbed her eyes, and then removed a card and wrote two phone numbers on the back of it. "This is my home number, and this is my cell. Call me anytime."

He took the card and motioned to the door. "Nothing will get done before the morning, I'm afraid. As you can see, the office is largely empty. But I'll put some people on it then, and you can expect a group to want access to your phone line so we can trace any new calls."

"Of course. I'll cooperate however you like," she said as she moved to the doorway. "Thanks again, *Capitan* Cruz. You're a good man."

Cruz escorted her to the elevators and, when she was gone, retraced his steps to his office, shaking his head. As though he didn't already have enough on his plate. But he couldn't refuse her.

Now he needed to make another round of calls and see what he could learn about the continuing closedown of the downtown area around the buildings, and see whether there was an alternative way into the hospital that he could use in order to free his wife and unborn child. There had to be some way in, either through ventilation shafts or, worst case, through the sewers.

But there was no way he was going to stand by and do nothing.

He was going through his Rolodex when his handset chimed.

It was Dinah.

"How are you, *amor*?" he asked.

"Everyone's settled in for the night. But it's a nightmare. They brought meals, but they were inedible, and they're still not telling us when this will be over. Have you heard anything?"

"No. Whatever is going on, it's being directed from higher in the food chain than I have access to. But I haven't given up. I'm going to find a way into the hospital tonight and get you out."

"How?"

"I haven't figured that out yet. But I will. I promise. Where exactly are you in the building? Everyone will probably be asleep by the time I get in, assuming I can, and I want to be able to find you without starting a riot or wasting time."

"They have guards patrolling the halls."

"Right, but I'm still the head of the anti-cartel task force. I'd say that trumps some private security goons."

She told him which floor she was on and the department name, and described its location. When she finished, Cruz was more determined than ever. "I'll come for you before the night's over, Dinah. I swear I will."

"I believe you, Romero. But don't get into trouble. Please. Be prudent."

"Absolutely," he lied, and disconnected.

The time for following the rules and operating through channels was over – he'd been doing that all day and had nothing to show for it, so he'd have to break some rules. His wife was all that mattered, and his job as a man, as her husband, was to get her out. He was her mate first, a cop second, and if he had to choose, there was no question which one would triumph tonight.

Now he just needed to come up with a workable plan to evade the entire Mexican army and police force.

He smirked at the thought. If Aranas could slip out of a supposedly impenetrable maximum-security prison right under the noses of the nation's premier security force, Cruz could certainly do the same for a hospital.

At least that was his hope.

He thought for a moment, flipped to the address card he was searching for, and began making calls.

# CHAPTER 38

*Charlottesville, Virginia*

El Rey and Dr. Hunt sat in his car, watching the fenced perimeter of the storage facility and the armed guards that patrolled it. They'd been there for two hours, and it was becoming increasingly apparent that the security was too rigorous for the assassin to attempt breaching. Hunt sighed and looked at her watch.

"Any ideas?" she asked.

"Not yet. I thought you said the security was lax."

"That was years ago. They must have upgraded since then. I don't think there were guards at night like this, just a few who sat around inside playing cards or whatever. Maybe there was some sort of a threat?"

"I might be able to cut through that fence and make it to one of the doors, but I'd be picked up by the surveillance cameras. You can just make them out near the roofline. See?"

She nodded. "Then what are you going to do?"

"I need to think."

She took the hint, reclined her seat, and closed her eyes.

El Rey could tell Hunt was still apprehensive about him, but he'd done everything he could to set her mind at ease and couldn't waste any more energy on reassurances. He squinted at the building in frustration – even if he managed to evade the security systems, both of them doing so was impossible. She was an untrained amateur, and all it would take was one slip to bury them both.

But then how to achieve his objective?

His mind felt fuzzy, whether from lack of sleep or the effects of the neurotoxin, he wasn't sure. But what was certain was that he was having trouble figuring out how to get inside, and the more he stared at the bunker-like building, the more despondent he felt.

*Think, damn it. You can do this,* he told himself. *You have no choice.*

If he had more time, maybe he could have gotten in through a ventilation shaft. He'd done so enough times before. But that still wouldn't get the woman in, and he'd have accomplished nothing.

Hunt stirred beside him. El Rey turned to regard her, an idea forming.

"What about walking through the front door?" he asked.

She blinked awake. "What? What are you talking about?"

"During business hours. Do they do any sort of tours of the facility?"

"No, it's closed to the public."

"How about for clients? Haven't they ever had any that want to see their plant? I'd think if the CIA was having them store antidote for them, somebody would want to look their systems over to ensure they're adequate."

"I don't honestly know. I mean, I wasn't involved in that level. Although…" She paused. "What are you thinking?"

"I can pose as a customer. A potential client with a substantial order. Or, better yet, pose as a security specialist who's been instructed to vet their facility before my group gives them the order."

"The problem is that they mainly deal with the government these days."

El Rey tilted his head and gave a small nod. "What about foreign governments?"

"I know they've done work like that in the past, as long as there's no national security threat to doing so."

"So if the Mexican government was considering hiring them to do something, I don't know, to create antidotes for something or generate some sort of specialized substance for it, that might work?"

She nodded cautiously. "It could. Why? Do you know someone in the government who could set that up?"

"I might."

"They'd want to verify it, obviously, before letting you in. But what about me?"

"I'd need a translator. Or a personal assistant. Would anyone recognize you?"

"I doubt it. I mean, it was years ago, and I wasn't at this facility very often. I used to wear my hair differently, too."

"So if we threw some glasses on you, there might be no issues?"

"I wouldn't want to chance it." She thought. "How about the Mexicans hired me as a consultant? That would fly. I do that sort of work, and that way I wouldn't need to pretend to be anyone else. And it would explain how you came to be looking at them – they'd know I'm familiar with their production capabilities, so it wouldn't be a shock if I recommended them as part of my diligence. In fact, we can say you're looking at two of their competitors, too. That would get the wheels turning faster. Make seeing this place almost an afterthought. Like, while we're at it."

"What would we need in order to get in?"

"I could contact corporate headquarters in the morning and tell them that I'm showing a client around. Tell them that it's their business to lose. But they'll still need to vet your identity, at the very least. That's not going to go away."

"I think I can get someone to vouch for me."

"They need to be legit. The company will check."

"Oh, he is."

"High level?"

"High enough. So now the question is, does this outfit make anything that the Federal Police might want to buy from them and have them store?"

Hunt considered the question. "Sure. I mean, it depends, but for instance if you were trying to build a stockpile of emergency antidotes for public health threats, like some bioagent, I could see it as plausible. They're big in that field."

"But why would we be interested in inspecting their facility?"

"What if you didn't have the capability of safely storing it in Mexico yet? There was a site planned for construction, but it won't be done for another year, so Mexico needs it stored in the interim?"

El Rey smiled. "That sounds good enough to get us through the door." He glanced at the time and retrieved a cell phone from his pocket. "I need to make a call. Don't say anything."

The assassin dialed a number from memory and waited as it rang, but it went to voice mail. He didn't want to leave a message, so he disconnected and dialed another number. When the switchboard answered, he gave the operator the name of the person he needed to speak to and crossed his fingers that the man was still in the office. There was a strong likelihood he would be, even late. He was a workaholic, and El Rey knew from experience that he typically clocked superhuman hours.

When his extension answered with a familiar voice, El Rey smiled and spoke softly in Spanish.

"Hello, my friend. You still owe me one. I'm calling to collect."

# CHAPTER 39

Cruz parked beside a CFE truck in the lot of a building three blocks from the general hospital. Two men wearing the power company's beige uniforms waited nearby, and Cruz walked over to them, slipping on his blue Federales jacket as he approached. The paunchier of the pair looked up at him and nodded.

"*Capitan* Cruz? I'm Adolfo Minos, and this is Bernard Trevino. We're at your service."

Cruz had gotten nowhere with his attempts to find a legitimate way to free Dinah, and so had contrived a plan that was an abuse of his office – but a necessary one. He'd notified the power company that he had an emergency action that required engineers to guide him into the hospital through the network of utilities tunnels that interconnected the area, and had used his blanket authority as the head of the task force to do so. Nobody had questioned him, which was as he'd expected. He was accustomed to receiving the full cooperation of any agency he approached, and this was no different.

"Pleased to meet you," Cruz said, and shook their hands.

"This way," Minos said, and led him to one of six windowless bunkers with fortified steel doors bearing the CFE logo. He opened it and led Cruz and Trevino inside, and then relocked the bolt before turning to a metal stairway that led downward into nothingness. Minos flipped several switches and the passageway lit with the dead white glow of fluorescent bulbs, and motioned to Trevino. "After you," he said.

Cruz followed them down three levels, and they came to another steel door, this one unlocked. Minos heaved it open and Cruz eyed the cables and pipes that occupied most of the narrow space, a walkway running along one side barely wide enough to accommodate a man's shoulders.

"This eventually leads into one of the hospital's basement utility rooms. The facility has a number of them, and they occupy the entire lowest level of the building, beneath the radiation oncology and radiology vaults," Minos explained.

"Why so far from the hospital?"

"This is the hub for the high-consumption buildings in the area. The rest run off standard cabling. Mostly hotels with convention facilities, and another hospital, private."

"Ah," Cruz said.

"Are you ready?" Trevino asked.

Cruz nodded.

The three blocks of tunnel ran in more or less a straight line, with only two bends in the span. Cruz tried not to think of the forty feet of earth and buildings pressing down on the tunnel ceiling as they slowly worked their way through the tight passage. The going was tight in many areas and filled with stagnant air. In several places the concrete-reinforced walls leaked mystery fluid.

"This was all lake bed, so everything is landfill, some of it from as long ago as the conquistadors," Minos said as he led the way. "There's still a lot of moisture in the ground even though the lake was drained and filled in by the Spanish centuries ago. And the frequent earthquakes don't help matters. We're constantly having to contend with damage from one of those hitting."

"Do the tunnels ever collapse?" Cruz asked, failing to keep the trepidation out of his voice.

"Oh, sure. But there haven't been any cave-ins for a while in the city center. Mostly in the outlying areas. You can guess the story — somebody's cousin gets the construction bid through nepotism and uses substandard products, cutting every corner he can so he can pocket more profit, and then an earthquake hits and, bam, flat as a pancake."

Cruz cringed at the sound of Minos smacking his hands together, his ability to imagine being crushed in a cave-in far too vivid for his liking. Trevino laughed at the graveyard humor and they continued their slog through the bowels of the earth. Minos looked over his shoulder at Cruz. "We lost sixteen workers last year from collapses where construction was thought to be the cause, but nobody ever goes to jail for it. Might want to talk to the higher-ups about that."

"I'll add it to the list," Cruz said. Corruption was a constant in every area of Mexican life, so the story of the cave-ins wasn't surprising or shocking to him. He'd file a report once everything was over, but it would just sit on someone's desk, he was sure.

They arrived at another steel door, this one weeping rust from its seams, and Minos fiddled with the lock, trying key after key, testing what little patience Cruz had after a night with little sleep and a day as demanding as any of his career. After an eternity, the heavy lock sprang open and Minos pushed the door wide, the chamber beyond it completely dark.

Trevino freed a flashlight from his belt, switched it on, and swept the walls with its beam. A complex tangle of pipes that led to oversized pumps the size of cars stretched as far as the light could penetrate in the gloom. Trevino moved into the room as Cruz and Minos trailed him.

Cruz could see that past all the pumps stood another door. Trevino found a switch and the room flooded with light. Minos retrieved his cell phone and brought up a blueprint of the hospital layout. He turned to Cruz and tapped on the screen.

"We're here. Outside this door is a corridor that ends at a stairwell. Two levels up is the lobby."

Cruz nodded. He had his own set of blueprints and had studied them at length. Dinah was on the fourth floor, halfway across the massive complex – the hospital covered four city blocks, and she was roughly two blocks away once he made it to her level. "Good. Wait for me in this room. Don't make a sound. I'd shut the lights off just in case – we don't want to attract attention."

The two CFE engineers nodded as though they had any idea what Cruz was doing. All they needed to know was that law enforcement wanted them to be discreet, which was sufficient. The call to help him had come from one of the top officials in the utility company, who had instructed them to give the captain all possible cooperation.

Cruz tried the handle and found the door unlocked. He pulled it open and grimaced at the groan of unlubricated hinges before stepping out into a drab gray hall lined with at least twenty identical doors. He made a mental note of the location and identification number of the pump room door and closed it behind him, the sound of the hinges as loud as a scream in the silence of the building's depths.

His footfalls echoed like drumbeats down the long corridor as he made his way to the maintenance stairwell, but there was nobody around to hear them. The stairway was dark, and he used his cell phone screen to illuminate the way, taking the steps two at a time, his sense of urgency increasing as he neared the fourth floor.

He was sweating and winded by the time he made it to the fourth-level landing, and he paused to catch his breath before covering the final stretch. After regaining his composure and blotting his face, he opened the door and found himself staring at two security guards lounging nearby. Cruz's expression didn't change. He approached the pair with his shoulders square and his chin high. One of the men, no older than twenty-five, stiffened at the sight of Cruz's uniform, but didn't release his grip on his baton.

"Nobody's allowed in the halls," he said, his tone conspicuously lacking in confidence.

"I know that. I'm with the Federal Police task force that's secured the building. Captain Cruz. I'm here to check on how you're holding up, and to transport a patient downstairs. Has everyone been behaving themselves?"

"They're getting pretty upset at being locked up," the second man said. "And nobody's really telling us anything. When will this be over?"

"We're hopeful by tomorrow."

"What's it all about?"

"I'm not allowed to say much, other than that we're going floor by floor, hoping to find members of a group that pose a threat to public safety."

"And this patient is one of them?"

"That's all I can say." Cruz glanced at his phone. "Where's the general practice ward?"

The pair exchanged a look. "Down this hall, make a left at the end, and then a right at the first hall you come to, and it's about halfway down on the left side. There's another guard stationed there who can open it for you."

"I'll be back with the suspect shortly. See to it that nobody passes this way other than me."

"Yes, *Capitan*."

Cruz stalked off, a busy man on a mission, leaving the two rent-a-cops to stare at his back as he disappeared down the hall. He could smell the nervousness coming off them, and was glad they'd deferred to his authority. As he'd suspected, the gravitas that came with his age and rank had worked magic; he just hoped that his good fortune held long enough to find Dinah and get her out of there.

The guard sitting on a chair outside the general practice ward stood as Cruz approached, and his tired eyes took in Cruz's uniform and holstered Glock without comment.

"I have to escort one of the patients you're holding in there downstairs for interrogation. Open the door," Cruz ordered, and the man shook his head.

"I don't have the key."

"What? I was told I would have access. Who does?"

"The shift supervisor."

"Damn. Well, get him up here, now."

"I'm not supposed to leave my post."

Cruz softened his tone. "Son, I'm a captain with the Federal Police. I'll stand watch. Just some advice, though – if a Federal officer tells you to do something, the correct answer is 'Yes, sir,' not 'I can't.' Do you understand?"

The guard nodded. "Yes. I mean, yes, sir. I'm sorry. I'll go find him."

"Good man."

He returned ten minutes later with an older man, perhaps thirty-something, who looked like he might pose a problem for Cruz. That impression was confirmed when the man stopped in front of him and spoke.

"My orders are that nobody goes in or out of there."

"Correct. Except me. I'm giving you a modification of the original order. I'm in charge of the group that's handling this emergency. I need to retrieve a patient and take her downstairs for questioning. Now open the door."

"How do I know this is legit?"

Cruz exhaled with frustration. The man obviously wasn't very bright. "Have there been a lot of high-ranking Federales walking the halls today, issuing orders? Are you confused about what authority a captain in the Federal Police has compared to a private security supervisor?" Cruz's tone hardened. "Now open the door, keep your mouth shut, don't let anyone out except me and my prisoner, or I'll place you under arrest and you'll spend a month in jail for your insolence."

The man tried to stare Cruz down and then looked away. "For the record, I don't like this one bit. You guys order us around and expect us to jump when you want." The supervisor hesitated, obviously working himself up. "And that's no way to speak to anyone. I've been on duty since before this started. I'm just trying to do my job, which is pretty miserable right now."

Cruz didn't push it. He wasn't looking to prove any points, just get his wife out.

"Very well. We're all pulling long hours. I'll be out of your hair in a minute. I just need to find this prisoner." He stared down at the door lever and raised an eyebrow, his hand on his pistol, just to underscore the real authority in the hall.

The man fumbled with his keys while Cruz waited beside him. When he finally unlocked the door, Cruz stepped into the waiting area, which was cool from the air-conditioning but heavy with the stagnant odor of too many bodies. He looked around the room as he pushed the door closed behind him and whispered as loud as he dared, "Dinah Cruz, I need you to come with me."

His order was met by snores and snuffles, and then a figure rose in the dark from one of the chairs by the reception desk. "Romero?"

"Dinah Cruz? Not a word. You're wanted for interrogation," he said.

Several sleeping forms stirred awake at the sound of his voice. He needed to get her out of there. Cruz crossed the room and took her arm, and then led her back to the door as he whispered to her.

"Stay quiet until we're in my car."

Dinah nodded, and he opened the door and they moved through the doorway, still holding her arm as though she was his prisoner. The supervisor and the pimply-faced guard considered them both, and Cruz gave the pair a curt nod. "Lock it back up. Nobody is to leave. Understood?"

The trip downstairs seemed to take forever even though only a few minutes passed, and she remained silent throughout the return trip in the tunnel. Once they reached his vehicle and the CFE technicians had driven away, he held her to his chest as tears streamed down her face.

"I love you, Dinah. I told you I'd come for you."

He felt her head nod against him. "I love you too. I knew you would." She lifted her face to his and gave him an exhausted smile. "Papa."

# CHAPTER 40

The grounds of the Museum of Anthropology in Mexico City were quiet at one a.m., the police presence required to maintain order far smaller than at the Federal building or the hospital. Those had turned into circuses, between the army, Federales, city police, and crowds of onlookers and vocal activists who weren't exactly sure what they were protesting, given the dearth of hard facts the government had provided.

The perimeter of the museum's verdant grounds was secured by army troops, their Humvees parked across the entry lanes, blocking all possible access and egress points. The handful of protestors who'd appeared mid-day had left once dusk had passed, and the outlying area was still, other than the armed soldiers patrolling the fence line.

Two demolitions experts had snuck into the building under cover of darkness; the risk of Aranas somehow watching twenty-four seven or having an informant in the building to alert him of the newcomers was considered remote enough to take the chance. They'd made their way in through the receiving area, hidden within two food carts the government team believed would fool any watching eyes into thinking that they were merely providing supplies for the people trapped inside – only a few dozen workers, thankfully. The carts were rolled to one of the service entrances, where they were left for the personnel inside the museum to retrieve. A moment after knocking on the door, several men's arms had appeared through the doorway and pulled the carts inside, technically complying with the demand that nobody be allowed in or out of the buildings.

The museum was equipped with portable X-ray equipment used on artifacts, and the two military demolition specialists had spent hours studying the bomb from every angle, including the guts of the mechanism, using the scanner. They'd concluded it was a minor miracle of engineering that lived up to Aranas's warning, designed to detonate with any movement, requiring no external power, and consisting of enough C-4 to level much of the building. Attached to the C-4 was a smaller secondary charge to detonate it, hooked up to a complicated bit of wizardry that could trigger it remotely…or if it was tampered with.

After much discussion and radio consulting with the American experts who had arrived that evening, they'd decided that their best bet lay in using a shaped charge to take out the secondary triggering explosive, the theory being that it could be accomplished with sufficient speed and accuracy so the main C-4 payload didn't detonate. Beyond that risky approach, there was no other way they could see to neutralize the device, and one of the Americans had commented that he was glad they'd never seen anything like it on their soil.

The president had been informed of the risks involved, and Norteño had again protested that an approach with a less than hundred percent chance of success was ill-advised. As expected, he'd been overruled, the president's political nose leading him to the compromise position his council members advocated in spite of the danger.

The bomb specialists in the museum had gotten the go-ahead a few minutes earlier and were busily making their preparations. They'd been ordered not to alert anyone else in the building, so they worked in silence as the rest of the staff slept.

Leo, the senior of the pair of demolitions experts, finished affixing the shaped charges to the side of the bomb's steel exterior in locations they'd marked with chalk based on the schematic they had created from the X-rays. He stood and stretched his arms over his head, the patience and detail required to get it right straining his physique as much as his intellect, and glanced over at Juan, the other instructor. Both men were old hands and knew the risks in dealing with a device unlike any they'd seen. They'd discussed in hushed tones the level of sophistication evidenced by the bomb maker after they'd studied the results of the scans, which had been far beyond anything they'd seen. A guard had located the device an hour after the museum had been locked down, and even the placement had been chosen to optimize the damage – there had been no other spot that would have been equivalent, which, along with the workmanship and the design, told them that they were dealing with a sophisticated operation.

"You ready to do this?" Leo asked quietly. His voice sounded relaxed, though he was anything but, having gone in a matter of hours from the safety of a senior instructor's job at the navy base in Veracruz to an assignment that could end his life.

"As ready as I'll ever be," Juan said. "Let's move to the max range of the wireless trigger. I have a bad feeling about this. Anyone who could build this baby should have foreseen the possibility of shaped charges being used to interrupt detonation."

Leo nodded. "Maybe that's why they ordered that nobody was to enter or leave the building."

"Let's hope so," Juan said doubtfully.

"You see any way it could be rigged to safeguard against it?"

Juan shook his head. "No. Or I wouldn't still be here."

"Then let's do this and go home to mama."

They moved to the next vault, one of fifteen storage areas used for artifacts that weren't on display, and took cover behind a heavy wooden crate. They knew that the attempt wouldn't mean much if their shaped charge failed – their only consolation was that the force of any blast would vaporize them instantly.

Leo ducked down as he retrieved a small radio transmitter from his pocket and armed the device. The handheld trigger was one he'd designed himself, which used encryption and transmitted on a military frequency so there was zero possibility of an accidental detonation signal from another source.

"Nice knowing you, buddy," he said, a grim bit of gallows humor that was an old joke between the seasoned veterans, and depressed the button.

# CHAPTER 41

The mood in the president's suite was somber as the Security Council watched the replay of the museum footage taken by a military helicopter five hours earlier. The dark outline of the building flashed orange and a massive fireball roared skyward, carrying with it debris that damaged structures as far as a quarter mile away.

"Enough," the president said as the glow from the explosion faded on the screen.

Norteño stopped the replay and waited in silence, opting not to belabor the obvious: that the result he'd predicted had come to pass.

The president rose and faced the gathering. "Gentlemen, we're out of options. If we're lucky, Aranas's greed will overcome his anger at our trying to disarm the bomb and he won't detonate the others. But I don't think I need to tell anyone in this room how disappointed I am in this performance. We've lost twenty-seven lives, as well as countless irreplaceable treasures."

The head of the council scowled. "While regrettable, it was the correct course."

"No, it wasn't, or we wouldn't be sitting here at Aranas's mercy," the president snapped.

The rest of the council members chimed in while Norteño sat back with an impassive expression on his face. After several minutes of bickering, the president turned to him. "Well, you were right all along. Any breakthrough ideas?"

Norteño nodded and the room fell silent. When he spoke, his voice was soft. "How would Aranas know we tried to disarm the bomb?"

The head of the council laughed humorlessly. "I'd say the smoking crater where the museum stood might be a giveaway."

Norteño offered a sad smile and fought to keep the condescending tone to a minimum. "You might say that, but I wouldn't."

"What are you getting at?" the president demanded.

Norteño scanned the table. "Look. All we know is that the bomb exploded. Nobody can be sure why. Not you, not Aranas – nobody. For all he knows, his bomb maker crossed the wrong wire. Or a small tremor set it off. We have two options here – we can either admit that we deliberately disobeyed his instructions, or we can go on the offensive, with our starting position being the assumption that he detonated it."

The men looked at each other, stunned by Norteño's suggestion. It had clearly never occurred to any of them to simply deny any wrongdoing and demand an explanation for why Aranas had acted in bad faith. Norteño's voice strengthened as he continued. "I've taken the liberty of pulling seismic data from last night. There was actually a small amount of activity about an hour before the bomb blew. Not big – a 3.8 shake – but that can serve as plausible deniability. Our story, after we pretend puzzlement at Aranas's accusations of tampering, will be that the tremor must have dislodged something, causing it to blow. We're just fortunate the other bombs didn't suffer from the same defect." Norteño paused, allowing his duplicitous suggestion to sink in. "We blame his bomb maker. That's where the fault lies."

The president shook his head. "You really think he'll buy that?"

"It's non-disprovable. He can't prove the tremor didn't dislodge something, and nobody's infallible, no matter how good – as we just learned by our top experts' failed attempt. I think it's a better gambit than admitting guilt. If I'm right and the money's most important to him, he'll want to go along with it." Norteño spoke directly to the president. "The art will be in the presentation. We should open with an accusation, which will put him on the defensive from the start. He'll fire back at us, and then you can advance the idea that a seismic event triggered it – that your experts warned you earlier that it was a risk given what we knew about the bombs, and that, sure enough, there was a tremor, and the rest is the bomb maker's shoddy workmanship. I think you can sell it," Norteño finished, and sat back.

The head of the council, seeing an out that would allow him to preserve his career, heartily endorsed Norteño's plan, and by the time the meeting ended, Norteño's gambit was the group's official recommendation. The men were polishing a statement for the press, alluding to terrorist animals taking innocent life, when one of the president's aides stuck his head through the door.

"Mr. President, excuse me, but you have a call."

The president glared at the young man, annoyed. "I told you I wasn't to be interrupted."

"Yes, sir. But the caller said you were expecting the call, and that if I didn't put him through, there would be hell to pay."

The president nodded and motioned to his advisors. "Everybody out."

Once the office emptied, the president sat behind his desk and stabbed the blinking line to life.

"Yes?"

"I warned you," Aranas hissed.

"*You* warned *me*? Then perhaps you can tell me why you blew up the museum when we're in the process of complying with your ridiculous demands?"

Aranas was silent for a promising second. "Why did *I* blow it up? What are you playing at?"

The president laid out his case exactly as Norteño proposed, and by the end of the exchange Aranas sounded, if not convinced, at least less sure of himself.

"I intend to check the seismic data. If there was indeed a tremor, you'll get the benefit of the doubt, although I still think you're being the shifty weasel we both know you are. I will call back shortly," Aranas said, and disconnected.

The president set the handset down softly and exhaled a long breath.

Twenty minutes later the drug lord was back on the phone.

"Very well. Here are my new terms. I can't prove that you

tampered with the device, although my instincts say you did. But in the spirit of putting this behind us, the new price for my silence is $1.5 billion – the extra half billion is for putting doubt in my mind. Have it ready by tomorrow morning or I will detonate the other devices."

"I...you'll have to give us more time. We're scrambling to assemble the one billion. Another half in that time frame is impossible."

"I thought you'd try to stall. But I'm in a generous mood. I'll give you twelve more hours. That's all. I'll be in contact tomorrow."

"We may not be able to get the–"

"Mr. President, make it a priority, or thousands will die. This discussion is over."

The president found himself listening to a dial tone, and this time he slammed the phone down, furious at the crime lord's dismissal. Aranas was treating him as if he were a common thug. The man's impertinence was not only insulting, but, the president suspected, designed to keep him off balance.

But two could play at that game, as Norteño had amply demonstrated.

He jabbed at the intercom button and barked into it. "Get Rafael back in here immediately. We have a press conference in half an hour, and I want his help with my statement."

"Yes, sir."

# CHAPTER 42

*Charlottesville, Virginia*

El Rey followed Dr. Hunt into the Bloomington Industries plant, wearing a suit that was less than an hour old, purchased that morning at a department store especially for the meeting. A tall man with salt-and-pepper hair and the face of a seasoned liar offered them a smile that never reached his eyes as he extended his hand in greeting.

"Dr. Hunt, a pleasure to finally meet you. I'm Carl Atkinson, the marketing director for Bloomington Biometrics division," he said, and then offered his hand to El Rey. "And this must be Lieutenant Briones of the Mexican Federal Police. *Buenos dias*," Atkinson said, his high school Spanish accent like nails on a chalkboard.

El Rey nodded, gave him a warm smile, and shook hands. He'd called Cruz and convinced him to swap Briones's photo with one of himself he'd taken on his cell phone, and inserted in his file that he was in the U.S. to inspect security arrangements at potential contractors. The ruse had worked, because when Hunt had called Bloomington first thing that morning to arrange for a last minute tour for a Mexican police official, they'd agreed and promptly requested the contact information for his office, as well as for a verifiable high flyer in the Mexican government – in this case, the highly decorated Captain Romero Cruz, easily checkable online from the media articles chronicling his startling career and exploits – and the man chartered with making a recommendation that could be worth billions of dollars of new business to some lucky contractor.

Cruz had spoken with Atkinson and affirmed that Briones was in the States for inspection tours, and that had gotten them an appointment at eleven a.m. Atkinson smiled at them again, and El Rey was reminded of a raptor, the man's eerily white teeth seeming to be too numerous for his mouth.

"I'm glad you decided to give Bloomington a chance, Lieutenant. We're not the largest in our field, but I daresay we're the best," Atkinson said, and El Rey nodded.

"Yes, well, the final evaluation will be based on the product and the terms," Hunt cut in. "The lieutenant here is evaluating security. It's mandatory for any company awarded these sorts of contracts in Mexico. It's how they keep their contractors honest."

"I think it was your President Reagan who said, 'Trust, but verify,' was it not?" El Rey asked.

Atkinson grinned again. "Very well, follow me. I'll give you a quick orientation and then you can hit me with anything I left out."

The tour lasted forty minutes, and by the end of it both Hunt's and El Rey's eyes were glazing over. It was obvious that the plant security was adequate, if not stellar, mostly standard procedures that had been put in place by an outside consulting firm. Atkinson bristled at Hunt's question about whether there had ever been a security breach and dodged it artfully, convincing her that something indeed must have happened after her brief stint with the company.

They wound up in the receiving area, where Atkinson regaled them with a long list of protocols that vendors had to follow when delivering supplies. Hunt moved a hand to her stomach as she flattened her blouse, and made a face. "Carl, I need to use the little girl's room. Did we pass one in the hall?"

"Yes, of course. I'll show you."

"No, we're on a tight schedule. You finish up with the lieutenant – don't let me interrupt. I'll be right back."

El Rey moved close to a pallet stacked with chemical containers. "You mentioned that if power was interrupted, you have backup generators that will kick in? What about if there's a natural disaster that cuts power for days or weeks? Like a super storm?"

"Well, first off, we rarely see storms like that," Atkinson began, nodding at Hunt as she made her way to the double doors that led to the corridor. "But if we do, we're covered. We have double backups that are natural gas powered, which can keep all systems operating round the clock for a week."

"Is the gas stored in tanks here at the facility, or are you reliant on it being piped in?"

"Good question. We opted for storage tanks that are fed by the utility company pipes, so that if there's an interruption in the supply, we go to the stored gas."

"Ah. And your alarm systems. You mentioned you have contacts on all the windows and doors. What about motion detectors? Pressure sensors? Infrared?"

Atkinson waved a hand, dismissing the question. "I can assure you that our systems are state of the art. There's no need for all that. We've got procedures that are industry standard and have been vetted by quite a few government agencies. For the types of products we manufacture, they're more than sufficient."

El Rey frowned. "I'm afraid I'll have to be the judge of that."

Minutes ticked by as the assassin peppered the American with detailed questions about the internal security of the various vaults, which amounted to locked doors and a few keypads he could easily bypass. He'd made careful note of the room where all the electrical panels were housed, and his practiced eye had seen several promising areas that might suit his purposes. Now it all depended on Hunt locating the antidote. But he was confident that getting into any of the vaults could be done.

After ten minutes had gone by, Atkinson glanced at the time and led the assassin back toward the corridor. El Rey tried his best to stall with another round of questions, which Atkinson pleasantly but firmly answered as he continued moving to the doors. They were footsteps away from the corridor when Hunt burst through, looking sheepish.

"I'm sorry, gentlemen. I hope you managed without me?" she asked.

"Absolutely, Dr. Hunt. I was just going to show the lieutenant our closed-circuit surveillance room, and then we were headed to my office."

El Rey caught the look in Hunt's eye. "I'm afraid we've stayed longer than I'd planned. Perhaps just the surveillance, and then we can be on our way?"

Atkinson seemed relieved to be so easily rid of them after fielding hardball questions for almost an hour. It was obvious that he was more of a salesman than an operations man, and many of his answers smacked of guesswork to El Rey's ear. Which was fine – he'd seen enough to know how to get past the cameras and the guards.

The security hub was impressive, with a bank of screens and a broad console loaded with comm gear, but El Rey was only marginally interested. He exhaled a sigh of relief when they passed through the gates and returned to the car, and leaned into Hunt as they neared it.

"So?"

"I got into the system. I'm pretty sure I know which chamber it's in."

"Pretty sure?"

"I'm extrapolating based on what I found. But yes, I believe I know what the agent's called, and where the antidote is being stored. So the question is whether you can get back inside without being spotted, and make your way into the vault without triggering any alarms."

El Rey gave a small shrug. "That should be the easy part. Now tell me what you discovered."

# CHAPTER 43

Flashes of dry lightning pulsed in a line of thunderheads brooding over a ridge of rolling hills, illuminating the night sky before fading back into the gloom. Muffled explosions followed from the distance, the clouds moving west, away from Charlottesville.

El Rey listened attentively, his car window halfway down, Hunt sitting beside him in the passenger seat. Earlier in the day she'd drawn a primitive layout of the plant from memory and marked the vault where the antidote was stored.

"It's in a climate-controlled room with other agents, but they'll have all the bins clearly marked. Yours will be TB2016LANG02. According to the system, there are ten vials – and you'll only need a quarter of one," she'd said. "Although…"

"What?"

"Well, in some of the animal tests, certain subjects required more than six shots. I recall that about nine percent required a seventh to return to an asymptomatic state."

"So I should take more than I need for this shot?"

She nodded. "It would be prudent."

"How long will it hold for?"

"I have no idea, but as long as the answer's at least six months and one day, that's good enough." She hesitated. "You probably won't even need it. But it would be silly to have access to it and not take more."

"How do I need to store it?"

"Room's at sixty-five degrees Fahrenheit, so just reasonably cool. Get a small wine refrigerator with a digital thermostat. That should do the trick. In the meantime, keep it in a thermos. That will protect it for a day or three. You just don't want any extremes – hot or cold."

"It's funny, because my first shot was in the tropics, and it was probably coffee temperature by the time I took it."

She nodded. "Which is fine, short term. But not if you're storing it for use six months later."

The plan was to use a syringe and drain several of the vials a few millimeters. If he drew it all from a single source, it might be noticed, but spread across a half dozen, the likelihood of anyone tripping to the theft was slim.

He'd given her a partial description of how he intended to bypass the elaborate security system and she'd made a face. "God, that sounds horrible."

"I've done it before. You may never get used to it, but you can get good at it."

"What about me?"

"You'll stay in the car. Once I'm done, I'll release you, and then you're free to go back to your daughter."

Hunt had seemed grudgingly satisfied with that answer, although clearly not happy, and she'd badgered him about her daughter at least every hour until he'd told her to stop – he had no updates, given that he was with her.

The day had passed slowly, and they'd busied themselves shopping for the supplies he would need to carry out his operation. Most of the equipment he'd located at a dive shop in a marginal neighborhood, where the owner hadn't shown the slightest interest in his specialized purchases. The rebreather wasn't absolutely necessary, but would make the unpleasant slightly more bearable. The rest was mandatory –fishing waders, night vision goggles, an array of tools with a neoprene satchel to carry them in, electrical connectors, batteries, and wire.

The final purchase had been two unopened syringes from a street dealer who threw them in with El Rey's hundred-dollar purchase of Mexican brown heroin. El Rey tossed the drugs into a dumpster before returning to the car, where Hunt sat, disgruntled at being bound while he scored.

"This really isn't necessary, you know," she complained.

"Perhaps. But it allows me to concentrate without worrying about whether you've had second thoughts."

"I did my part."

"Which I appreciate, and once I'm satisfied you told me the truth, and didn't invent the location of the antidote so I'd release you prematurely, I'll drive you to your daughter myself."

"You can tell me where she is."

"I will. Right before I go in tonight." He gazed off into the distance. "Just in case something goes wrong. A deal's a deal, and if I get myself shot, well, you've still done your part."

They ate Chinese food at a restaurant in town and then, seated in the car a quarter mile away, waited as the plum sky faded to black, the plant's lights glowing in the otherwise dark wooded area.

When the shift changed at ten p.m., they watched a line of cars retreat from the facility, and then El Rey had moved to the trunk and begun suiting up. Hunt watched nervously as he donned the waders and strapped on the rebreather, and then he approached her with a length of yellow nylon cord.

"Time for the final binding, Dr. Hunt."

"To think that some women dream of this," she observed as he went to work on her wrists.

"I can assure you that nothing in our brief time together has been pleasurable for me, other than your scintillating company. Soon you and your daughter will be free, and I'll be out of your lives."

"I just hope she isn't scarred for life."

"She wasn't abused, if that's what you're implying. I told you – she hasn't been harmed."

"Other than being tied up by a stranger and imprisoned with no food and water, you mean."

"Again, an exaggeration. I left her with two liters of water and some food. Her wrists are bound like yours, and I used chain for her ankles so she couldn't get far, but she'll be fine. Children recover quickly. She'll be frightened, but that couldn't be helped. As you know."

"I'm not saying it could have been. But I also can't ever forgive you."

He nodded. "Nor do I expect you to. What you'll do is free her, comfort her, perhaps go on a long vacation somewhere nice, and put this behind you. I'm confident you won't do anything foolish like contact the authorities – I would hate to see you spend the rest of your life behind bars for aiding and abetting. You strike me as smarter than that."

Once he had secured her, he pocketed the car keys, left the windows rolled down a few inches, and gave her a small nod of his head. "I disabled the horn, so no point in trying that."

"You promised me you'd tell me where Courtney is."

"So I did. She's still at your condo. Chained to the bathroom pipes, well hydrated and fed, as I mentioned. I put cushions from your sofa in with her so she's comfortable."

"And...she's alone?"

"Yes. I didn't leave her with someone who would rape her. She's unharmed, probably scared, but will be relieved when it's over. As will we all, I assure you."

"Good luck," Hunt said as he closed the passenger door.

"Luck won't come into play."

Ten minutes later he was crawling along the inside of a sewer pipe in over a foot of noxious fluid, making his way the four hundred yards to where waste water emptied from the plant. That whoever had set up the security had ignored the possibility of an intruder using the sewer system didn't surprise him. It was an approach most wouldn't attempt, and one he'd been happy to see would get him past the perimeter fortifications that served as ninety percent of the facility's security. It was his good fortune that the designer of the defenses hadn't considered the threat of someone penetrating beyond the alarms, sensors, and fencing seriously – the internal safeguards were manageable, if not easily defeated. The building was much like an egg: all the protection built into the shell, leaving the contents vulnerable.

The surroundings glowed a familiar neon green in the night vision goggles as he worked his way to the iron grid that protected the plant's master evacuation pipe. At the grid, he studied the locked shackle and spotted a single cable that armed a contact sensor mounted to the barrier. He removed a long wire with a metal clip on each end from his bag, and after attaching one end to each side of the sensor, used a pair of bolt cutters to snip off the rusty padlock hasp.

El Rey cracked the grid open wide enough to crawl through and inched into the gap, careful not to dislodge the clips that maintained the connection for the alarm. He left them in place, mindful that he'd be returning the same way, and continued forward, scanning above him for motion detectors. Confident there were none, he continued until he arrived at the base of a vertical shaft with a metal ladder leading upward into nothingness.

Once inside the pump room, he quickly stripped off the rebreather, the fishing waders, and the heavy rubber gloves, his nose wrinkling at their stench. A pair of metal doors stood at the opposite end of the vault. He ignored the din of the machinery and made his way to the entrance, relieved to see that there was no deadbolt on the doors.

He removed a coil of yellow nylon cord from his kit and tied it to one of the two lever handles, leaving the other end hanging loose. His preparations complete, he stood motionless with his ear pressed to the metal barrier, listening for any sign of guards patrolling the hallway beyond.

Three minutes later he'd located the chamber where Hunt believed the antidote was stored and was studying the keypad beside the door. As he'd noted on their tour with Atkinson, the units were of a commercially available variety favored by budget-conscious contractors – and one that fortunately was relatively simple to work around.

More clips and wires, and after prying the cover off, he dismantled the keypad within seconds and short-circuited the mechanism to instruct the lock to open. A click sounded from the bolt and he nodded to himself. If only all his problems were so easily overcome.

Inside the chamber he moved quickly along the alphabetized racks of agents. He found the bin he was after and eyed the handful of vials. After such lengths, the tiny containers were almost anticlimactic.

He checked the labels and noted that all bore the same expiration date – fourteen months in the future.

The assassin selected a vial and drained a tiny amount of the precious honey-tinted fluid into a syringe. He replaced it and repeated the process with the others until both syringes were full, the levels of the vials down no more than a few millimeters. After sliding one of the syringes into his bag, he unbuttoned his shirt and pulled one shoulder off, exposing bare skin. His face didn't change when he drove the tiny needle into his vein, nor when he emptied the contents of the syringe into his system.

El Rey waited, and when he didn't convulse or black out, shifted the bin containing the antidote vials back into position. He was edging back through the door when he heard the pounding of running boots from around the corner.

The assassin took off at a dead run, any need for subterfuge gone. Something had triggered the alarm – it could have been the lock or an undisclosed sensor in the room that had notified a slow-to-react security team of an intruder.

A klaxon wail sounded when he was halfway down the corridor, and he poured on the steam as he sprinted for the stairwell that led to the maintenance levels. Footsteps echoed behind him, and then a man's voice screamed at him, "Stop, or I'll shoot!"

He ignored the warning and ducked through the stairwell door, figuring they wouldn't fire unless they were complete idiots, given the danger of a ricochet, and took the stairs three at a time, putting as much distance as he could between himself and the guards. At the lower level hall he bolted to the pump room door, hoping his pursuers would be slowed some by having to search the rooms closer to the stairwell first – they couldn't know behind which door he'd disappeared.

He slipped into the room and secured the cord, which would further delay the guards – at least until they could cut it. Seconds counted in making his escape, and if the simple knot bought him twice the time it took to tie it, it was a good investment.

He pulled on his gear and returned to the sewer, moving as fast as he could in the confined space. Now it would be a race against the guards' competence. There was slim chance employees getting paid low wages would follow him into the pipes without breathing gear, so that left them with locating a blueprint of the system and isolating the points where he could exit. If they were on the ball, he'd be the loser. If they didn't have the relevant schematic at their fingertips, he stood a better than fair chance.

Near the road, there was no sign of a welcoming committee when he emerged from the manhole he'd left open, the metal cover invisible in the darkness. He shrugged off all his gear except his night vision goggles, ignoring the glare from the emergency lights that blazed at the nearby plant, and ran for the clearing where he'd left the car.

When he arrived he got his second surprise of the night – Dr. Hunt had managed to work loose from her bindings and escape. He peered into the surrounding trees and made an easy decision: he'd have to leave her. He could be on a plane jetting south long before she could make it to civilization, assuming she decided to chance reporting him, which he didn't think she'd risk.

"Good luck, Dr. Hunt. Take care of your daughter. Family matters most," he called out, and then slid behind the wheel and twisted the ignition, the biggest challenge now getting to the airport from the rural road before all hell broke loose.

# CHAPTER 44

*San Miguel de Allende, Guanajuato, Mexico*

*Don* Aranas reclined on his plush leather sofa, the wood frame ornately carved by regional artisans famous for their skill, and took a generous measure of steaming coffee. Getting clear of DF had been simple, a matter of a charter flight under an assumed name. For all the government's sound and fury, like all bureaucracies, it was inept at the things that mattered – which he'd proved countless times in his criminal career. There had been roadblocks in place, of course, but a few pesos to the right security men and his flight had been cleared for takeoff with no fuss.

His new cell phone warbled from the table beside the couch.

"Yes?" he answered.

"I'm glad to see everything appears to be going according to plan," an American voice said in accented Spanish.

"It's always nice when hard work pays off." Aranas paused. "I trust you've had a chance to discuss my proposal with your masters?"

"I did, and they agreed, at least in principle. But they weren't happy with the reduced cut."

"It's not a reduced cut, and you know it. It's the same as it's been for the last four years. Which has worked well for everyone."

"It's a reduction from what was negotiated with Agundez."

"Who had no authority to make the commitment. And for which he paid with his life."

"Well, the deed is done, so you got what you were after."

"It seems extraordinary to me that it was such a struggle. All I want is what's fair for the job I do."

The American switched topics. "Do you think the president will pay off or try another gambit?"

Aranas took another swig of his coffee and set the cup down carefully on the saucer before answering. "I don't suppose it much matters, does it?"

"Well, a billion is a nice payday."

"Achieving your objective is a nicer one. I can't help but believe there will be promotions on your end for engineering this."

"I live in hope. What do you think went wrong at the museum?"

"Oh, without question they tried to disarm it. And then they didn't have the balls to admit it. But I let them out gracefully...for a small surcharge."

"Do you plan to detonate the others?"

Aranas was a reasonable man. "Not if they comply. I still have to do business here, so there's no reason to agitate things further. Even in your new environment of increased international cooperation."

"Terrorism is a global threat. They're everywhere," the American said, and Aranas barked a laugh.

"Of course they are. I think I saw one out by the woodpile earlier. Sneaky bastards."

It was the American's turn to laugh.

"Just let us know if you plan to blow them."

"Will do. I don't think it will be necessary, but I've learned to never underestimate the stupidity of civil servants or politicians. No offense."

"None taken."

Aranas hung up, satisfied with another successful negotiation concluded with his longtime partners in the U.S. –the largest market on the planet for illegal drugs. Without their cooperation, trafficking into the country would have been far more difficult, and they were worth the percentage of profits he paid; but only to a point. This current round of talks had ended as favorably as he'd hoped, with everyone getting what they wanted: his cartel maintained its margins, and the Americans got to increase their reach.

It was a good bargain, with a billion and a half bonus at the end of the rainbow for him – a worthwhile expenditure of effort.

Perhaps most importantly, it had given him the chance to get even with the president for his betrayal, and remind him where the real power rested. The silly peacock strutted around like a pint-sized statesman, but it didn't serve Aranas's purposes to allow him to believe he actually ran things. The president's double cross, which Aranas had used to put his current scheme into motion, had been unforgivable, and balance needed to be restored.

Now that the administration understood the true order of things, Aranas expected matters to settle down and to be able to conduct business in the usual fashion: he paid off politicians at the mayoral and governor level, owned most of the senate, and would mobilize his massive wealth to determine which candidate got to be the next president, as he had for the current worm. It was only when the servants forgot their place that he set them straight. The rest of the time he had no interest in what they did, as long as they followed his direction and used the military and law enforcement to gut his rivals. Let them loot the country – they'd been doing it since before Aranas was born, and he had little doubt that the larceny would continue long past his expiration.

It was the way of the world. How anyone in the neighborhood to the north believed that any candidate who could raise the billion dollars it took to get elected wasn't wholly owned by the special interests that funded the campaign baffled him. In Mexico it was understood that gaining public office was a license to steal.

He shook his head at the wonder of it all and finished his tepid coffee.

"Maria! *Mas café, por favor*," he called, and debated whether it was too early for his first cigar of the day. He opted for discipline, but patted his breast pocket, where the four he allowed himself each day fit snugly.

A woman in a white smock and loose trousers hurried in with a coffee pot. "Here you are, *Don* Aranas."

"Only half a cup. Oh, and I'll be having our favorite guest over for lunch. Please make his usual. You know how he values consistency – I fear this latest adventure has been a bit much for him, but a good meal should go a long way to calming his nerves."

Maria nodded. She knew exactly what to make. And as always, plenty of it.

Because for all his social ineptness, El Maquino enjoyed his food.

# CHAPTER 45

Carla looked up from her tea to find El Rey standing in the doorway of her dining room, watching her as she responded to early morning messages on her cell phone. She gasped in surprise as he moved toward her, covering the space between them in a few long strides. She rose and he took her in his arms, holding her close as she battled conflicting impulses. After several moments she looked up at him.

"Did you get what you needed?" she asked.

He nodded and lowered his lips to hers. She tilted her head back and they shared a long kiss, and then she pulled away and slapped him as hard as she could.

"You miserable bastard. You promised me, and you lied."

He raised his fingers to his reddening face and nodded. "I couldn't allow your stubbornness to interfere with my survival chances. I'm sorry."

"And what about your commitment to me?"

"You would have slowed me down, Carla. I didn't want to risk my life in order to make you happy – because those were the stakes. I did what I had to do in order to be successful." He paused. "I hope you can forgive me."

"I've been up with worry since you left," she countered, the hurt coloring her tone. "You have no idea how affected I was when you didn't show up. I got you the visa, everything, and you didn't even bother to call."

"I was busy. I had to interrogate several scientists, break into a

210

top-secret lab, that kind of thing. I didn't see where having a long argument over the phone would help my focus." He paused. "All I can say is I'm sorry."

"You're sorry you did it, or you're sorry about the effect lying to me had?"

"The latter. I was able to get the antidote, so whether or not you agree with me, going it alone was the right call."

He allowed that to sink in. While he knew he could have handled the situation differently, his methodology had been successful. He didn't bother to tell her about the kidnappings or the near miss in the lab or the violence he'd used to achieve his objective. Keeping her out of that was part of the reason he'd misled her. What she didn't know couldn't hurt her, and seeing his operational side wasn't something that would do either one of them any good.

She sat and stared at her tea. "I took the job in Spain. I leave in four days."

He nodded, unsurprised. "That's great news for you, Carla. It's the right thing for your career."

"Don't try to butter me up. I'm furious with you."

His lips twitched with the hint of a smile. "I couldn't tell."

Carla couldn't help herself, hating the grin that leapt unbidden to her face. She looked away, but not before he'd caught it. "I *am* glad you're not dead," she conceded.

"So am I."

He took a seat across from her and they sat in uncomfortable silence until she finally spoke. "Are you going to tell me about it?"

He did, leaving out the worst. When he finished, she shook her head. "Then it's finally over?"

He nodded. "I hope so. I got an extra dose, just in case. Apparently there are a few types who require seven shots instead of six."

"How do you feel? Any more symptoms?"

"No. I'm tired, but that's from lack of sleep, not anything else."

"Do you want to try to grab a little here?"

"If you'll have me."

She appeared thoughtful. "You're really going to have to make this up to me."

"I plan to. You name it, I'll do it."

"That's the way to a woman's heart. Be careful what you promise."

This time he smiled broadly. "Be careful what you wish for."

He trudged up the stairs to her bedroom and was kicking off his shoes when his cell rang. Nobody had that number...except one man. El Rey freed it from his pocket and glared at the screen before answering.

"Hello."

"I presume our little subterfuge worked?" Cruz opened with.

"Yes. Thanks." El Rey frowned. "Is that why you're calling?"

"Not entirely, although I'm overjoyed that your time was well spent."

"What do you need?"

"So suspicious."

"I know you, *Capitan*."

"Yes, I suppose you do. Just to remind you, I put my neck on the line for you. Now I need some help."

"With?"

"Nothing for your considerable skills. I just need to track down *Don* Aranas and figure out how to disarm a pair of bombs he's using to blackmail the government."

El Rey laughed. "Are you serious? That's Aranas? The news is all about terrorists."

"That was a cover story. I was brought into the loop by the president early this morning. I'm risking charges of treason telling you this."

"Then why are you doing so?"

"Because you're the only one I know who could find him in time."

"I'm afraid you're overestimating my abilities." The assassin hesitated. "What's 'in time,' anyway?"

"By tonight."

"You must be joking."

"I wish I was."

"It's impossible."

"I wouldn't jump to conclusions. We think we've located the bomb maker's facility."

"Then arrest him."

"It's not that easy. He blew it up. It's in pieces all over a Mexico City street."

"Then how do you know it was him?"

Cruz recounted his ordeal with the drones. El Rey listened wordlessly. When he was done, the assassin grunted. "That proves nothing."

"Perhaps not. But the downed drone was equipped with C-4. I don't suppose I need to tell you how hard it is to get your hands on C-4."

"It can be done."

"There was also C-4 found in the ruins of the building that exploded." Cruz let that register. "That's an awful lot of coincidences on a day where there are two C-4 equipped bombs deployed in the city, wouldn't you agree?"

"Fine. But how does that help?"

"We're running the traffic camera footage as we speak. It appears a van was used as a getaway vehicle. We tracked it to a house on the edge of town. A car left shortly after the van arrived. We followed it to a rural airfield near Puebla. Briones contacted the tower for a flight plan – a prop job took off ten minutes after the car arrived."

"Sounds like you already know more than enough."

"This is where it gets dicey. Aranas read the president the riot act. Said that if anyone shows up anywhere near him, he'll detonate the bombs."

"An effective preemptive measure, you have to admit."

"Yes, and that's where you come in. I need you to help us…under the radar."

"How?"

"Travel to where the plane landed and see if you can find either Aranas or the bomb maker."

"Why not add walk on water while you're at it?" El Rey sighed. "I haven't gotten more than three hours of sleep in the last three days, *Capitan*. I'm not up to this."

"I wouldn't ask you if I had any other options. You're the best. If anyone can pull this off, it's you." Cruz lowered his voice. "I did you a solid. I need you to do one in return."

"I was calling in my favor, so we're even. Besides, that's considerably more than switching some photos and backing my story."

The line hummed faintly as Cruz considered his response. "I have no choice."

"Why should I help you? Risk my life — for what?"

"If he detonates the bombs, thousands of people will die."

"Then don't screw him. Problem solved."

"We can't be sure he still won't," Cruz said. "There are women, children, and pensioners in those buildings."

El Rey didn't speak for a long moment.

"If I do this, we're through, correct? No more reaching out for just one more thing, is that clear?"

"Crystal."

"Nobody can know of my involvement. I'm officially dead, even to CISEN. I do this as my parting gift, I walk off the edge of the earth, and we're even. Deal?"

Another long pause. "Deal."

# CHAPTER 46

*San Miguel de Allende, Guanajuato, Mexico*

The colonial charm of San Miguel's quaint streets, lined as they were with touristy kitsch and façades painted every color of the rainbow, was undeniable, and El Rey admired the view through his distraction as he walked toward the towering spires of the hill town's famous cathedral. He had a meeting set up with one of the local Federal Police informants at a café on the square, who had been told that he was a logistics specialist from Mexico City. The man, Ignacio Lorna, was a small-time loan shark who augmented his income by snitching on his competitors to the police, and the assassin knew his type well enough to understand that he'd be just as likely to sell them out as provide them information.

The trip on a private puddle jumper had been arranged by Cruz in the time it took for El Rey to get to the airport, and the 140-mile flight had taken less than an hour. Cruz had arranged for a car to be waiting, and El Rey had received the keys from a man who'd been standing on the tarmac when he'd arrived. The man had directed him to the car, a battered Nissan Altima that looked on its last legs, before he'd continued to a pickup truck parked in the shade afforded by a tree's spreading branches and driven away without looking back.

El Rey parked the Nissan several blocks from his rendezvous and was making the rest of the journey on foot – the less the informant knew about him, the better. Cruz had agreed with him and told him that he had carte blanche with how he handled the operation. As far as the world was concerned, the assassin didn't exist, and he was therefore deniable. Short of blowing up the entire town, whatever he deemed appropriate was fine – with the clock ticking as the government scrambled to meet the ransom demand, expedience was the order of the day.

Normally the assassin would have allowed more time so that he could reconnoiter the meeting area beforehand and verify he wasn't walking into a trap, but due to the urgency, he was risking going in cold, a practice he detested, but there was no viable alternative.

The café's sidewalk tables were mostly empty due to an earlier cloudburst. El Rey pushed past the vacant seats and into the interior, where a man in a green soccer jersey sat at a table in the back, nursing something with foam on top. El Rey sat beside him and, when the waitress came over, ordered a cup of decaf. Once she'd gone to the kitchen to get his drink, he turned to the man.

"Olivero?" he asked.

"The one and only. Arturo, I presume," Olivero said, using the alias he'd been provided.

El Rey nodded. "You mentioned to a mutual friend that you might have something for me?"

"Yes. There's a ranch outside of town, maybe fifteen minutes, that's been empty for months. Yesterday a group showed up and ordered the propane tank topped off, bought enough food to feed an army, and had a water truck deliver a pipe full."

"Hardly suspicious," El Rey countered.

"They said you wanted anything that raised eyebrows. That did. Then today, a plumber went out to work on the cistern and said that there were guards posted on the grounds."

The waitress arrived and set the assassin's coffee in front of him. El Rey offered her a smile, which she returned with a flash of mahogany eyes and white teeth. He took a swallow and set the cup down to cool.

"Many high-net-worth people have bodyguards," he observed.

"These guys look hard. That's how the plumber described them – and he was in the army."

"I wouldn't expect bodyguards to look soft."

"Nobody knows who owns the ranch. It's always been a source of mystery around here. You know how small towns can be."

"You mentioned that it had been empty for some time. Who was there before?"

"Nobody knows – they kept to themselves. I just know they were there because the guy who delivers their groceries told me. But he said they went through a lot of tequila and Tecate."

El Rey took a swallow of coffee and nodded. "Hardly earth-shattering. Where is this ranch located?"

The informant scanned the restaurant nervously. "I could use a little bonus. I'm short on cash."

"That's reasonable," El Rey agreed. The arrangement was that Olivero would be paid the usual way, by his handler; but Olivero was angling for more, and El Rey was short on time and patience. "Say, two thousand pesos?"

"Three would be better."

"Twenty-five hundred's the maximum I can expense." El Rey reached into his pocket and withdrew a wad of five-hundred-peso notes and counted them out. "Now stop stalling. Where's the ranch?"

"About six kilometers outside of town, on the road to Alcocer." Olivero finished his drink. "There's a roadside shrine just before the turnoff. You can't miss it – it's fairly elaborate. Family of four, popular in the community. Very sad. Drunk driver never saw them."

"Right or left side?"

"Right if you're heading to Alcocer." He rose. "That's all I have. Might help if I knew who you were looking for."

"If I told you, I'd have to kill you," El Rey said, deadpan.

Olivero laughed nervously and waved a hand at him. "Okay. None of my business."

"That's right. Oh, but Olivero? If you breathe a word about our discussion to anyone, you'll discover I wasn't kidding." The assassin's tone could have frozen fire.

The informant's eyes locked with his for a moment and then he quickly looked away. "Yeah, yeah. I know. Don't worry. Your secret's safe."

El Rey drained his cup and debated following Olivero and neutralizing him. He put the odds at fifty-fifty that the man would sell them out. A glance at his watch convinced him to abandon the idea and go for a drive to Alcocer. He needed to move fast and didn't have the luxury of tying up that loose end, as he would have if he'd been working on a hit.

The assassin placed a call to Cruz as he walked from the café and warned him about Olivero. "I'd have him picked up and locked away for the day, *Capitan*. I don't need to tell you that we can't afford a leak."

"I'll order the local office to send a car out to his usual haunts."

El Rey told him about the ranch. "Can you pull up anything you can find on satellite and send it to my phone? It would save me time if I knew the layout."

"Will do. Figure ten minutes."

"Make it five."

"I just got a piece of good news. The government bought us a little more time. They negotiated for delivery of the goods tomorrow by ten a.m. – apparently it's not all that easy to locate a boatload of diamonds on short notice."

"That will make it easier, assuming he's there. Going in when it's light out would be suicide."

"I figured you'd be relieved."

"Relieved would be when you tell me I don't need to pursue this anymore."

"Sorry."

"Sure you are."

He hung up and strode down the cobblestone street to the parking lot, his senses on alert. He was unsurprised when a man wearing the stained clothes of a laborer emerged from a doorway and began tailing him. As he'd suspected, Olivero was playing both ends against the middle.

The assassin continued past the lot and ducked down a side street, and then took off at a run. He disappeared into an alley and sprinted until he reached a cross street, and then rounded the corner and stopped, listening for running footsteps.

It was the laborer's lucky day. He'd lost the trail and, in the

RAGE OF THE ASSASSIN

process, saved his own life.

El Rey circled back and was on the road minutes later, no sign of anyone following him now.

Which didn't give him much comfort, because if he was right, there might well be a welcoming committee waiting for him at the ranch – one intent on ensuring he never made it back alive.

The drive only took ten minutes. El Rey rolled past the closed ranch gates without slowing and kept going for another kilometer before pulling off the road behind a grove of trees to make his approach on foot. He skirted a decrepit brick building with a partially collapsed roof near the property perimeter and continued through the tall grass with cautious steps. Something glinted by one of the wooden fence posts, and he froze when he spotted a motion detector. A breeze stirred the foliage around him and he relaxed a little – they'd have the detectors set with reduced sensitivity or receive false alarms all day. Still, it told him what he needed to know – ordinary ranches didn't typically boast sophisticated electronics for security.

He continued along the fence line, noting that the barbed wire gleaming in the sun appeared new – it would be dull in another week, which meant that someone had only recently taken pains to get the ranch prepared for habitation.

Further along he noted a trip wire strung at ankle level beyond the fence, which told him still more.

Once back in the car, he called Cruz to give him a terse report, and then told him what he'd need. Cruz said nothing for a moment when he finished. When he finally spoke, his tone was sarcastic.

"Anything else? Maybe a suitcase nuke?" Cruz asked.

"No, just what I requested. Call me back to confirm."

# CHAPTER 47

*Mexico City, Mexico*

The Mercado de la Merced, one of the largest indoor flea markets in Latin America, was bustling in the early evening as bargain shoppers of all stripes meandered down the aisles. Yelling vendors hawked every imaginable contrivance, and the din was akin to the roar of a jet on takeoff. A home electronics salesman bellowed through a karaoke system at passersby, while across from him a group selling car stereos demonstrated the bone-crushing bass of one of their premium setups.

Mrs. Godoy stared straight ahead, her eyes determined behind her dark glasses and her face set in a frown as she negotiated the rows of junk. She clutched a green nylon suitcase in one hand and a scrap of notepaper in the other. Pausing at the end of the aisle to look around, her gaze settled on a string of *piñatas* hanging from a steel frame. She swallowed hard and moved to where the vendor was sitting to ask about prices.

The merchant was eager to make a sale and haggled with her for five minutes before she waved him off and continued down the aisle, her bag abandoned at the edge of his booth, where it went unnoticed for several minutes. When she'd disappeared around a corner, a young barefoot street urchin sidled up to the suitcase and, after glancing around, made off with it, moving fast, but not so quickly he'd attract attention.

He darted outside the building and made a beeline to a gray Nissan Maxima double-parked on Calle Rosario. A swarthy man wearing a striped blue polo shirt stepped from the passenger side, a handheld scanner gripped tightly in one hand, and did a quick sweep of the bag before taking it from the boy in exchange for a five-hundred-peso note. The urchin ran off, delighted at his newfound riches. The passenger tossed the bag in the backseat of the car and climbed back in.

He removed a cigarette from a soft pack in his breast pocket, lit it, and then blew a long plume of gray out his window before turning to the driver. "It's clean."

"Positive?"

"The scanner doesn't lie. It would have detected a tracking device."

The driver nodded and put the car in gear. "At least she's playing straight."

"Given her husband's position with the police, she's got to know how useless they are."

The driver laughed. "It would be better than even odds that if they caught us, the money would just disappear."

The passenger grinned. "Beats working."

After a glance around, the driver forced his way into traffic and began the long drive to the suburb where his boss was waiting to count the ransom money and verify it was all there.

Briones sat in the cockpit of a Bell 206B JetRanger helicopter that was hovering two thousand feet above ground level three blocks south of the flea market. In the rear of the aircraft, a pair of technicians sat with portable consoles, watching the screens intently. Briones checked his watch and switched his headset radio to transmit.

"Still waiting for the party to start. They made the grab," he reported.

"Patience, Lieutenant. They won't get far," Cruz replied in his headphones.

"I know. But this is always the worst part – the waiting."

One of the technicians interrupted him. "We have a signal."

Briones nodded. They'd used a tracking chip that didn't turn on for half an hour, expecting the kidnappers to check for one when they had the bag. "Okay. It just went live. Signing off." He turned to the technician. "Where?"

"Moving west on Emiliano Zapata."

"Intersection?"

"Coming up on Manuel-doblado."

Briones looked at the other tech. "Cameras?"

The tech tapped in several commands and then nodded.

The first technician's voice rose. "Turning north on Manuel."

"See what we have on the cams."

The second tech scowled. "Too many vehicles to be sure. Probably a half dozen. Could be any of them."

Briones grunted and looked to the pilot. "Let's maintain a decent amount of distance. Say half a kilometer. Don't want them getting spooked."

The Maxima wended its way north until it stopped outside a pharmacy in a residential area of Emiliano Zapata, a lower-middle-class neighborhood known for high crime and one which the police were reluctant to patrol. The two men got out of the car and retrieved the bag, and then walked around to the back of the building. A heavyset man with a conspicuous bulge in his pocket nodded to them as they approached the rear door, where three more thugs waited.

The door opened and the new arrivals entered, bag in tow, and then the heavy wooden slab slammed shut, leaving the men to watch the alley.

"They're stationary now," Briones said into his headset microphone.

"Address?"

Briones gave Cruz the information. He spoke to someone in the background and returned to Briones. "The SWAT team's ten minutes out, no more. Can you set down somewhere they can pick you up?"

"There's a soccer field we passed a minute ago. In Popular Rastro. How long till they get there?"

"Figure five to seven."

"Then I'll be waiting."

The pilot executed a turn and banked toward the field. There was nobody in the deserted area to watch the helo drop from the dusk sky, its blades thumping rhythmically as it descended to a soft landing at one end of the expanse. Briones hopped down from the aircraft and ran in a crouch until he was clear, and then the helicopter rose again, its downdraft flattening the grass around him. When silence had returned to the grounds, he raised a handheld radio to his lips and spoke into it.

"I'm on the ground."

"Roger that."

Luis Hierro took a long drag on the joint he was enjoying as his right-hand man counted the stacks of hundred-dollar bills, feeding them into a bank bill counter that rifled through them at machine-gun speed. Every so often he stopped the counting and checked several of the banknotes at random, eyeing the magnetic strip with a seasoned eye and studying the watermark with a jeweler's loupe.

"What you think, man?" Hierro asked, holding the smoke in as he spoke.

"All good so far."

"How much longer?"

"Dunno. Maybe ten?"

Hierro nodded. "Okay. I'm going to grab some *asada*. You want some?"

"Sure."

"When you're sure it's all there, pack up and let's get ready to hit it. I want to be in Puebla by tonight."

"What about the cop?"

Hierro shrugged. "Pop him. Bastard asked for it."

# CHAPTER 48

Briones sat in the situation van as the SWAT team deployed, circling the building where the tracking chip had remained stationary for the past twenty-five minutes. Four snipers had taken up positions on neighboring roofs, the darkening sky making them impossible to spot in their black helmets and balaclavas, their sound-suppressed rifles equipped with night vision scopes, removing any chance of a miss.

The radio in the van hissed and the quiet voice of the squad leader came over the air.

"We're ready to go in. Just say the word and we'll move."

Briones leaned forward, eyeing the screens before him where the leader's helmet camera broadcast a high-resolution real-time image. "Wait until the bad guys are down before taking the door. I'll give the signal, and I want the roof shooters to take them out simultaneously."

"10-4, Lieutenant. Ready?"

"On my count. Three…two…one…fire!"

Up on the roofline the snipers' rifles popped in unison, the special load subsonic cartridges barely louder than champagne corks. The cartel watchers died in silence as the sniper rounds hit home, all of them easy chest shots at the sub-hundred meter distance. The pair framing the door tumbled backward and the snipers fired again, ensuring that they were dead by the time they hit the pavement.

Running boots filled the alley as one of the officers cut the building's phone line, and then there were two dozen heavily armed men standing by the back door as the squad leader tried the handle. He glanced at the nearest officer, shook his head, and stepped back. The officer removed three charges from his satchel and attached them where the hinges opened inward. He gave a thumbs-up, and after inserting triggers, stepped away. The men pulled back a respectful distance and the leader nodded.

The charges detonated and the door blew inward. The leader tossed a pair of flash bangs through the opening and waited until they exploded, and then the men followed him in, weapons sweeping the room as they went in low.

Three men lay stunned on the floor, a blanket of dollars strewn everywhere around them by the blast. One reached for his belt and had a Beretta 9mm free when a hail of rounds punched into him. The other two were holding their heads and groaning. Four officers moved to them, assault rifles trained on the stunned men's torsos, and quickly disarmed them.

The leader pointed to the two interior doors and trotted to the first. He tilted his head at the second and held up five fingers. His men closed in on the door, the remainder taking up position behind him, and a voice crackled over his helmet comm system.

"Front office is secured," reported the head of the team that had gone in through the front door.

He nodded and took a breath, and then reached out and gently twisted the lever. To his surprise, it opened, and he pushed the door wide and ducked back behind the safety of the cinderblock wall in case anyone fired from within the next room. The other door swung open and his men moved through it, guns at the ready.

They found themselves in a dark room, empty except for a form huddled in a corner. One of the officers hit the light and the leader approached the naked, shivering man, his face crusted with dried blood and his skin discolored by bruising. The leader knelt down, and the man dared a look at him through eyes swollen nearly shut, and even in his brutalized condition the leader recognized Eduardo Godoy of the Federal Police.

The leader activated his earbud and reached Briones.

"We've secured the building. Victim's in bad shape. We're going to need an ambulance to get him to a hospital immediately."

"Three are standing by. I'll send them in," Briones said. "Any survivors?"

"Two. Want to handle the interrogations?"

"I wouldn't miss it for anything. I'll be there in a minute."

"We'll need to secure the cash, too. Room's full of loose bills."

"I'll bring two men to handle the money. I want it all accounted for. No slipups. Everyone leaving the scene will be searched."

"I understand." It wasn't unheard of for tens of thousands, or even hundreds of thousands, to go missing in a chaotic crime scene. "Ounce of prevention."

"That's right. Any familiar faces?"

"Negative."

"I'm coming around the corner. Be there shortly."

The leader motioned to one of his men and pointed to Godoy. "Get a blanket and cover him up."

Briones arrived and strode to where Godoy lay awaiting medical attention, curled beneath a navy blue field blanket. Briones crouched beside him and spoke softly. "Sir, help will be here in a moment. Just hang on. We got the kidnappers – you're no longer in danger."

Godoy's mouth worked, but no words came out. Briones winced at the sight of his ruined teeth and averted his eyes. Godoy tried again, and this time managed to croak a few halting words.

"Hierro. Did…you…get…him?"

Briones's brow furrowed at the name. Luis Hierro had been the bane of the task force's existence for years, but they hadn't heard much about him for at least six months.

"Hierro? He's involved?"

"He…did…this."

Briones rose and crossed into the other room, where the squad leader was standing over the two cuffed survivors. Briones leaned into him and whispered, "Luis Hierro. Is he one of the dead?"

The leader's brows rose. "Hierro? No. I'd have recognized him. Can't mistake that ugly mug."

Briones nodded and moved to the prisoners. "Where's your boss?" he demanded.

Neither of the men spoke. Briones knelt beside them and lowered his voice. "The man you tortured to the point of death? He's a top

Federal Police official. Which means that you can expect that to look like a massage compared to what we're going to do to you. So you either talk, or you're going to suffer ten times what he's been through – and I'm not exaggerating. We have a special place in our hearts for scum who target cops, and you're the only ones left to take it out on." Briones paused to let his words resonate. "Now here's the deal. One of you talks, and the other gets the full treatment. I don't care which. Neither of you talks, I'll personally put the word out that you rolled over on Hierro and told us everything you knew. Which means you won't live more than a few minutes once you're out of the infirmary for your multiple injuries sustained while resisting arrest and attempting to escape during the interrogation. That's the only deal you're going to be offered, and when I leave, the offer's off the table."

Briones stood. "So which of you is still going to be breathing this time next week?"


Hierro heard the muffled reports of the sniper fire as he was rounding the block with two bags of freshly grilled carne asada and hand-rolled tortillas. He didn't even blink and continued straight rather than approaching the building, his steps unhurried, a worker on his way home to his family with a late dinner.

He cursed under his breath as he walked, aware that he was suddenly not only a million dollars poorer, but would be the target of a renewed manhunt within the hour, leaving him precious little time to get out of town. To complicate matters, he'd set up a buy that evening and had planned to use most of the ransom to pay the supplier.

Hierro fished a burner cell from his back pocket as he neared the parking lot where he'd parked his Chevrolet Tahoe. The supplier would be angry but might be willing to advance a portion of the product – Hierro was at least warning him that there was a problem, which would count for something. How much remained to be seen, but any goodwill, combined with the several hundred thousand he had stashed in one of his apartments, should help alleviate the worst of the disappointment.

He'd live to fight another day.

Which at this stage was all he could hope for.

# CHAPTER 49

*San Miguel de Allende, Guanajuato, Mexico*

The high-altitude night sky was clear, the stars bright and seemingly close enough to touch as a Cessna 182, its running lights extinguished, droned along six thousand feet above the mountain town. The pilot checked his GPS and turned to where El Rey waited in the rear of the plane.

"Figure thirty seconds. You ready?"

El Rey gave him a nod and settled his night vision goggles into place. When he switched them on, the dark interior of the plane blinked to yellow daylight. The assassin adjusted the parachute strapped to his back and rechecked the H&K MP5 submachine gun secured to his chest, more to kill the remaining time than out of necessity.

The pilot's voice rang out. "Fifteen seconds."

El Rey twisted the handle on the fuselage door and was instantly buffeted by cold air. Even at only a hundred and twenty knots airspeed, the wind hit him like an arctic fist, and he shuddered as he waited for the pilot's final count. When it rang out, he waited an extra instant and then threw himself into the inky void as the plane banked hard left for its return to the airstrip at Santiago de Queretaro, where he'd boarded it an hour and a half earlier.

Cruz had come through with all the weaponry and equipment he'd requested, including the black Special Forces rectangular glider-parachute that would enable him to land with pinpoint precision within the fortified enclave below. As with the Bloomington plant in Virginia, he was certain that the defenders of the hacienda had never

229

contemplated their defenses being penetrated without detection, and his plan was to make it into the house unseen, locate Aranas and take him prisoner, and then call in the cavalry once he was secured. Cruz had a hundred men waiting in the brush surrounding the ranch for his signal, and their instructions were to only engage when he gave the word. These were the best of the best Cruz could muster, elite shock troops of the Federal Police, who had been transported after dark to a remote staging area so as not to arouse the attention of the locals, any of whom might be an early warning system for the drug lord.

That Aranas would have the local police on his payroll wasn't questioned – it was impossible for the most wanted man in the world to come and go as he pleased without detection unless he owned most of the politicians and cops. That he had the resources was also a foregone conclusion; at one point, *Forbes* magazine had named him one of the hundred richest men on the planet, and his wealth had only ballooned since then. It was assumed that he spent generously in order to capture the very apparatus charged with catching him, as his miraculous prison escape had more than adequately demonstrated.

El Rey freed his chute and braced as his fall abruptly slowed with sufficient G-force to rattle his teeth. It had been some time since he'd last jumped, but like riding a bicycle, it was a skill one never lost, and he smiled behind the night vision goggles as he gripped the pair of handles that enabled him to glide to within footsteps of the expansive ranch house's back door.

The complex of buildings came into sharp focus as his speed fell off, and he spotted the area he'd chosen based on the satellite images – a flat depression behind one of the structures that lined the drive, presumably a four-car garage next to the last shape, which was no doubt a barn, given its size. The air grew warmer as he neared the ground, his descent soundless in the moonless night.

When he touched down, the rubber soles of his boots made no noise on the hard-packed dirt. He shrugged off his chute, stowed it beneath a pile of refuse, and freed his submachine gun. The surroundings glowed in his goggles, and he could see three of the six men he'd noticed patrolling earlier now standing no more than a hundred yards from him, smoking, their AK-47s held loosely as they enjoyed their cigarettes and conversed in low voices.

Only one of the windows of the house glowed at the late hour. He made his way to the rear door on catlike feet, careful not to make any sound. Once at the door he found it unlocked; unsurprising, given the perimeter security. He inched it open and slipped through the gap, then closed it softly and flipped the lock shut – for what he intended, it was best to limit the likelihood of being interrupted. He held the suppressed H&K at the ready as he crept along the hallway that led from the empty kitchen into the depths of the house, which was silent as a tomb.

The first door he came to was open a crack, and he eased it wider and peered in through the space. An empty bedroom, large, the king-size bed a postage stamp in the massive space. He stepped into the room and made his way to the far door, which turned out to be an equally deserted bathroom large enough to accommodate a tour bus.

That had to be the master suite, and given that it was empty, Aranas might not be there after all. Unless it wasn't his place, in which case all of the stealth had been in vain. The thought slowed the assassin, but he shook it off and continued his mission – now that he was past the guards, there was no reason to abandon his search.

Three more bedrooms were likewise empty, which left only the room with its light on. El Rey approached, pressed his ear to the door, and frowned in puzzlement at the sound that greeted him: an atonal humming.

He twisted the knob and opened the door a few centimeters, flipping his goggles up and out of his sightline. He waited a few moments as his eyes adjusted, and his frown deepened.

A small mountain of a man wearing farmer overalls sat at a table with a look of intense concentration on his face, an array of tools spread before him. He was staring through an oversized magnifying glass supported by a table-mounted arm. The atonal humming was emanating from him as he rocked slightly back and forth, working on something on the table.

El Rey recognized the shape of an aerial drone at a glance, but it took him several beats to appreciate that there was something wrong with the man – aside from the humming, his expression was oddly vacant, even as his brow scrunched while he manipulated the delicate instrument in his bear-sized hand.

El Rey had seen that look before, once, years ago, while on a mission.

Aranas might not have been in the house, but his bomb maker was. The surprise for El Rey was that the man was clearly touched in some way, a way the assassin suspected he understood.

El Rey pushed the door open and the man looked up, his slack expression never changing as the assassin took measured steps toward him, his machine gun now pointed at the ground.

"How's the project going?" El Rey asked with an easy smile.

The man gave a small nod. "Good."

"You think it'll work?"

"Should."

"That's great. Then what?"

"Next project. Always have one. Idle hands are bad. Best to keep busy."

"Yes, it is. And it looks like you've settled right in. Shame about the last place."

"A shame," the man agreed. "I liked it there."

El Rey smiled again. "Sorry to bother you, but I need your help."

"Me?"

El Rey nodded. "The bombs. It's time to defuse them."

"Already?"

"We're doing it early. But nobody knows how."

"I told Uncle."

El Rey didn't blink. "He forgot."

The big man shook his head. "I told him three times."

"He says he's confused. Wants to make sure he does it right, so he sent me. Can you show me how?"

"Oh, it's easy. I gave him the control."

"Right. But it broke."

"Broke!" the big man said. "Oh no. That's bad. Bad, bad, bad."

"It is indeed," El Rey agreed. "So what can we do?"

"Well, I have another. A just-in-case one."

"He hoped you might. That's smart."

"You never know."

"No, you don't. Can you show me how it works? I'll even write down the instructions so your uncle doesn't get confused again."

"Write it down. Good idea." The man stood, his hair askew, and lumbered over to a pile of parts and motors. He rooted around in it, talking to himself in a low murmur. "Write it down. Write it down. Good idea. Write it down."

The bomb maker was a case of arrested development, El Rey guessed, or perhaps more accurately, of different development, where certain talents were wildly exaggerated while others atrophied. A part of him recognized something of himself in the big man, who clearly saw nothing wrong with building doomsday devices for his uncle. El Rey was quite sure that if he asked him what happened when the bombs blew up, he'd get the same blank look – it was obvious what happened: the bombs worked!

"Gotcha," the big man said and turned to El Rey with a hint of pride.

The assassin eyed the metal box. "Oh, that's really nice. You made it?"

"Sure did. It's my prototype. Not as good as the one I gave Uncle, though. That one was much nicer."

"How does it work?"

"Coded radio. Three buttons. Here on the back? Switches. On, off, on, active. Off, off, off, inactive."

"Those little toggles? Off, off, off?"

The bomb maker nodded. "Off, off, off."

"Why, I can remember that! You're a genius."

The man handed him the console. "Write it down."

"Oh, I will. As soon as I leave. I have a pen in my car, and I'll definitely write it down. Wouldn't do to forget, would it?"

"No. And be careful. Don't break it."

"I won't." The assassin eyed him. "How far away does it need to be for it to work?"

"Uncle's box, up to two kilometers. This one, maybe…five hundred meters. I could increase the range if you give me more time."

"Uncle said to hurry. So I'll tell him the closer the better," El Rey confirmed.

El Maquino moved back to the table, uninterested in any further interaction. El Rey understood. There was no reason for more discussion. And the big man had a project to complete.

The assassin returned to the door and slipped out. He paused at the threshold to slide the console inside his jacket and zip up, and then returned his goggles to the active position.

Fifteen minutes later he placed a call to Cruz. "I have the means to disarm the bombs."

"You found Aranas?"

"No. The bomb maker."

"How did you get it out of him? He might have lied."

"No. He probably doesn't know what a lie is."

"What do you mean? How can you be sure?"

El Rey told him, and when he was done, the silence on the line stretched for a half minute. "He just gave it to you?" Cruz finally asked.

"Why wouldn't he? It's for his uncle."

"Just like that?" Cruz demanded, disbelief in every syllable.

El Rey shrugged. "Just like that. But we better disarm the bombs before Aranas detonates them. I'm down at the main road. You can have someone pick me up whenever you want."

"How did you get clear of the ranch?"

"I disabled all the surveillance gear at the source. It will take a day or two for them to figure out the systems are disconnected, because I just cut the wires carrying the signals to the alarms. That way, if Aranas calls, the guards will tell him everything's fine – because their systems are telling them it is." El Rey paused. "Now, what's the fastest way to get me back to Mexico City so we can save a few thousand people from certain death?"

# CHAPTER 50

*Mexico City, Mexico*

Cruz met the assassin's helicopter at the landing pad, the morning sun lightening the sky as the chopper touched down. El Rey stepped from the copilot's side of the cockpit and moved in a crouch to where Cruz stood. They shook hands, and then Cruz led him to a squad car, its rooftop emergency lights flashing. El Rey strapped into the passenger seat and Cruz slid behind the wheel, and moments later they were racing for the nearby cargo gate.

"I want to do the hospital first," Cruz said. "You're positive that thing will work?"

"The bomb maker was. I'm taking him at his word."

"Explain to me how you got him to cooperate. I'm still not following that."

El Rey gave him a more detailed account, and when he finished, Cruz shook his head. "Amazing. But you realize we're going to have to get him off the street, right? Can't have him building doomsday devices for Aranas."

"Just see to it that he's in a good facility. He isn't a criminal, at least not in any sense he'd understand. He's just really good at making things, and his uncle directed his talents in an ugly way. He'd probably be just as happy working on engines or computers."

"One of his gizmos killed over twenty people at the museum. He'll have to pay for building it. No way will anyone let that slide."

"I understand. All I'm saying is that he doesn't deserve to be in some shithole. Do your best to see that he winds up somewhere safe. You have the clout, Cruz."

"Not for much longer. After this, I'm done."

El Rey gave him a sidelong glance. "You'll never leave."

"Never say never. I made a promise to my wife last night, and I plan to honor it. Things have changed. I'm going to be a father, and I'm not going to risk my family, living like gypsies, wondering whether today's the day their heads arrive in a box."

The assassin was familiar with the story of Cruz's past, so he didn't comment. After a long pause, the only sound the roar of the car's engine and the squeal of its tires as Cruz pushed the vehicle to its handling limits, he turned the conversation back to the bombs. "How do you plan to get us into the building?" he asked.

"You said five hundred meters, didn't you? Why do we have to be inside?"

"He said the closer the better. Doesn't seem like he spent a lot of time on the prototype, so it's probably just jury-rigged. I'd rather be right next to the bomb with it, if you don't mind."

"You don't have to do that. I have twenty men who will gladly volunteer for the job."

"I'm not in the habit of farming out my projects. If I'm right and it works, there's no danger."

Cruz didn't argue. "I have a way in." He described the maintenance passageway.

"Okay, then call your CFE guys so they're waiting for us when we arrive. Time's not our friend this morning."

Cruz looked at the dash clock. "The deadline is two and a half hours from now."

"That'll be tight. Figure, what, half an hour each direction into the hospital? Then we have to get to the Federal building in morning rush hour. It'll be close."

"More like twenty minutes each way, but we also need to allow time to get to the device, so you're probably about right. Still, we can make it." Cruz paused. "Let me worry about getting us across town."

They arrived at the utility buildings where Adolfo Minos was waiting by his truck, sipping coffee from a foam cup, his expression sleepy. Cruz nodded to the man and didn't introduce El Rey. Minos didn't seem to care, nor did he appear curious about the assassin's backpack.

"Couldn't stay away, huh?" Minos joked.

"It's like a drug," Cruz said dryly. Both men chuckled, and Minos unlocked the utility building door.

Once in the passageway nobody spoke, the earth around them silent except for the occasional tremble from a truck rumbling by overhead, busy with the morning rush, as they passed beneath the streets. Cruz glanced overhead as the passage vibrated, still distrustful of the construction even though he'd been through the tunnel recently – but that had been late at night, with no traffic.

"That doesn't worry you?" he asked Minos.

Minos grinned. "Nah. If I let it get to me, I'd never go down the hole." He kept moving and looked back at Cruz. "Do you worry about getting shot every day when you put on your uniform?"

Cruz had to give the man credit. "Good point."

They reached the hospital vault door and Minos unlocked it. "I'll just wait here again, right?"

"That would be great. We'll be through in a few minutes."

"Or vaporized," El Rey muttered.

Cruz ignored the comment and led him into the pump room. "The bomb's on the third floor, in an elevator maintenance room. Aranas did his homework – according to the experts, that's where it would inflict maximum damage. All the facility's gas pipes run next to it, as well as the pressurized air lines. The blast would set those off, too. It would be ugly."

"Then best if we don't set it off."

They took the stairs to the third level and moved along the corridor to where a group of security guards lounged by the elevators. Cruz greeted the men and told them to clear the area, and they did so without protest. Rumors had been racing through the hospital like wildfire as tensions heightened, and one of the more popular was that there was a bomb in the building.

Cruz stopped the supervisor as he was preparing to leave.

"I need you to unlock this door."

The man fumbled for his keys and tried several, his hands unsteady, and finally found one that fit the lock, which sprang open with a clunk. Cruz stepped toward the door. "Thanks. You can go now, but I don't want anyone disturbing us – is that clear?"

"Yes, *Capitan*. Of course."

El Rey waited until the man had disappeared before moving to Cruz. "You going to open it?"

"Might as well see what we're dealing with, right?"

"Although there's not much we can do by looking. Either the switches work, or they don't."

Cruz pulled the door wide and they stared at the container, which was large enough to easily accommodate a V8 engine and had a single red LED blinking on its side. "There's a lot of C-4 in that thing. Hundreds of kilos," Cruz said. "I saw the X-ray images of the museum device."

"You can say what you like about our bomb maker, but he's good at what he does."

"I hope so, given that you have his work in your hands."

El Rey had removed the console from the backpack and flipped the toggle switches on all three channels to off. His mouth twitched as a thought occurred to him. "Hope he remembered to put new batteries in recently."

"You didn't check?"

The assassin shrugged. "Here goes nothing," he said, and pressed the button marked *Hospital*.

The LED blinked a final time and went dark.

Cruz exhaled in relief, and El Rey smiled. "See? Easy."

"Let's get moving. I'll have the bomb squad move in once we've disabled the other one."

The assassin glanced at his watch and then back to Cruz. "Lead the way. But we're not going to make it if there's any traffic."

"I told you I've got it covered," Cruz said.

El Rey slid the console back into his pack and leveled a neutral gaze at Cruz. "It's your party."

# CHAPTER 51

When Cruz and El Rey emerged from the CFE building into the morning sunlight, Cruz pointed at a skyscraper at the end of the block. "That's our ride."

El Rey blinked. "That's a building."

"I know. Come on."

They left Minos in the lot and trotted to the lobby of the edifice, where two serious Federal Police officers waited. "Everything ready?" Cruz asked, and the nearest one nodded.

"On the roof."

They rode the elevator to the thirtieth floor, where two more Federales framed a steel door. One of them held it open for Cruz, who led El Rey up the stairway to the roof. As they neared they heard the whirring of a helicopter turbine. Cruz pushed open another door and stepped outside, where an unmarked helo idled, its rotor orbiting slowly.

"I figure we can put down on one of the nearby buildings. This should buy us fifteen minutes, at least," Cruz called over his shoulder to the assassin as he jogged toward the aircraft.

The helicopter lifted into the sky seconds after the doors were closed, and the pilot ascended to just above the tops of the highest surrounding buildings. "All air traffic's been shut down along the route, but why attract attention?" Cruz explained.

El Rey closed his eyes as if napping.

Five minutes later the chopper touched down on the roof of a bank several blocks from the Federal building. El Rey dropped from the helicopter and Cruz trailed him to where a Federal policeman stood by an iron door.

"We're going to have to use the sewers on this one, unfortunately," Cruz announced as they neared the officer. "I've arranged for protective clothing."

"Not like I haven't done it before," El Rey said. "But an important question: how many people know about all this?"

"I've deliberately kept the circle small. Briones, whom you know. A handful of others, people I trust completely. Why? You can't be worried about a leak…"

"That's exactly what I'm worried about."

"My men are loyal."

El Rey didn't respond, but his expression indicated that he wasn't impressed by Cruz's assurances.

*Don* Aranas punched his cell phone off with a curse. His deputy, Ramirez, looked at him from over the rim of his coffee cup.

"What is it?"

"Another double cross. Stupid bastards are forcing my hand."

"But we're in the process of picking up the diamonds. What's the point?"

"I don't know, but we've been screwed." Aranas's face darkened. "I'm going to detonate the bombs."

Ramirez set his cup down and formed his words carefully. "Maybe we let them blow themselves up without our help?"

"No. This is about control. I issued exact instructions. They've violated the agreement, and they'll pay the price."

"But we'll have the diamonds in a few more minutes."

Aranas stood. "Which is about how long it will take me to make it to the attic," he snarled. "This was never about the money. It was about…never mind. Somebody still hasn't learned their lesson. But they soon will."

A roadwork supervisor pointed at an open manhole and looked Cruz and El Rey up and down. "You sure about this?" he asked doubtfully.

Cruz nodded. "We don't have a choice. You have the blueprint of the network?"

"Don't need it. I've been working the pipes for twenty years. Know every inch of 'em."

El Rey took in the man's boots and gas mask, twins of the ones he and Cruz wore. "Let's get going."

The supervisor took the hint, slipped the mask and his bright yellow hard hat on, and lowered himself down the manhole. When the top of his head disappeared beneath the rim, El Rey followed him into the gloom, and Cruz brought up the rear. The supervisor switched on his helmet light and El Rey did the same. A channel containing odious fluid coursed along the bottom of the tunnel, and an army of cockroaches scuttled from their lamp beams. The supervisor kept to one side, motioning with his hand to indicate that they should do the same.

A rat scurried away, its coat gleaming dark brown, wary of the intrusion into its dominion. They continued along, the floor sloping downward at a gradual angle, until they reached another shaft above them, the only marking a spray painted number in what had once been bright yellow but was now caramel from years of astringent fumes.

The supervisor gestured at the rungs leading upward, and El Rey wasted no time climbing them, his backpack hanging by a shoulder strap. At the top of the shaft he encountered a metal hatch, rusted along the edges, and he pushed up with all his might. The plate groaned and rose, and he continued his ascent. Cruz followed him into the large maintenance room, their helmet lamps lighting the area, and they removed their masks and the rubber boots that covered their shoes and trousers.

"This way," Cruz said, moving to the door.

"We're running low on time," El Rey reminded him.

Cruz's face darkened. "I know."

*Don* Aranas mounted the steps to the top floor as he dialed the president's number. He wanted the fool on the phone when he detonated the bomb. One of his police informants had tipped him off about an irregular helicopter flight to the Federal building, and he'd connected the dots – it had taken off within a few blocks of the hospital, and he could think of only one reason anyone would be making that trip with such urgency it required flight.

His phone beeped, indicating an incoming call. He switched lines, and the voice of his courier sounded from the phone.

"I've got the stones. We're pulling away. We'll be taking evasive maneuvers while we switch them to new bags."

"How long until you're clear?"

"No more than five minutes, tops. I have a crew running interference. Nobody will be able to follow us – the way is blocked by a truck. And we'll change to the motorcycles once we're in the underground parking area."

Aranas did a quick calculation and grunted. "Call me when you're through." He terminated the call and eyed the attic door. He could afford to wait a few more minutes for his newfound fortune to be secured. Not that he needed the money; it was to drive home the point that crossing him carried a high price.

He freed the attic hatch and the wooden steps lowered into place.

Aranas was strangely ambivalent about what he intended to do. His hand had been forced by the president's stupidity. What happened next was simply the inevitable conclusion of a series of disastrous decisions by a man with the moral qualms of a heroin-addled street prostitute.

He climbed the steps and moved across the attic to the console. His hand felt at his breast pocket and he retrieved a pair of reading glasses from beside his trove of cigars. After slipping them on, he squinted at the box and flipped up the cover on the final button – the one that would obliterate the building he could see from his balcony, a symbol of the government's authority – and soon to be another glaring example of its inability to protect its citizenry.

Cruz and El Rey emerged into a long hall, at the end of which was the room where the bomb had been discovered. They made their way toward it, only to find themselves facing a group of eight guards, all of them obviously exhausted and agitated.

"Stand aside. We need to get in there," Cruz said, fingers resting loosely on his Glock for emphasis.

"Why?" the largest of the men demanded.

"That's none of your business," Cruz snapped back. "Move out of the way."

"So you can blow us all up?" another belligerent guard said. "We haven't slept in days, and you show up barking orders? Who the hell do you think you are, anyway?"

"Look – I know this has been a difficult situation, but let's keep it simple: I'm a captain in the Federales, and you're a rent-a-cop. Now move aside."

The large man glowered at Cruz. "We were good enough to keep everyone from rioting, but now we're grunions? Screw you. How do we even know you're really cops? For all we know, you're terrorists."

The color rose in Cruz's face at the overt refusal to yield to his authority. His hand gripped the Glock as he stared the men down. "You realize that I can have you all locked up for a very long time for obstructing a federal officer, right? That outside of your little make-believe world in here, I can have you jailed for years?"

El Rey saw the fire in the men's eyes and edged away from Cruz. Going head to head with an exhausted, panicked group wasn't getting them anywhere, and only footsteps away was a bomb that could turn them all to fine mist.

"Hey. Where are you going?" the big guard demanded, but the assassin remained silent as he kept moving while freeing the console from his backpack. "Did you hear me?" the guard barked, and then his eyes widened in fear. "Wait – what's that?" he yelled, pointing at the console in the assassin's hands. The guards moved in a rush toward El Rey as Cruz drew his weapon an instant too late.

Aranas's cell trilled. When he answered it, the courier spoke the words he'd been waiting to hear. "We're clear."

He hung up and dialed the president. An aide answered and Aranas growled into the phone. "Tell your idiot boss to go stand by the window and look at the cost of his betrayal."

"What? Who is this?" the aide stammered.

"Tell the president that his day of reckoning is at hand," Aranas hissed, and then pushed the console's third button.

# CHAPTER 52

Cruz stood outside Federal Police headquarters with Dinah, dressed in street clothes instead of his uniform. He looked down at his trousers and then back at his wife.

"It'll take a while to get used to being a civilian," he said.

"You have about seven and a half months before you can add being a civilian daddy."

He smiled. "Both will take some adjustment."

"How did the meeting go?"

"As I expected. They tried everything to get me to commit to at least another six months so they could find a successor and ensure a smooth transition. I refused. They wanted to stick some politically connected hack into the job, but I told them that they already had my replacement working in the ranks."

"Briones," she said with a nod.

"Of course. He's ready. And more importantly, he's got youth and idealism on his side. He'll put in the necessary hours, see things through, and won't make the kinds of compromises that erode the effectiveness of any government organization." Cruz shrugged. "Of course they hated the idea."

"Some things never change." She took his hand. "How long do we have the condo for?"

"Two weeks."

"And your pension?"

"They tried holding that over my head, but I told them if they screw with me, I go to the press about what actually happened. That would shut down the administration, which they realize. So they agreed to my full pension, plus an additional 50% as long as I live for honorable service rendered."

"Hush money, huh?"

"Exactly. Which I'm not too proud to take. I want to spend that time with you…and our baby."

"That's the right response."

"Sometimes even I figure it out." He squeezed her hand. "I'll still have to put in some time over the next week helping Briones come up to speed, but he's already involved in most of the cases, so it shouldn't require much. And then we're out of here. For good."

"What about the Aranas task force?"

"I quit. This time there was no argument. It was always a farce, so nobody fought me."

She smiled. "Then where to?" They'd discussed possible living destinations, but hadn't come to any conclusions.

"How about Cozumel? Beaches and the ocean, but remote enough so nobody will recognize me. And slow, so no rat race."

"Only if you agree that if I don't like it, we can move."

"Of course." He looked down the block and spotted a familiar figure standing by a hot dog vendor preparing meals from a grimy cart. "Can you give me a minute? I have some unfinished business."

"I'll just stand here and pretend to be a call girl or something."

"Won't be long. And for the record, I'd be your best customer."

"Your pension isn't that big."

Cruz made his way down the block to where El Rey waited, his baseball cap pulled low over his brow, his wraparound sunglasses further disguising his appearance. Cruz eyed the hot dog vendor's wares and made a face.

"You eat that?" he asked.

"Of course not. I live dangerously enough without tempting fate with that poison. You think I have a death wish or something?"

Cruz laughed. "I heard from my sources that Aranas was on the line with the president while we were in the building. Apparently he tried to detonate the bomb."

"That must have been an awkward call."

"I'd think so. But you saved the day."

"Somebody had to. The way you were going, we were going to be there all afternoon arguing."

The big guard had snatched the console away from him, and for his trouble gotten a throat strike that felled him like an oak. El Rey had dived for the console as it tumbled to the ground, and caught it no more than a few millimeters from the hard floor. He'd depressed the button as three of the security men had moved in on him, and it had only been Cruz's warning shot that had stopped the men in their tracks. The reality of his Glock had won the day, and after verifying that the bomb's LED had gone dark, he'd radioed headquarters while holding his weapon on the guards.

"So this is it. We're square," Cruz said.

"Technically, you still owe me one, but I might let that slide seeing as I'm out of the life."

Cruz nodded. "Not like I could do much for you anymore. I quit, like I said I would. So now I'm a free man."

"Lot of that going around."

"And you? Now that you've gotten your antidote – now what?"

"To be determined. I have one final bit of business I need to attend to, and then I'll disappear. Since everyone believes me dead, I have nothing but options."

"Sometimes I wish everyone believed me to be, too."

"For the right price you can paper that and create a whole new identity that will withstand scrutiny. I can give you some contact names, if you like."

"You have my anonymous email?"

"I'll send it by the end of the day."

The two men stood awkwardly. After a long moment Cruz extended his hand. "Nice working with you. Stay out of trouble."

"That will be my life's goal."

He looked back over his shoulder at where his wife stood, carefully avoiding glancing in her direction. "There are worse ones."

# CHAPTER 53

Rafael Norteño closed his briefcase with a snap, glad the long day was finally over. After the odd call with Aranas, where the drug lord had indicated he was going to detonate the bomb, the president had been in a notably upbeat mood. When no explosion ensued and Aranas had abruptly hung up, the ugly episode was officially over, with a press conference announcing that the terrorist threat had been neutralized. The president had shone at the media event, all refined seriousness and determination.

"Mexico is a global force, and as such it has become a target of the same terrorism that plagues other civilized countries. We have been fortunate to avoid it for so long, but the regrettable events of the last days underscore that the twenty-first century brings with it both opportunities and risks. As long as there are extremists willing to do the unthinkable, to sacrifice the lives of the innocent in order to achieve their deplorable goals, there will always be a danger, which the museum bombing brought home."

Cameras had clicked and whirred as he'd delivered an impassioned speech that had been carried by every network, and by the end of the day the popular consensus was that Mexico needed a resolute response to terrorism that would include new immigration measures, security checks, the creation of a database of high-risk individuals, and the establishment of a paramilitary law enforcement organization chartered with defending the homeland.

"Of course, safety comes at a price, and vigilance will require sacrificing some of our rights in order to counter the terrorism threat. But we must take appropriate steps as a player on the world stage, and I know that every Mexican will agree that nothing is more important than ensuring a safe and stable future for our children…even if that comes at a cost. I am committed to doing everything in my power to respond to this new challenge, and with the cooperation of our lawmakers, I am confident that we will persevere no matter what, as we have since our forefathers fought the revolution that created our sovereign state. In this war, there can be no middle ground – you are either with us, or against us."

In the question-and-answer period after the speech, the inquiries had been mostly benign, dealing with the initial measures that would be taken. Toward the end of the interrogatives, a journalist from Television Azteca had pitched a hardball at the president that Norteño and he had discussed in advance.

"Mr. President, what did the terrorists hope to achieve with the bombing?"

"Good question, Renaldo. The terrorists issued a demand for Mexico to sever all ties with the United States, which they blame for a host of evils, none of which are legitimate. But the attack had the opposite effect – it brought us together as a nation and strengthened our bond with our neighbor to the north, who provided considerable assistance to us during this dark time."

The response, a patent falsehood, had been eagerly lapped up by the media, and Norteño knew that within days it would be broadcast so often it would become the accepted truth. He understood from studying the Americans that it was possible to create a completely mythical official account of anything, and that most would believe it to be true if the press echoed it as reality. As a student of human nature, the approach had privately fascinated him, and he'd seen the technique used time and time again throughout history by governments intent on manufacturing enemies so they could justify their actions. The Soviets had done so, as had the Nazis, as had Japan, Italy, and the UK…but the U.S. had upped the ante and perfected the approach to the point it was considered treasonous to question even the most unlikely official explanations of events.

Now it was Mexico's turn. About time, he thought with

satisfaction, as he recalled the minor triumph of his ascendance to power, all within less than three days. He'd often dreamed of being the right-hand man to the throne, but his performance during the crisis had sealed it, and he could now do no wrong.

"Good night," Norteño said to his secretary, and then worked his way down the long marble hall, his footsteps the confident ones of a man of consequence.

The drive to his high-rise condo was the only annoyance of the day, traffic snarled as was typical of the huge city, but even that couldn't ruin his high. He'd pulled off a coup few would have had the audacity to dream of, much less spearhead. And his future was sealed as one of the men who would steer the nation's fortunes, at least for the next few years. That gave him time to develop his standing within the party, which would be ably supported by the president's endorsement.

Who knew? Perhaps he might be persuaded to run for office. Stranger things had happened.

He parked in the underground security garage and rode the elevator to the eighteenth floor, his mind a whirl of conflicting thoughts. While the condo was lavish for a single man, he'd start looking for something larger, in a more elite building. After all, he was now rich – his third of the one and a half billion dollars of diamonds would trickle into offshore accounts as Aranas liquidated the stones, so if he wanted a penthouse that ran five million dollars or higher, what of it? He could more than afford it and had the plausible deniability of his family's fortunes to account for where the means to buy it had come from – not that anyone would dare to probe too deeply.

He unlocked his condo door and stepped inside, paused to set his briefcase down in the foyer, and moved into the living room, the panoramic view of Mexico City's lights one of his simple pleasures. At a small bar near a wall-mounted flat-screen television he poured himself a healthy portion of Don Julio 1942 tequila before shrugging out of his suit jacket and plopping down on the contemporary sofa to watch the news.

He nearly jumped out of his skin when a voice spoke from behind him.

"Quite a day, no?"

He bolted to his feet, spilling his drink down the front of his slacks, and spun. A young man he'd never seen before leaned against the doorway with his arms crossed, a slight smirk on his face.

"Who the hell are you, and how did you get in here?" Norteño demanded.

"Ah. You don't recognize me. Of course not. Why would you?"

The intruder took a step toward Norteño and drew a small pistol from his pocket. Norteño stood frozen as the intruder screwed a sound suppressor into place.

"I…I have money in the safe," he blurted.

"That's good to know."

"And gold. Coins. Kruggerands."

"A prudent investment," the gunman said. "But that's not what I'm here for."

Norteño's expression registered confusion. "No?"

"No. I'm here to watch you jump from your balcony."

Norteño's mouth worked, but no sound came out other than a hoarse choking noise. He found his voice, and his grip on the brandy snifter he was clutching tightened. "I don't understand."

"Allow me to explain. You authorized my execution with CISEN. I am known by many names, but the one you'll recognize is probably El Rey – the King of Swords."

The blood drained from Norteño's face. "I…I have no idea what you're talking about."

"I don't blame you for lying. I suspect it's a way of life for you, and so far you've largely gotten away with it. Until today."

"You have the wrong man."

El Rey's countenance could have been carved from granite. "It's not working. Make your peace, because you don't have long."

A rivulet of sweat ran from Norteño's hairline and traced a course down his cheek. "I swear it wasn't me."

El Rey glanced at Norteño's nearly empty tequila glass. "You know what I hate more than a privileged snot who thinks he owns the world and can do whatever he likes with no consequences? Go ahead. Guess."

"I…"

"A liar. I'd down the rest of your drink."

"Please. I can make you rich."

"I'm already rich."

"Not like this, you're not. I can give you a hundred million dollars."

"The strange thing about having enough is that once you do, you don't really care about getting more." El Rey motioned with his gun. "Last chance to savor your cocktail. Shame for a good tequila like that to go to waste."

Norteño hurled the glass at the assassin, who easily dodged it as Norteño lunged at him. El Rey sidestepped the clumsy attempt and clubbed him on the back of his skull with the pistol butt. Norteño landed hard on the polished floor but managed to break his fall with his arms. El Rey delivered a brutal strike to Norteño's neck with his free hand and he groaned before going limp.

When Norteño came to, his upper body was hanging over the terrace railing. The city's twinkling lights spun dizzily as he fought in vain to orient himself, the street beneath him dark save for the street lamps' faint glow. Sour bile rushed into his throat as vertigo overcame him and he retched.

"Have a nice trip," El Rey said from behind him, and then his legs followed his body over the railing and the street rushed toward him at impossible speed as his mouth formed a silent no.

El Rey didn't watch Norteño's fall from grace, preferring to let himself out of the condo and slip down the stairs. The apparent suicide would create sufficient chaos so that he could escape unnoticed, and he didn't want to chance the elevator in case someone boarded it on his way down.

It took him three minutes to make it to street level, and by the time he did, the doorman and the two security guards were out on the street, yelling into their cell phones.

None of them noticed the slim figure emerge from the building and saunter away.

# CHAPTER 54

*Culiacán, Sinaloa, Mexico*

*Don* Aranas ran a hand through his steel-gray hair and took a puff of his first cigar of the day as he watched the news. An earnest young man with the fake sincerity of a televangelist was reading the teleprompter while attempting to make the words sound like his own.

"The president announced today that he has arranged for the United States to house antiterrorism Special Forces troops in Mexico City, Guadalajara, and Monterrey as part of his comprehensive reforms in Mexico's battle against terror. The troops will begin to arrive next week and represent an unprecedented step in international cooperation between the two countries. This culminates negotiations with United States antiterrorism to provide funding, weapons, and training. During the morning press conference, the president pointed out that many American corporations have manufacturing enterprises in Mexico, so it was in both nations' best interests to ensure that there were adequate precautions in place against terrorist threats. In light of the recent bombing of the anthropology museum, the majority of the Mexican Congress applauded the historic peace pact."

The newscaster paused and his tone grew somber. "Critics of the move called it a de facto invasion force and the next step in Mexico's loss of sovereignty, which they say began with the acceptance of funds and equipment to fight America's war on drugs – turning Mexico into a battleground and endangering its population to advance the U.S.'s agenda. The president didn't address the concerns, instead underscoring that the forces would be under Mexico's control and would only be used if a threat presented itself."

Aranas chuckled and shook his head at the notion. He was quite sure that there would soon be another terrorist incident, even if he had no active part in it. He understood how the game was played, and another event was entirely predictable – the only question was when.

"In other news, the ministry of the interior announced that several key bids in the ongoing privatization of Mexico's petroleum industry had been reviewed and nullified, and that an investigation was being launched into bidding impropriety. The companies in question are Haoyun Petroleum, Sun Strike Oil, and Shanghai Gas, all Chinese."

A clip of a Mexican bureaucrat speaking ran. "We cannot allow a corrupted system to determine who will be our partners in harvesting our oil. There is sufficient evidence of widespread payoffs in the bidding process that we've canceled the agreements with these firms and held a second round of bids. It's of paramount importance that the process be fair and impartial, and that the contracts go to the most qualified candidates."

That drew a laugh from Aranas.

The broadcast switched to a beautiful brunette with blazing green eyes.

"Still no progress in the hunt for *Don* Aranas, the head of the Sinaloa Cartel. A well-publicized recent sighting, on a bus bound for Guatemala, turned out to be a false alarm after Mexican authorities, working with the Guatemalans, stopped the bus at the border and found nothing. Experts believe that the crime boss has taken refuge in Eastern Europe, where his organization has developed strong relationships with the Russian mafia."

Aranas couldn't help but roll his eyes. His disinformation campaign continued unabated, the lies repeated by a press that had never heard a whopper it didn't believe. Next they'd place him on a flight to Mars.

His phone buzzed from its position on the coffee table, and after setting his cigar down, he reached for it.

"Yes?" he answered.

"Looks like you won that round," the American said in accented Spanish.

"Life is nothing more than a series of obstacles to overcome."

"Yes, well, it's come to my attention that two of the three contracts went to companies that you have an interest in. Only one went to an American firm."

"This is a land of compromises. Promises were made. It was impossible to do it any other way." Aranas paused. "Of course, if you want to have greater participation, I could always arrange for a percentage of the companies to be sold to your friends. At a fair price, of course, representing their new status with the Mexican government."

"That's remarkably generous of you," the American said dryly.

"Just as it was generous of you to waste no time renegotiating with my adversaries – at more favorable terms for you."

The American cleared his throat. "We all do what we must. I'll pass your thoughts along to the appropriate parties."

"Yes, do so. Oh, and congratulations on achieving your objective of establishing a military presence within our borders."

"It's time for old-fashioned geographic distinctions to go by the wayside. We're all in this together, after all."

"I'm sure we are. But the track record for countries that have had American military helpers, for whatever reason, hasn't been stellar."

"Not everyone will be happy in all circumstances. As long as your interests are safeguarded, what do you care?"

Aranas sighed. "I fear the world is becoming too small for this old man."

"Let us know if you plan to retire. We are heavily invested in you at this point."

"Not quite yet."

Aranas signed off with a frown and returned to his coffee. He took a sip and set the cup down in disgust.

"Coffee's cold. Bring another cup," he called out, and sat back to contemplate the grounds of his estate, his cigar as his companion, the distant whinnying of his horses music to his tired ears.

# CHAPTER 55

*Mexico City, Mexico*

Rows of prisoners sat at a line of long wooden tables, working on tasks they'd been assigned by the prison administration. A bell chimed, and then a metallic voice rang over the prison public address system.

"Shift over in ten minutes. All prisoners prepare to return to their cells in five."

El Maquino looked up from the collection of parts he was assembling and nodded slowly, his hair now trimmed close to his head. Aside from having to be around the other inmates, he didn't mind being incarcerated – the routine had been easy for him to get used to, and his uncle had arranged for a private cell in the overcrowded facility with many of the same comforts of his old loft.

Four of his uncle's jailed allies shadowed him everywhere he went, and not much had changed from his prior existence, other than the food, which he hated. He'd mentioned it to one of the guards soon after arriving, and the next day an older convict with a flat nose and a face that had seen its share of fights introduced himself as El Maquino's new private chef, and asked for a list of his favorite meals.

That had temporarily stumped the big man, who eventually conveyed that he really only had one favorite meal and enjoyed eating it every day for breakfast, lunch, and dinner. The chef had been taken aback at that and had been convinced that El Maquino was toying with him until he'd seen the dull gray of his unwavering stare and understood he was serious.

Since then he'd gotten along well, no sense of how long the twenty years he'd been sentenced to was, just as he couldn't have told anyone his age. It simply didn't matter, and he'd never bothered to keep track.

The mind-numbing sameness of each day that wore down even the hardest prisoners had been a dream come true for the big man, and he looked forward to each morning with the anticipation of a child for Christmas. He'd been assigned to the prison labor pool that dealt with repairs to the facility's crumbling infrastructure, and he was quickly prized by the maintenance supervisor as the preferred person to handle anything mechanical or electrical.

Even the best prisons in Mexico were chronically underfunded and therefore constantly falling apart, and this one was no exception, so El Maquino was never short of work. He thrived on the challenge of troubleshooting and fixing the various pumps and gizmos he was brought, and had seldom been happier. Freedom had never been more than increased responsibility to him, and freed from the requirement to do anything but his repairs, he was thriving in the unlikeliest of circumstances.

The inmate next to him slid closer and leaned toward him. "Can I borrow that hex driver?" the prisoner asked. "You aren't using it right now."

El Maquino turned his big head toward the man and gave him a glare. The inmate froze as he was reaching for the tool and abruptly reconsidered. He moved back to his position on the bench and El Maquino resumed assembling the pump, humming quietly to himself, looking forward to dinner in his cell alone before spending his remaining hours before lights out drawing schematics for advanced drone guidance systems his uncle's guards then ferreted out of the prison for shipment to the patent attorneys that handled his inventions.

Aranas had set up a shell company to license the intellectual property, and if El Maquino had been capable of appreciating irony, he would have been delighted to know that his biggest customer was the U.S. military, which would make him wealthy enough by the time he was released early for good behavior to eclipse all but the cartel bosses in his uncle's employ and, of course, the great man himself.

~ ~ ~

*Cozumel, Mexico*

Cruz jerked the tip of the fishing rod skyward and set the hook on the third yellowfin tuna of the day. Forty-pound test monofilament stripped off the screaming reel for a good twenty seconds until he gradually tightened the drag for the battle to come. Ten minutes later, the exhausted fish was making its last run after seeing the bottom of Cruz's skiff and deciding that no good could come from being hauled aboard.

He waited until the fish had burned all its resources and then pumped and reeled with all his might. The school he'd come upon were all forty to sixty pounders, and this one felt like it was at the upper end of that range as he cranked it to the surface.

Once the fish was landed, he stowed his tackle and prepared to head in. He'd caught enough to last a week, at least, even after giving half of the take away to Ramón, his boat cleaner and the marina jack of all trades, who ensured that his twenty-six footer was always ready for a run out to sea.

The outboard caught on the first try. He swung the bow around and directed it at the beige island that rose from the turquoise sparkle of the Caribbean in the near distance. After a month in a rented house in the main town, he'd settled into the slow pace and was finally sleeping normally. Turning off his brain hadn't been as easy as he'd hoped, and the first nights there he'd start awake, his heart palpitating, reaching for the Glock he kept in a nightstand drawer. Dinah hadn't said anything, though he knew that she had been worried; but over the last week the anxiety had melted away as he'd spent his days on the water, the boat a kind of therapy that had worked a minor miracle.

The hull sliced through the mild chop as he accelerated to twenty-five knots, and within no time he was pulling up to the dock, Ramón moving on spindly legs to help tie off. Cruz killed the engine and the pair of them made short work of fileting the tuna, the meat pink and nearly translucent.

He was bagging his share when he spotted Dinah's sundress by the parking lot, her lithe form only now beginning to change with pregnancy.

"Take as much as you want, Ramón, and feel free to sell what you can't eat," Cruz said as he finished with his chore. "But don't forget to hose off the boat. Be a shame for it to reek when I show up tomorrow."

Ramón nodded and offered a gap-toothed grin. "No problem, boss man. Thanks for the fish. Goes a long way in lean times like these."

"My pleasure."

Cruz carried two bags, each weighing an easy fifteen pounds, up the gangplank to the shore. Dinah watched his progress with a half-smile, her hair stirring in the soft sea breeze.

"What's for dinner?" she asked as he neared.

"Ahi. I'll cook it, if you like. Pan sear it for a few seconds, blackened, of course."

"Mmm, sounds delicious." She tiptoed and kissed him, then wrinkled her nose. "You smell like you swam in it. Shower time, *Capitan*."

He grinned as he took in her sun-kissed face and nodded. "Your wish is my command."

They made their way up the path that led to the main shorefront street that ringed the island and Cruz stopped suddenly.

Dinah turned to him. "What?"

"Weren't you going to the doctor today?"

She nodded slowly. "Very good. You remembered. I was sure you'd forgotten."

"Never. So? What's the news?"

She smiled again, and Cruz's breath caught in his throat. At that moment she was the most beautiful woman he'd ever seen, flushed with the exertion of the walk, and...something else. Well-being, perhaps. "Well, *Capitan*, congratulations are in order. Soon you're going to have a son to help you with the fishing."

Dinah began walking again, as though she'd done nothing more than tell him the time, leaving Cruz standing on the curb, an expression of wonder on his face as he watched the mother of his child make her way home. She glanced over her shoulder at him and furrowed her brow. "Are you coming, or are you just going to stand there with a bunch of rotting fish?"

Cruz shook his head and began moving again, visions of a smaller version of himself sitting in the bow of the boat, black hair swirling in the wind, his son's eyes dancing with a world seen for the first time.

# CHAPTER 56

*Madrid, Spain*

The Plaza de Cascorro was bustling on Sunday morning as El Rey made his way along one of the tributary lanes leading to the square. Every weekend the area became a giant flea market, and one of the ways he killed time when Carla was occupied on a breaking story was to stroll the endless rows of stalls, where enterprising vendors sold trinkets, used books, produce, antiques, cheap clothing, soccer jerseys, and every variety of memorabilia.

Graffiti covered the roll-down steel awnings of the shuttered shops that had surrendered the square to the swarm of street merchants. Old women walked with arms intertwined as they argued over which sellers had the least unfair prices – that they were all criminals, gypsies, and thieves went without saying, but some were less larcenous than others.

The two months the former assassin had spent with Carla in the city had gone by in a blur as they'd settled in, she to her new job, he to being completely aimless for the first time he could remember, with no enemies to fear, no targets to pursue, nothing but the blank canvas of a new existence with a woman who continuously surprised and delighted him.

He spotted a pickpocket bumping a pair of Germans whose distinctive vacation-wear and obvious prosperity practically cried out for robbery, and shook his head as the male's wallet disappeared into the thief's hoodie pocket. Before the Germans were aware of the theft the slender grafter quickly turned a corner and vanished like smoke into the throng. Like Mexico City, Madrid was a metropolis with high unemployment and scarce resources for the jobless, and the residents did what they had to do to make ends meet. Most were honest and law abiding, but with twenty-five percent of the country out of work, morality tended to be elastic, especially on an empty stomach.

A bright green and yellow hand-painted sign in one of the doorways caught his eye, and he slowed at the image of a tarot card: a stylized image of the moon depicted with intricate brushstrokes. He drew nearer, and an ancient woman with a threadbare red bandanna over her white hair nodded to him from where she sat on the stoop behind a small wooden table and a single vacant collapsible camp chair.

"Come, young man. Allow me to tell your fortune. Señora Campos sees all in the cards – love, riches, success or failure – there are no secrets from me," she said, her words thick with a Basque lilt.

"No thanks, Mother. Perhaps some other time," he replied, although he didn't move past the table. A vision of a different fortune teller, so many years ago, sprang into his imagination as vividly as though it were only hours before, and he blinked it away.

"For you, I will make a special price, for today only. I can see you are in need of guidance," the woman pressed.

That brought a smile to his lips. "Very generous of you, but I'm afraid I must be going."

She shuffled the cards as though she hadn't heard him, and began turning them over. He reluctantly withdrew a few coins from his pocket and placed them on top of the first card. "That's very kind of you," she said, collecting the money with fingers twisted by the ravages of arthritis and time. "But I haven't named a price."

"I have no need to see any more of the future than I already have," he said, and offered a small bow before turning and moving into the stream of humanity, unremarkable in his drab garb, just another of thousands of young men out on a balmy morning with nothing much to do.

He hummed as he walked along cobblestones worn smooth by centuries of feet, strangely at peace with his surroundings even in the midst of the market's hubbub. He'd seen the face card as he'd laid the coins upon the table and didn't doubt the old gypsy's talents, but in the spirit of reinvention with which he'd accompanied Carla to Spain, his interest in what the future held lay beyond the deterministic universe that the tarot implied governed him. He was a different man from the impressionable young boy he'd once been; and the image beneath the tarnished metal coins he'd so casually left for the crone – the monarch's regal glare, sword clutched in one determined hand – meant nothing to him any longer.

The cards had no sway in what was to come.

# About the Author

Featured in *The Wall Street Journal*, *The Times*, and *The Chicago Tribune*, Russell Blake is *The NY Times* and *USA Today* bestselling author of over forty novels, including *Fatal Exchange*, *Fatal Deception*, *The Geronimo Breach*, *Zero Sum*, *King of Swords*, *Night of the Assassin*, *Revenge of the Assassin*, *Return of the Assassin*, *Blood of the Assassin*, *Requiem for the Assassin*, *Rage of the Assassin The Delphi Chronicle* trilogy, *The Voynich Cypher*, *Silver Justice*, *JET*, *JET – Ops Files*, *JET – Ops Files: Terror Alert*, *JET II – Betrayal*, *JET III – Vengeance*, *JET IV – Reckoning*, *JET V – Legacy*, *JET VI – Justice*, *JET VII – Sanctuary*, *JET VIII – Survival*, *JET IX – Escape*, *JET X – Incarceration*, *Upon a Pale Horse*, *BLACK*, *BLACK is Back*, *BLACK is The New Black*, *BLACK to Reality*, *BLACK in the Box*, *Deadly Calm*, *Ramsey's Gold*, *Emerald Buddha*, and *The Day After Never – Blood Honor*.

Non-fiction includes the international bestseller *An Angel With Fur* (animal biography) and *How To Sell A Gazillion eBooks In No Time* (even if drunk, high or incarcerated), a parody of all things writing-related.

Blake is co-author of *The Eye of Heaven* and *The Solomon Curse*, with legendary author Clive Cussler. Blake's novel *King of Swords* has been translated into German by Amazon Crossing, *The Voynich Cypher* into Bulgarian, and his JET novels into Spanish, German, and Czech.

Blake writes under the moniker R.E. Blake in the NA/YA/Contemporary Romance genres. Novels include *Less Than Nothing, More Than Anything*, and *Best Of Everything*.

Having resided in Mexico for a dozen years, Blake enjoys his dogs, fishing, boating, tequila and writing, while battling world domination by clowns. His thoughts, such as they are, can be found at his blog: RussellBlake.com

# Books by Russell Blake

## Co-authored with Clive Cussler

THE EYE OF HEAVEN
THE SOLOMON CURSE

## Thrillers

FATAL EXCHANGE
FATAL DECEPTION
THE GERONIMO BREACH
ZERO SUM
THE DELPHI CHRONICLE TRILOGY
THE VOYNICH CYPHER
SILVER JUSTICE
UPON A PALE HORSE
DEADLY CALM
RAMSEY'S GOLD
EMERALD BUDDHA
THE DAY AFTER NEVER – BLOOD HONOR

## The Assassin Series

KING OF SWORDS
NIGHT OF THE ASSASSIN
RETURN OF THE ASSASSIN
REVENGE OF THE ASSASSIN
BLOOD OF THE ASSASSIN
REQUIEM FOR THE ASSASSIN
RAGE OF THE ASSASSIN

## The JET Series

JET
JET II – BETRAYAL
JET III – VENGEANCE
JET IV – RECKONING
JET V – LEGACY
JET VI – JUSTICE
JET VII – SANCTUARY
JET VIII – SURVIVAL
JET IX – ESCAPE
JET X – INCARCERATION
JET – OPS FILES (prequel)
JET – OPS FILES; TERROR ALERT

## The BLACK Series

BLACK
BLACK IS BACK
BLACK IS THE NEW BLACK
BLACK TO REALITY
BLACK IN THE BOX

## Non Fiction

AN ANGEL WITH FUR
HOW TO SELL A GAZILLION EBOOKS
*(while drunk, high or incarcerated)*

Made in the USA
Monee, IL
11 October 2023

44406557R00159